The slumped figure might almost have been sitting. One leg was bent at the knee and splayed slightly to one side, the other stretched out awkwardly away from me. It was not a natural pose. The torso leaned back against the rock face with the head tilted slightly to one side. Although it was dark enough now that I would not have been able to see the rise and fall of the chest, I was certain that it was motionless. The coppery smell of blood was faint but noticeable.

The head was partly obscured because the jacket's hood had been pulled up, perhaps to keep the bugs away. I had been waving my arms intermittently to drive them off ever since we left the house, which had bug zappers at either end, but they were persistent and numerous, even more so here because they sensed the blood.

Managansett Press

Don D'Ammassa is the author of:

Horror
Blood Beast
Servant of Chaos*
Caverns of Chaos*
Wings over Manhattan
The Gargoyle
That Way Madness Lies*
Little Evils*
Passing Death*
Date with the Dark*
The Devil Is in the Details*
Living Things*

Science Fiction
Scarab*
Haven
Narcissus
Translation Station
The Sinking Island*
Alien & Otherwise*

Mysteries
Murder in Silverplate
Dead of Winter*
Death at the Art Gallery*
Death on the Mountain*

Fantasy
The Kaleidoscope*
Elaborate Lies*

Nonfiction
The Encyclopedia of Science Fiction
The Encyclopedia of Fantasy and Horror
The Encyclopedia of Adventure Fiction
Masters of Detection Vol I*
Masters of Detection Vol II*

*published by Managansett Press

DEATH ON THE MOUNTAIN

Don D'Ammassa

Managansett Press First Edition 2015

DEATH ON THE MOUNTAIN

The trail was narrow and winding and the sunlight was disappearing quickly, sending shadows creeping out to lap at our feet as we walked. It wasn't a particularly steep climb but it was steady and the backs of my calves were beginning to complain. I hadn't used the treadmill as much as I should have lately and I was getting soft. If my two companions were similarly discomfited, they gave no sign; in fact, we had barely spoken since we'd set out on our short but necessary journey.

We were probably making good time but I felt as though some invisible force was clutching my ankles, retarding my progress, and while I realized that it was simply my reluctance to reach our goal and find what I was almost certain we would find, realization didn't make it any less effective. None of us had been enthusiastic when we had set out and our moods had darkened as we drew closer to our goal. I had never come this way before so I didn't know exactly how far we had to go, but it couldn't be much longer now and I felt a constriction in my gut.

This was going to be very unpleasant.

I'm one of those people who loathes parties of any kind, even or perhaps especially the occasional one where I'm the host. I don't enjoy sipping cocktails and trying to make conversation with people in tailored suits and designer dresses, or informal barbecues where both sexes wear expensive jeans and pretend that they enjoy beating off mosquitoes and eating hamburgers that are charred or undercooked, or sometimes both. As a child I dreaded the inevitable gathering of my school chums in the basement my parents had converted to a "family room" during which we played carefully vetted games under the watchful eyes of our elders and as an adolescent I failed to see the attraction of meeting a group of friends so that we could all drink ourselves silly and then vomit in the bushes – if we made it that far. I attend the annual office Christmas party because my employees seem to enjoy it but I always make a joke about the difficulty of relaxing around the boss and skip out as early as I can. Dusty, my significant other, calls me the original Party Pooper and I guess she's right. I'm not antisocial but I prefer my interactions with smaller groups and with more spontaneity. Parties offer neither and they are frequently disasters.

Particularly the ones where a dead body turns up.

I guess I'd better start closer to the beginning. My name is Paul Birch and I run an admittedly somewhat stuffy detective agency, Birch Investigations. We don't track down Maltese Falcons, shoot bad people, locate secret passages, or exchange insults with organized crime figures. Mostly we do skip tracing, security evaluations, statistical analysis and audits, missing persons, and sometimes divorce work and repossessions, although mostly I subcontract those last two. It probably sounds rather boring, and in fact it generally is, but I prefer it that way, although Dusty keeps trying to convince me that I'm in a rut. I like my rut.

Dusty and I had been together about a year and a half, and for the last eleven months we'd been sharing quarters. I had previously bought a house that was far too big for me on the advice of my accountant and most of the second floor had been closed up until Dusty moved in. We had separate bedrooms even though we usually spent the night together but when she first arrived I figured she needed her own space and she didn't seem to find the arrangements awkward. At the time I hadn't realized how much space she really needed. Dusty was a fairly successful novelist although few people had heard of her because she used several pseudonyms in addition to her own name. I liked her books, but I was prejudiced. She also had an unusual way of working out the details of her stories. Or at least I thought it was unusual; I'd never lived with a writer before.

Dusty's first thriller had done well enough that the publisher wanted a sequel, but Dusty had balked, at least for the time being. Her new interest was epic fantasy and she was plotting what she liked to call a "four volume trilogy". "I have to create a whole new world," she told me over supper one evening. "Can I use the attic?"

Some writers create detailed outlines and draw maps, but Dusty was more ambitious. While writing her spy novel, she'd converted the dining room into a crude model of Paris – at least she said it was Paris. To me it just looked like piles of wooden blocks, canned vegetables, and plastic toys. She saw it as a physical metaphor. Technically speaking we didn't have an attic. The third floor was semi-finished with bare walls and plank floors and the ceiling sloped down on either side so that you had to crouch if you moved too far from the center. It consisted primarily of one large room with three smaller ones, closets really, one in each corner except for the last, which was the top of the staircase. As far as I could remember at the time she asked it was completely empty – I'm one of those people who dispose of stuff when I'm done with it – but I hadn't been above the second floor in at least a year.

"No air conditioning up there."

"That's okay. Most of Pullenia is desert. It'll add atmosphere."

"Take one of the fans. There can be windstorms in a desert. I warn you, it probably needs a good cleaning."

"Already done, mostly. I started this morning, actually. I knew you wouldn't mind."

Nor did I, but I didn't get to see the metaphorical Pullenia until a week later. It was a Friday night and I'd quit early, planning to take Dusty to Al Forno's for supper, but the house seemed to be empty even though her car was in the driveway. I had just about decided that she'd gone out for a walk when I heard a thud from overhead and realized she was on the third floor.

I made a point of treading heavily on my way up the narrow staircase so that I wouldn't startle Dusty, who is often so immersed in her imaginative process that she's oblivious of the real world. That afternoon she was completely submerged, so it was kind of a tossup which of us was more surprised when I reached the top.

Dusty was on her knees, wearing sweat pants and a halter top, with her hair gathered into an unruly ponytail. Her back was to me and I couldn't quite see what she was doing, but I did see the large empty space beyond. Except it wasn't so empty now.

The entire far end was covered with sand. It was only a light covering, and I could see the edges of the drop cloths beneath, but it spread across almost the entire width of the room. There were three small bowls of water situated apparently at random, but otherwise it was an unbroken expanse. The near left wall was lined with piles of folded towels which I recognized as the ones Dusty had brought with her when she gave up her apartment. We had never used them. I felt mildly guilty about that, but they really didn't match the bathrooms and Dusty didn't seem to care. When Dusty stood up, I could see that there was a large stack of wooden blocks with smaller piles surrounding it in the exact center of the sandy area, and I assumed that was probably a city though it didn't much resemble the dining room Paris I'd lived with for three months. I must have made a sound then because before I could look at anything else Dusty spun around and flashed me a smile.

"You're too early. I'll have it finished by tomorrow. I have to go to the toy shop and buy some monsters."

"I see you've been busy."

"Pullenia is shaping up. I'll be able to start writing next week. What do you think of it?"

I searched for the right words. "Maybe you should explain it to me before I express an opinion."

She stood up. The attic was warm and she'd been perspiring. The halter top clung to her body and the last thing I wanted right now was a guided tour of Pullenia. ' That's the desert, of course," she gestured toward the sand. "And we have three oases." Those were the bowls of water. "The towels are going to be the mountains of Trepidor. They still need some work."

I noticed a feature I had missed before – a teddy bear sandwiched between two towels. "Who's he? The hero?"

"Mountain troll. And these are going to be orcs." She held up a plastic bag of green toy soldiers.

"At least they're the right color."

"Orcs aren't green."

"How many have you met?"

She sniffed at me. "This is the city of Solenia. It doesn't have its moat yet."

"How would a city manage to have a working moat at the edge of a great desert?"

"It's a fire moat. No water."

"You're not going to burn down the house, are you?"

"I'll use salad oil and I won't light it.."

"No forest either. What do they use for fuel and building materials and to make paper?"

"They use people who ask tedious questions. It's magic fire, a kind of eternal flame that ignites when danger threatens. And they trade for what they can't get locally. I haven't worked out all the details yet. So what do you think?"

"I think you need a break. How about supper at Capriccio's?" I put my arms around her.

"I need to work up an appetite first." She gave me a lascivious smile.

She had a mighty big appetite by the time we were ready to go out.

It was while we were sipping wine and waiting for our food to arrive that Dusty sprung her surprise on me. "We're invited to a party."

"I'm thrilled to death."

"I know you won't want to go but this one is important. It's even job related so I can claim travel expenses on my taxes."

"Travel?" I was already marshalling excuses for why I couldn't go to wherever it was, whenever it was.

"It's in New Hampshire. Southern New Hampshire. Two or three hours drive. I made a motel reservation already."

"What kind of party?" Our dinners arrived, shrimp scampi for me, some kind of fancy chicken for Dusty.

"It's nothing elaborate. Less than a dozen people, most of them writers or editors."

I'd met some of Dusty's writer friends. All they wanted to talk about was either a detailed synopsis of their latest book or how horribly they were being treated by their publishers. They were probably right, but that didn't make it any more interesting for the rest of us. "When is this supposed to happen?"

"Two weekends from now. I thought we could drive up Friday night, go to the party on Saturday, and do some sightseeing on Sunday if you want before we come home. Culloden is supposed to be very pretty, at least according to the town website. It's a little north of Keene."

As usual my first impulse was to find or manufacture a reason not to go, but Dusty always came along when I was trapped into social events with people she didn't know. She seemed to enjoy herself most of the time, but I knew she would have gone even if she'd been bored to distraction. "All right. I'll clear my calendar for Friday and we can take our time on the trip up."

"Great."

We ate for a while. The shrimp was very good and that cheered me up some. "What's the occasion anyway?"

"The party? It's actually really special. Have you ever read anything by Martin Edison?"

I shook my head. "The name sounds familiar though."

"You need to widen your horizons. He's only the greatest living fantasy novelist."

"Only until yours gets published." I was pretty pleased with that line but Dusty ignored me.

"He's a very private person. Never does book tours or interviews, won't attend conventions, doesn't even have his photograph on his book covers so when he does go out no one recognizes him. There have been rumors that he sometimes travels under another name. But somehow his agent and his publisher talked him into attending a small gathering to celebrate the publication of his fiftieth novel on the 50th anniversary of his first book, *The Wildings of Westhall*."

"But he wouldn't agree to go to New York so the party is coming to him." I'm a trained detective; I can figure out the obvious.

"Right. And he insisted that it be limited to a few other writers and professionals and that he had final approval of the guest list."

"Not that I don't think you're a marvelous person and a brilliant writer, but how did you make the cut?"

"I owe that to Damon."

"Damon? Your agent?"

She nodded. "He's Edison's agent as well, his cash cow, in fact. Or at least he was. There have been rumors that Edison isn't going to renew their contract when it runs out."

"I thought Damon was supposed to be very good." Dusty had been thrilled when he agreed to take her on as a client.

"He is. Edison apparently changes agents every few years as a matter of course. Anyway, one of the people Edison invited declined to come, a western novelist who uses the penname Dusty Trails."

"Cute," I said. Dusty's birth name was Dolores but she'd changed it when she turned eighteen.

She made a face at me. "Anyway, Damon knew I was starting a fantasy series so he decided to pretend he'd gotten the name wrong. If he pissed Edison off, it wouldn't matter if he's being fired anyway. That's the story, and I really really really want to go. I know you'll be bored but it's only for a few hours."

"Boredom is rarely fatal ," I said. "I'll survive."

I did survive, in fact, but another person at the party would not, and the weekend would be anything but boring.

The drive from Providence to Keene is just long enough for you to feel as though you've really gotten away from the city and just short enough not to be overly wearying, particularly if you break up the trip with a coffee stop, which we did. Dusty and I had spent several weekends together in this area and nearby Vermont, and once drove all the way up to Mount Desert Island in Maine for a full week. This particular trip passed all too swiftly for me because I wasn't looking forward to spending any extra time hobnobbing with people I didn't know, although I did try to convince Dusty that I was feeling convivial. I shouldn't have bothered. We've brushed up against each other's nuances often enough that we could read moods readily. But she was really enthusiastic, almost bubbly, and I tried to set aside curmudgeonly thoughts.

"So tell me about this Edison person. Is he any good? What's his background?"

She was curled up in her seat as best she could manage with a seat belt on and still a bit sleepy despite the coffee. "I don't know much about him personally. He's in his late sixties, never finished college. Wrote his first novel as a teenager in 1963 and became reasonably popular within the genre, although his career didn't really take off until 1970, when the Tolkien craze had publishers looking at fantasy in a whole different way. *Revenge of the Necromancer* was the first fantasy novel to make the *New York Times* bestseller list. His early stuff got reprinted and he started turning out a new book every year or so. By 1980 he was the most successful American fantasy novelist of all time."

"Is he just popular or is he good?"

Dusty wrinkled her forehead. "That depends, actually. His early stuff certainly was original and nicely done though occasionally awkward, but during the 1980s he just started cranking out sequels and variations of his earlier stories. A lot of writers run out of steam somewhere along the line. His books were always readable and his fans kept buying them, but the critics were less kind. He was doing two or three books a year by the late 1980s and they all felt the same."

"Why work harder than you have to if the public is willing to pay for stuff that's just okay?"

"I guess. Anyway, about twenty years ago he turned the spigot off. There were no new books for three years and people began to think he was going to do a Salinger."

I knew about Salinger. "So he became reclusive."

"No, he'd always been like that, kind of remote and mysterious. I told you he stays out of the public eye. The only picture of Edison that I've ever seen was taken about the time his first novel came out."

"Obviously he started writing again."

"Recharged his batteries, I suppose. He slowed down to his previous pace though, one book per year, and everything was new. He dropped all of his recurring characters and settings and started off fresh. Wouldn't allow his publisher to reprint anything from his manic period, although the early work had nice new editions with matching covers. The new stuff was great. He's created a whole mythological background for his Merrivale series and a clever magical system for the Father Auburn stories. He even started getting a lot of attention in academic circles. They call him J.K. Rowling for adults."

"I thought most of her readers WERE adults."

"Don't be picky."

Culloden was only a few miles past Keene but there was no highway and it took half an hour to get there through a series of secondary roads. Damon had provided the phone number and address of the Culloden Inn, which was in what passed for a downtown, just across from a butcher shop and next door to a gas station/convenience store. Unlike most rural New England towns, Culloden did not have a central green or a white painted church with a tall spire, just a boxy little building for the Methodists and a hideous concrete and glass structure for the Episcopalians. The town had only been incorporated during the 1940s and had sprung up around a nearby mill complex, currently falling into ruins. A picturesque brook cut the commercial district in half. There was a covered bridge, boarded up and festooned with warning signs, and adjacent to it a completely characterless modern construction with rusting handrails.

The Inn, which was actually just a motel with a fair sized diner and a tiny bar attached, had seen better days as well. There were no cars in the parking lot when we arrived, but it was the middle of the day so I would have been more surprised if it had been full. A rather bouncy young man with an improbable southern drawl checked us in, insisting upon calling us "Mr. and Mrs." even after Dusty corrected him, and gave us two keys, though only after an extensive search for the second. I suspected that most of the paying customers were couples who only required a single key and an hour or so of privacy, but the room was clean and almost pleasant looking.

"Are we likely to meet other party guests here?"

Dusty was busily unpacking. She refused to live out of a suitcase even if we were only spending a single night and I knew better than to suggest otherwise. For want of anything better to do, I imitated her, burying the Gideon Bible under some clean underwear. There were the usual bits of paperwork on the desk including a menu for the diner – there was no room service – advertisements for local businesses masquerading as helpful information, a chart of the fire exits, a list of helpful telephone numbers, and an empty envelope marked "housekeeping gratuity" that looked like it had been sitting unused for years. Checkout time was nominally eleven.

"Yes, we are." It had been so long since I had asked the question that I had to do a mental rewind to figure out what she was talking about. "A couple of people are staying at the house but it's not big enough for all of us."

"Edison's not entirely a hermit then."

We ate lunch at the diner. The fish and chips were edible enough, to my great relief. We hadn't seen anything but fast food places for the last half hour of the drive and I didn't want to go all the way back to Keene just to get a decent meal. Dusty somehow managed to engage the waitress in conversation and asked her if she knew who Martin Edison was and if he ever ate there.

"I guess most folks out here know of him, but we don't see him very often and I don't think he's ever been here. His housekeeper, Mrs. McCone, comes in once in a while for coffee and pie. She likes her sweets, though you'd never know it by looking at her. His son is around from time to time and the young girl goes to school here in town."

Dusty frowned. "I didn't know Edison had a daughter."

The waitress laughed loud enough that heads turned in the adjacent booth. "She's not his, dear. His new secretary brought the baby along when she moved in with them. The story is that he wasn't any too happy about it either. Seems the mother forgot to mention that detail when she applied for the job. But he gave her a trial and it must have worked out because she's still here fifteen years later."

I smiled at the concept that someone who had lived here for fifteen years might still be considered "new" but then again, compared to most people in Culloden, that was probably accurate.

The waitress wandered away and we ate for a while without talking.

"So what's the agenda for tomorrow?" I asked.

"We're invited over any time. They're doing a big brunch outside and a barbecue in the afternoon. The formal part isn't until evening. I guess there'll be some reporters and photographers but probably not a whole lot of them. Damon says it was very hard to convince Edison to have his picture taken and he only agreed because he has some secret announcement he wants to make at the same time."

"I can hardly wait."

After lunch we drove around town, which did not live up to the promises of its website. Once we were away from the town center, the trees were pretty, not turning yet but starting to show hints of color around the edges. The sky was bright blue with just a handful of thin white clouds as an accent. Mount Brandoch, where the reclusive Mr. Edison made his home, was picturesque but not impressive, worn down by time and the elements, inclined away from us so that the peak seemed like a secondary rise in the distance. The brook babbled nicely. The town itself, however, was even uglier than its first impression had suggested. Most of the houses were in need of roof repairs, new siding, or both. Several had windows boarded up. Older model cars sat in driveways or more often in backyards, sometimes without tires. Four of the ten shops in town were closed, apparently not just for the season – if Culloden actually had a season. There was a donut shop in town to provide the only competition for the Culloden Diner, the Methodist and Episcopalian churches, a coin operated laundry, a combination police station/post office tucked up beside the Culloden Volunteer Fire Department, which had one engine and one ambulance. Martin Edison might be making a lot of money with his writing, but he wasn't spending it here. No theater, no library, no playgrounds except a tiny enclosed one at the Cullodon Combined School, kindergarten through 12th grade. A practice schedule for the Culloden Highlanders basketball team was posted near the front door, but it was a year out of date.

Dusty suggested we return to our room and amuse ourselves there, and since I had a pretty good idea what she meant, I agreed enthusiastically. Unfortunately, we were waylaid in the parking lot, which now contained half a dozen cars, all from out of state. One of them was parked next to our slot and a tall man with longish but immaculately coifed hair was just locking the driver's side door when we arrived. Dusty was out of the car the second I stopped.

"Hey, Damon. Welcome to New Hampshire."

The view from the trail must have been impressive during the daylight. I could see for miles in every direction but only two or three building protruded above the tree line. We were on the opposite side of the mountain from the closest town and this area was partly state park, partly undeveloped woodland. I'm not really fond of heights and the trail was quite narrow from time to time, but there was a wide ledge a few feet below us that extended out toward the abrupt drop off, and it was reassuring to know that a misstep would not send me plunging hundreds of feet to my death.

Our guide had slowed suddenly but there was no change in the terrain, so I assumed we must be near our goal. We had been given an approximate description but so much of the trail seemed the same to me that I had given up trying to anticipate the end of our climb. The tension was palpable; I felt it in my upper back and shoulders now.

There was a sudden dip in the trail and then a level stretch. We were moving at only half our previous pace despite the easier going. A few seconds passed and then we stopped. No one spoke but our guide raised an arm and pointed to his right. I glanced down onto the ledge and saw the outline of a dark shape hunched over and leaning back against a half buried boulder worn smooth by rain and wind. Without thinking I moved closer to the edge so that I could see better, but the figure was in shadow and all that I could say for certain was that it was a human being.

All four of us were motionless for a moment, and then three of us moved.

Damon Wright turned in our direction and I saw the rather leonine face of a man who looked to be in his late fifties or early sixties. I was sure he was coloring his hair. He raised one hand in greeting and his face broke out in a broad but artificial smile that I instinctively found offputting. "Ready for the big day, Dusty? Remember, if you're disappointed in the great man, it's not my fault. I warned you he has feet of clay, not to mention an unpredictable but usually bad temper."

Dusty took him by the arm and led him over to where I was deliberately taking my own sweet time locking the car manually rather than using the remote. "Damon Wright, this is Paul Birch, the most important person in my life. Paul, this is the second most important, my agent."

Wright's smile seemed to falter slightly but he made a quick recovery while shaking my hand. "Ah, the detective."

"Investigator," I said quietly. "More like a forensic accountant. Dusty likes to tell people I'm Sam Spade or Philip Marlowe so they're almost always disappointed when they finally meet me."

"Nonsense. Every job has its own kind of romance. Even mine. Sometimes a little too much in fact." He looked momentarily thoughtful. "Are you just arriving?"

"No," said Dusty. "We drove up this morning. We've been out seeing the sights."

"That should have taken about five minutes. If you travel about twenty miles north from here or drive around to the other side of the mountain, the countryside is much nicer. I used to have a little house up that way, but I never seemed to find the time to make use of it so I finally sold it to a friend." Wright glanced toward Mount Brandoch. "Martin's house is quite nice actually and he has a great view because he's high enough that you can't see the dingy details. And his place faces in the other direction."

"As though he'd turned his back on the town," I ventured.

Wright gave me a startled look. "More truth than jest. I don't know where he spends all of his money, but it's certainly not here." He walked around and opened his trunk, removed a large suitcase and a briefcase. "I've got some work to do but why don't we meet for dinner? The diner isn't going to win any awards but the food is decent."

"We had lunch there," said Dusty. "It was fine."

"It's a date then. 6:30?" He looked back and forth between us and we both nodded. "See you then." His room was two doors down from ours. He probably hadn't gotten inside before Dusty and I were in our own and halfway undressed.

Dinner was slightly awkward. I couldn't quite put my finger on what was wrong, but Wright seemed vaguely uncomfortable. When Dusty started talking about her new novel, he excused himself for a trip to the men's room and when he came back he had someone else with him, a tallish man who was in danger of becoming seriously overweight and who combed his long, graying hair into an odd pattern to insufficiently conceal a bald spot. "Look who I found."

Since neither Dusty nor I had any idea who the man was, this elicited no response. Undeterred, Wright plowed on. "This is James Patrick." Both men looked back and forth between us but the name rang no bells for me and apparently not for Dusty either. "You know, *Danger is My Duty*, the Demolisher series."

Dusty perked up. "Oh! Remo Williams. I saw the movie." I still hadn't a clue.

"That's the Destroyer," said Patrick quietly. "My hero is named Griff Standish."

Of course he is, I thought, but tactfully refrained from saying.

Wright decided to minimize a festering faux pas. "James is going to join us if neither of you mind."

"The more the merrier," I said, trying to get into the spirit of things.

"James is a neighbor of yours," said Wright.

"Are you from Providence?" Dusty asked.

Patrick, who looked somewhat embarrassed by now, shook his head. "Boston, actually. New Yorkers assume that anything outside the city is close together."

We all pretended to laugh.

"So what's your connection to Martin Edison?" asked Dusty.

Patrick glanced away. "Actually I've never met him and I don't read or write his sort of story. I think it might have been arranged by a mutual friend."

I had the distinct feeling that Patrick was not telling the truth, or not all of it, which had its usual effect. I was more interested now than I had been. "You share the same agent, don't you?" I glanced at Wright, who immediately shook his head.

"James is not one of our clients, although I keep telling him he'd do better with us. Thrillers and men's action are our specialty."

Patrick seemed more at ease now, although his laugh was forced. "I've been with Mike Lanyard ever since I started in the business. He does all right by me and he stuck at it when I couldn't sell a thing. He's kind of a lone wolf, only has a handful of clients. I'd be leaving a pretty big hole in his income."

"You have to put your own interests first, James. Writing is a very competitive business. Aren't I right, Paul?"

"I wouldn't know," I said tactfully. "I've only known one writer up until today."

The food came shortly afterward and the conversation became more general. The steak was overdone but not fatally. Wright kept trying to talk about publishing and Patrick kept changing the subject. At one point the latter asked me if I'd ever done any hunting. "There's some good deer country north of here."

"I was brought up in a city and no one in my family hunted so I never thought about it."

Wright dismissed the subject. "A bunch of yahoos running around in the woods with guns. I don't see the attraction. I wouldn't have one in my house."

Patrick shrugged it off. "It's not for everyone."

Everyone did, however, seem to enjoy the food and conversation died off. Patrick was the first to take his leave. "I have some calls to make." Wright started to follow but Dusty put a hand on his arm.

"I don't know how busy things will be tomorrow so maybe we should talk about my new project now."

Wright looked decidedly uncomfortable and I had a feeling that I should make myself scarce. "If you two are going to talk business, I think I'll walk off some of my dinner. Catch you back at the room, Dusty."

I poked around for half an hour or so. It was a pleasant night and in the dark the area didn't seem quite as homely. A man and a woman with British or Australian accents were arguing loudly in one of the rooms I passed on the way back but I tuned them out. Dusty wasn't back yet so I took off my shoes and lay down on the bed with the new John Sandford novel. I only managed to get through four pages before the door opened and then closed with moderate violence.

"I take it your conversation didn't go well." I could tell that Dusty was mad even before I saw her face. The position of her shoulders, a general stiffness in her body, the way she clutched her bag were all pretty good clues. The fact that she slammed the door was pretty telling as well. Dusty never slammed doors.

"Damon Wright is an unimaginative, condescending, jerk. He wouldn't recognize a good idea if it reared up and bit his nose off. No wonder publishing is in such a sorry state." I opened my mouth, then closed it. Dusty's fury was self sustaining and as long as it wasn't directed at me, I wasn't going to meddle. "He told me that fantasy readers don't want originality just more of the same, preferably with cookie cutter characters, and that I shouldn't waste my time on it. Then he suggested a three book deal for more Dan Craig spy thrillers. No wonder he's been courting James Patrick. He wants to fill my slot in someone's publishing schedule."

"But you said he represents Edison, didn't you?"

"Edison isn't just a fantasy writer. He's a certain bestseller and bestsellers are a kind of super genre of their own. Damon doesn't have to work to sell the next Martin Edison fantasy. He just announces its existence and solicits bids." She laughed nastily. "He won't have much luck replacing Edison on his client list if the rumors are true. There's only one of him in a generation."

"Then it's not Wright dumping Edison?"

She sat down on the bed beside me, her anger dropping to a dull simmer. "Damon would put up with almost anything to keep Edison as a client so it has to be the other way around. I told you, Edison is notoriously fickle about agents, even though he's never really had anything to complain about that I've ever heard. Except the movie maybe, and that was before Wright."

"The movie?"

"Yeah. *The Wizard of Wayfare*. It was the first in the Corsus the Wanderer series. Some European film company wanted to buy the rights and do a big budget version back when all the studios first started looking for long term franchises. Edison refused to even consider a deal at first but his agent at the time – I don't remember her name – finally talked him into it, promising that there would be all sorts of safeguards in the contract to preserve the integrity of the story. Edison was to be script consultant."

"I can see where this is going. Consultant is one of those wishy washy words that doesn't imply any actual authority."

Dusty nodded. "Theoretically Edison had the right to be on the set and veto things if he wasn't happy but Edison never goes anywhere voluntarily and the film company wasn't anxious to have him around anyway, for obvious reasons."

"Did the movie have anything to do with the book?"

She laughed. "Well, most of the character names were the same and there was a wizard in it, but instead of being a thoughtful, scholarly type he was played by some muscular blonde guy who never covered his chest during the entire film. The young girl who wanted to be the first female wizard was ten years old in the book, about twice that in the movie, and she had two topless scenes. The war with the barbarians - mostly offstage in the novel – became a thirty minute long battle scene."

"So the movie tanked and I take it Edison disapproved."

"Actually, the movie did very well. But Edison was so outraged that he wouldn't sell rights to the sequels or any of his other work and he fired his agent." She shrugged and started to undress. "I guess Edison and I have more in common than I realized."

"How's that?"

"I just fired my agent."

"How did he take it?'

She gave me a half smile. "I'd like to say he was devastated but truthfully he seemed relieved. My stuff hasn't done badly but my last three books were in three different genres and that kind of pattern doesn't generate a following. None of them were bestsellers, although I came close once. Agents, like publishers, are fixated on the few who can generate the big dollars, even if that means publishing fewer books – though in larger quantities. If one writer is lost there are hundreds of wannabes to take her place. It's all product. There's some really bad writing coming from publishers who should know better, and the self published stuff is generally even worse."

"So will you get another agent?"

She nodded. "I was approached by another agency a few weeks ago. I still have their card."

"So is tomorrow still on or not?"

Dusty looked surprised. "Of course it is. I can't wait."

One of us was going to have to climb down to the ledge and even though I hesitated I knew it was going to be me. It wouldn't be physically difficult. I could see the ghost of a path where other hiker had descended in the past. I wasn't really dressed for this kind of adventure; I was wearing my new suit and I had visions of tearing a sleeve or falling and ripping the pants, but I wasn't going to suggest that either of my companions take my place. I could almost read their thoughts. I was the detective so presumably I was used to physical exertion. It wasn't true; I wasn't that kind of person, but I would have felt like an idiot trying to argue the point.

None of this took very much time to work out in my mind. There was always the chance that this was a false alarm, that the motionless figure below us was simply caught up in the beauty of the countryside or had fallen asleep. But I knew that wasn't what had happened, even if I didn't know anything else.

I tested the ground with one foot. It was firm and didn't appear at all slippery. "I'll go down and take a look," I said quietly. No one answered.

I didn't sleep very well. Cars came and went constantly, or so it seemed. I would doze off for a while, then wake up feeling as though something had just happened that I needed to deal with. Around two in the morning, my right leg cramped and I couldn't find a comfortable position. I stood up very carefully and walked around in my bare feet for a while, kneading the muscle in my thigh with one hand. I'm not sure why I went to the window because it was quiet outside, but I did so and parted the curtains slightly.

The parking lot was brightly lit and, at first sight, completely deserted. The darkness beyond was impenetrable, like a solid wall, and I could barely make out the base of the motel's sign, which had been turned off for the night. I was about to turn away when a spark of light caught my attention, winking at me from the base of a flagpole that probably hadn't seen Old Glory in years. It moved slightly and I realized I was looking at the end of a cigarette. Someone was standing with his or her back against the flagpole, having a smoke. It seemed innocuous enough, even when I spotted a second figure that emerged from the shadows and joined the first.

The newcomer was clearly a woman with very long hair but I couldn't make out her features. Idly curious, I watched as they appeared to speak to one another. The smoker suddenly tossed down his cigarette and the two of them became one figure briefly. The embrace went on for quite a while and I would have turned away even more quickly than I actually did if I hadn't briefly seen the man's face. It was a face I recognized.

I slept much better after that.

Dusty is usually a grump in the morning so we didn't say much before breakfast. A cup of coffee smoothed some of her inner wrinkles and she actually made conversation with the waitress – the same one as before - when her scrambled eggs arrived. "I never sleep well in a strange place," she complained.

"But you like to travel."

"I am large. I contain multitudes."

"Not all that large, but I get your point. We've got a couple of hours to kill. Want to do anything in particular?"

"I think we saw all the local tourist spots in about ten minutes yesterday. Did you have anything else in mind?"

The diner was filling up. A couple took the table next to us and the man had a distinct British or Australian accent. His wife, if that's who she was, said nothing. She had very long hair. James Patrick had already been there when we arrived, but he was sitting at the counter staring into a cup of coffee and I don't think he'd noticed us. I felt no urge to invite him to our table. There was no sign of Damon Wright, but he hadn't struck me as a morning person, which is just as well. Dusty has a talent for inventive sarcasm which she exercises freely when she is cranky. If we got ourselves banned from the diner, we risked starvation.

"How about a scenic drive to clear our heads?" I'd been up well before Dusty and used my laptop to do some research. There was some pretty country not far away, well within range for some slightly too early leaf peeping before we met the great man.

"Works for me."

We circumnavigated Mount Brandoch using the GPS to avoid getting lost. There was a Girl Scout Camp on the opposite side, and a couple of antique stores nestled against the base of the mountain. I had turned up a connection to Edison thanks to Google. "Edison used to own almost half the mountain. He filed a complaint against the Scouts back in the 1980s because they were straying onto his property, then had a change of heart about ten years later and donated a huge chunk of land to them on condition that it not be used for any purpose other than scouting during his lifetime." I had spent an hour looking into the past of our soon-to-be-host, looking for conversational gambits if they should become necessary. There was a great deal online about his books. There wasn't very much about him as a person. The only pictures I found were a couple from the 1960s and one very grainy snapshot taken by a fan at a book signing in 1983.

"Can we stop at that antique store? I promise I'll only be a minute." Dusty was addicted to antique stores, but fortunately rarely bought anything. "Damon told me once that Edison gave a lot of money to charities but generally avoided publicity." The drive had finished the job the coffee started and Dusty seemed to have returned to her usual jauntiness.

I remembered the previous evening's eavesdropping. "That reminds me. Do you know if the infamously obtuse ex-agent is married?"

"Divorced. He once told me that he made the mistake of mixing business with pleasure early in his career and married one of his clients. I don't think it lasted very long."

"How about lately?"

She shrugged her shoulders. "Why are you so interested?"

"Because last night I saw him smooching with someone in the parking lot. Maybe he brought a girlfriend with him on the trip."

Her eyebrow went up. "If he did, why didn't she join us at supper last night?"

"Maybe she hadn't arrived by then."

"What did she look like?"

I shook my head. "She was facing away when they weren't in a clinch. A bit on the short side, long hair, average build."

"Could be almost anyone. Rumor has it that Damon is insatiable." She paused. "Interesting though." I parked and we went inside. Everything was old and dusty. By the time we left, even Dusty was dusty, but at least she didn't buy anything.

We arrived at the Edison estate at 10:30. The last couple of miles were over a gravel covered road barely wide enough for two cars to have passed one another, particularly since the forest closed in from both sides as though to bar our passage. The branches formed an impenetrable canopy overhead and turned late morning into early dusk. They also muffled sound, apparently, because traffic noise and other audible hints of civilization ceased almost immediately after we turned off the paved highway. The road wound back and forth quite a bit, usually rising before us, following natural features, and Dusty once insisted she'd seen some deer in the distance. I was concentrating on not running into a ditch too intently to look where she was pointing.

After a few minutes we emerged into a grassy meadow that extended down the slope to our right until scrub growth reasserted itself, and up to our left where it eventually reached a line of pine trees so uniform that they looked as though they'd been manufactured. We saw the house a few seconds later, also surrounded by meadow as well as a sprinkling of pine and spruce. There was an extensive garden on a level shelf just above the main building, with a greenhouse and some kind of shed. The house didn't seem all that grandiose to me but in part that was because the landscape dwarfed it. Edison, I later learned, had built it during the 1970s, inspired by Rudyard Kipling's home in Vermont, although on a somewhat larger scale. There were three floors with seven bedrooms and three baths. The ground floor consisted of a kitchen that would have serviced a small restaurant, a dining room that could comfortably seat two dozen, a living area with an elaborate fireplace, Edison's office and a good sized library, along with one of the three bathrooms. The other two baths were on the second floor with all of the bedrooms. The top floor consisted of a billiard room, a secondary library which held multiple copies of each of Edison's novels, and some general storage space, mostly filled with furniture and off season clothing. There were two staircases, one at the center of the building, the other at the kitchen end of the house. There was a balcony at the opposite end of the house with a narrow spiral staircase that served as a fire escape.

There was also an extensive porch that ran around the front and the side lacking the balcony, a portion of which could be closed off from the elements during the winter. There was a laundry room and more storage under the porch. The "garage" was a stable that Edison had renovated when he tore down most of the original house and it could have easily accommodated up to eight vehicles. A man in his thirties came out of the house when we drove up and gestured for us to take one of the stalls, which I did.

He was standing, shifting his weight from one foot to the other, while we got out and I automatically locked the door. His face had what I can only call a "hunted" look, as though he wasn't used to dealing with strangers. "Everyone is in the house. Go right on in."

There was a sliding glass door at the rear and we stepped through into a small hallway. The main staircase was directly in front of us with a polished wood banister and carpeted steps. The narrow corridor to our left led into a narrow pantry. To our right was the dining room with a fully stocked bar at the far end. Most of the furniture looked like it belonged in a museum. The only person in sight was a tallish woman about sixty years old wearing a dark gray pants suit. She was frowning when I first saw her, but her expression immediately changed to faux heartiness and she waved at us.

"Come on in. I'm Naomi. You must be James Patrick." She ignored Dusty completely and reached out to shake my hand.

I smiled but shook my head. "Sorry, but I'm just supercargo. My friend here is the writer."

"Dusty Rhodes, but I currently write as Dorian Snow." The women nodded to each other but neither extended a hand.

"You write westerns?" Her expression suggested skepticism.

"No, my last book was a spy novel. I'm working on a fantasy series at the moment."

"Oh, that's nice. I never read that sort of thing but I'm sure you're very good at what you do."

This wasn't going very well but I was smart enough not to inject myself while they were pawing at the turf.

"I didn't catch your name."

"Naomi. Naomi Winstead. I write children's books. You might have heard of the Poppy White series?"

"I'm afraid not."

Actually, I had bought one of them as a Christmas present for my niece a while back, based on a store clerk's recommendation. I could mention it and ingratiate myself with Winstead while annoying Dusty or I could remain tactfully silent. Not being stupid or suicidal, I chose tactful. I was pretty sure that Dusty knew about the Poppy White books despite her denial.

"Well, follow me and I'll introduce you. Martin has nominated me as acting hostess."

There were two parallel passages to the next room and we took the one to the right. Several people were scattered among two couches and a handful of chairs. The room was dominated by the oversized fireplace, in which a low fire was crackling merrily away. An older man stood leaning against the mantle, hair and moustache gray, his clothing obviously expensive but somehow old fashioned. He was sucking on a pipe that didn't appear to have been lit and looked like an aging Sherlock Holmes. At the far end of the room, a narrow table offered a variety of food and drink. A teenager with long blonde hair was refilling a pitcher with what I assumed was lemonade under the watchful eye of the darkest woman I had ever seen. Her skin was so black that the word "ebony" came to mind, and she was wearing a scarlet dress that would have looked lurid on most women. The contrast was eye catching. She leaned down and said something softly to the teenager, who nodded and left by the far passage. The black woman glanced over the table for a second or two and followed.

Predictably, the only person I recognized immediately was Damon Wright, who sat on a couch engrossed in conversation with a very thin man with pale skin wearing an ascot and vest. Whoever the latter was, he seemed uncomfortable or bored or both. I would later discover that he always looked this way, as though his inner transmission had failed and he could no longer shift gears. I suspect he practiced in front of a mirror.

The woman with long hair whom I'd seen in the restaurant sat in a chair alone, her expression glum, eyes focused on some distant object invisible to the rest of us. The second couch held two men, one of whom was the one with the British accent I'd notice in the diner. He wore a turtleneck and jacket while the other sported a three piece suit and looked like a generic business executive. A woman sat in a chair next to them, apparently listening intently. She had long blonde hair with a hint of gray that hid most of her face. I guessed – correctly as it turned out – that the man at the mantle was Martin Edison and that the blonde woman was his secretary and mother of the teenager. I could never have identified Edison from the pictures I had turned up. There was no sign of James Patrick.

At the time I expected them to be a dull, even tedious group. I might have thought differently if I'd realized that one of them would be dead before the end of the day.

It wasn't quite as easy a descent as I'd expected. A twisted spruce tree dropped its shadow across the slope and I couldn't really see where I was placing my feet. At one point a rock turned under my heel and I momentarily lost my balance, but I recovered in time to save myself a fall. Then I put my weight on a slippery patch and twisted awkwardly, reaching out for something to hold onto. My right knee scraped across an exposed root and I said something impolite under my breath.

Finally I reached the ledge. I glanced up at my companions and gave a little wave to indicate I was all right and to delay by another few seconds the moment when I would have to approach the hunched figure a few feet away. I called his name and asked if he was all right, but of course there was no answer. I hadn't expected one.

I had not wanted to come to this party. I had not wanted to meet these people, however inoffensive they might be. And I most definitely had not wanted to face a dead body high on a mountainside in the moments when dusk turned to darkness.

But here I was.

Wright spotted us and excusing himself from his companion stood up and came across the room, although I noticed he didn't meet Dusty's eyes. He ignored Winstead, who gave him a look that should have caused internal hemorrhaging, and took Dusty by the arm. "Folks, this is Dusty Rhodes, better known as Dorian Snow, and her friend Paul Birch." He turned and did the introductions clockwise. "That erudite looking gentleman is Arthur Wolfman, who writes insightful if sometimes inciting reviews of some of our books. Next is Peggy Johnson, the producer, who is currently working on a project up in Maine with her husband, who is directing. That's him in the turtleneck sitting next to Hillary Austin, Senior Editor at Pikestaff books, publisher of Martin Edison, among others. Meredith Fallon there is Martin's secretary and right hand woman. And of course the man himself is standing there glowering at me." He glanced at Naomi Winstead . "I assume you've already met Naomi."

Edison did not appear to be happy. "I thought we were expecting someone else. There was apparently some miscommunication between Damon and myself." His tone and expression suggested that he imagined no such thing. "Nevertheless, you are quite welcome Ms. Rhodes and Mr. Burke. Please make yourselves at home and sample the sideboard. Mrs. McCone has taken great pains with it, as she always does on those rare occasions when I provide her the opportunity."

Dusty said something that I didn't quite catch and the individual conversations resumed immediately, with Wright returning to the man in the ascot, Wolfman, while Dusty and I picked our way through to the refreshments, which were in fact quite appealing. I took some shrimp cocktail and cheese on a wafer thin plate while Dusty tried the caviar and some fruit cut into elaborate shapes. The teenager reappeared and I decided she was older than I had originally thought, probably at least sixteen. McCone was right behind her. "The regular coffee is fresh but we're making another pot of decaf." Her voice was firm and confident, not even remotely deferential. "Tracy will bring it out as soon as it's ready."

"Regular is fine," I told her.

Patrick arrived just then, apologizing repeatedly for being late, which he wasn't, and the round of introductions fell to Wright again. He was apparently used to taking charge, obviously enjoyed it, and no one cared enough to interfere, apparently not even Winstead, who was perhaps just as happy to cede her hostess duty to someone else.

We mingled a bit as people began to get up and move around. Actually, Dusty mingled and I smiled and nodded a lot. We got separated for a while after Meredith Fallon took us on a tour of the house and I found myself sitting next to Wolfman, the critic. He was drinking tea and scowling a bit. "A tedious group of people, aren't we?"

I refrained from nodding. "It's always interesting meeting new people."

He snorted. "These aren't new people. They're old inside. Fossilized. So am I, for that matter, but at least I know it. I make my living writing formulaic reviews of formulaic novels because those are the kinds of novels that people buy and those are the kinds of reviews that the editors want to run. They tell me to use phrases that publishers will reprint as blurbs rather than try to actually cast any illumination on the subject matter. Some of my fellow critics have read the 'best book of the century' several times each year."

"Most business is built on some kind of pretense. That's the whole basis of advertising."

Wolfman reached over with his free hand and patted my knee. "That's exactly the problem, you see. Writing has become a business. It used to be that writing was an art and publishing a business, but the line of demarcation got blurry and faded away. I have a doctorate in literature and I use all of my sophisticated training and long years of study to find thematic nuances in stories about feisty young woman with shapeshifting lovers, sturdy men who are immune to hostile gunfire and who have dedicated their lives to bringing the lawless to justice, or nosy women of varying ages who solve murders by happenstance while engaging in crafts or gourmet cooking. Do you know what the subject of my dissertation was?"

It was a rhetorical question so I didn't answer.

"Spiritual Metaphors in the Poetry of Edmund Spenser." He sipped at his tea. "That's Spenser with an S, like the detective." He chuckled at what he thought was a private joke. I've read the Robert Parker novels, but I didn't want to spoil his fun. "What do you do for a living, Mr. Birch?"

"I run a small consulting firm. Security systems, audits, that sort of thing. Minor crimes where the possibility of adverse publicity makes it difficult to use the police." I was not going to identify myself as a detective.

"Sounds boring."

"It often is."

"Life sucks."

I decided to change the subject. "Have you ever reviewed any of Edison's novels?"

"Oh yes. He sells a great many books."

"So what did you think of them?"

I could tell he was considering a clever rejoinder, but he visibly reconsidered. "He writes well enough, but his subject matter is childish. He engages in too many revenge fantasies and his characters are almost always sexually dysfunctional. His invented societies are complex and even original, but they lack context and are sometimes internally inconsistent. So my reviews echo with praise of his limitless inventiveness and mature themes and the depth of his well realized characters." He smiled. "After my last review, he sent me a letter. A note, really. All it said was that he found my invariable veiled sarcasm refreshing. That's probably why I'm at this little get together. It rarely shows up in his fiction unfortunately but I suspect Martin has an impish sense of humor."

Dusty showed up then and rescued me from the need to reply. She and Wolfman shook hands and she complimented him for some review of his she'd read. I cringed but he accepted the praise politely and excused himself to use the bathroom. "Have you seen the gardens yet?" Dusty asked. I had not. We did a brief walk through, during which I was complimented on my patience, and we returned to refill our plates at the sideboard.

The man who had directed our parking appeared a few minutes later and nodded to Edison, who turned and addressed us all. "Ronald tells me that the fire is ready. Shall we go outside?"

The slumped figure might almost have been sitting. One leg was bent at the knee and splayed slightly to one side, the other stretched out awkwardly away from me. It was not a natural pose. The torso leaned back against the rock face with the head tilted slightly to one side. Although it was dark enough now that I would not have been able to see the rise and fall of the chest, I was certain that it was motionless. The coppery smell of blood was faint but noticeable.

The head was partly obscured because the jacket's hood had been pulled up, perhaps to keep the bugs away. I had been waving my arms intermittently to drive them off ever since we left the house, which had bug zappers at either end, but they were persistent and numerous, even more so here because they sensed the blood.

One arm was twisted slightly away from me, but the nearer crossed a thigh. I came closer enough to reach out and touch that hand. It wasn't cold, exactly, but it wasn't warm enough either.

"Is he still alive? Should we come down?"

I glanced up toward the trail and cleared my throat. "Stay where you are. There's nothing we can do for him now."

It was all pretty elaborate. There was an enormous fire pit filled with glowing coals in the center of a slight depression that suggested a miniature stadium, emphasized by the placement of lounge chairs that all faced approximately toward the center. Tables had been set up in strategic locations and there were steaks and chicken breasts waiting to be grilled. Mrs. McCone and the blonde teenager began ferrying food and drink from the house while we admired the flowers again and found places to sit or stand. I had a brief conversation with the editor, Hilary Austin, but since I wasn't anyone who could advance his interests it was superficial and quite short.

Dusty managed to corner Edison, who initially looked annoyed, but when I glanced back a minute or two later he was smiling and even laughed at something she said. I involuntarily eavesdropped on part of a conversation between Peter Johnson and Meredith Fallon. He was trying to convince her to intervene in some indeterminate matter with her boss, Edison, but she kept shaking her head and insisting that there was nothing she could do to help him. Johnson's wife was glaring at them but I couldn't tell who she was targeting.

Noon had passed a while ago and it had warmed up a bit, so I decided I could justify a beer. There were two coolers plus a large stainless steel tub full of cans and bottles surrounded by ice. I found something dark with a twist off cap and opened it.

"Would you like a glass with that?"

I turned and found myself facing Mrs. McCone, who was even more impressive from near at hand than she had been from a distance. She was remarkably attractive and one sensed that her smile was genuine rather than manufactured, although she might be smiling at a private joke. I had thought her about my age but I realized now that she was at least ten years older.

"This is fine. Quite an impressive layout."

"We don't get to entertain very often. Mr. Edison tends to be rather obsessive about his privacy. So when the occasion arises, we do our best."

She acted more like a guest than a servant. "Have you been with him long?"

"Since 1991. I just did the cleaning and dusting and laundry back then, but when Mrs. Wilson died he told me her job was mine if I wanted it, and I did."

"So who does the cleaning and dusting and laundry now?"

"I still do a lot of that, but Tracy helps now and then." She nodded to where the teenager was arranging pastries under a series of mesh domes to keep the insects away.

"It looks like a beautiful area to grow up in."

She gave me a doubtful look. "It's pretty lonely. She has a few friends in town but they never come out here. Mr. Edison doesn't welcome company and I think he scares them away."

"They're probably convinced he has a troll chained in the basement."

Damon Wright came over for a beer and McCone slipped away, but not before I saw her frown. She clearly didn't care for Dusty's former agent.

The next couple of hours are still a bit of a blur. I talked to a number of people but it was that kind of zombie buzz that one produces when speaking to strangers with whom you have no discernible common interests. I do remember trying to speak to Ronald, who spent most of the time watching over the grill. His pained look edged toward acute distress when I asked if he'd been with Edison for very long. He nodded, but didn't speak. In fact, I don't recall him saying a direct word to anyone except Mrs. McCone. Austin mentioned that he had hunted as a boy but no longer had time for it, Winstead told us that her father had wanted sons but had ended up with daughters, and Peter Johnson recommended that we consider vacationing in New Zealand. Those were the memorable bits, believe it or not.

The food was good, however, and I ate rather more than I had intended. Dusty seemed to be having a good time, but that didn't mean anything. She seemed to have a good time at the dentist. I wish that some of the investigators I employed had half her talent of blending in and getting people to say things about themselves that they wouldn't tell close friends. Maybe I should hire her.

Just after two, Hillary Austin announced the schedule for the rest of the day. The photographers had already arrived and were unloading equipment. "The formal reception starts at five, but you're welcome to stay the afternoon, or leave and come back at any time before then. The press conference and photo session are at six and any of you who know Martin will not be surprised that it's going to be very brief. Dinner is at seven. I'd like to thank you all once again for coming and helping to make this special occasion even more special."

Dusty tracked me down a few minutes later. "Why don't we go back to the motel for a while? I need to change into more comfortable shoes."

We hadn't even left the property when Dusty turned to me. "What did you think?"

I was certain that I was in the presence of death and almost certainly a homicide. There was a splatter of blood down one sleeve which looked not quite dry. This was a crime scene and prudence and professional ethics told me that I should leave immediately before I inadvertently contaminated it any further. There was a kind of horrid fascination about the posing of the victim— I was certain it had been moved after the assault, possibly when the body had first been discovered and reported to us, although that seemed unlikely. It had not been an act of concealment. If the killer had been so inclined, it would have been simple to just topple the corpse off the ledge and let it fall into the deep woods below us.

I wasn't going to touch anything, just look around. It was dark enough that I wished I had a flashlight, but not so dark that I couldn't spot anything obvious. A good sized piece of jagged rock lay about three feet away. There appeared to be a dark stain at one end but I couldn't be certain because it lay in shadow. Nothing else was suggestive so I turned back to the body. The hood of the jacket had been pulled up over the head so that I could see most of the face, but nothing else. The eyes were closed, the mouth slack, no real expression. There might not have been long enough to feel any pain.

Although I knew better, I decided to bend the rules just slightly. I reached out slowly and with the back of my hand I slowly lifted one edge of the hood away from the face.

Dusty and I were still in sight of the house when I spoke up. "An unusual mix of interesting people and stuffed shirts."

"Arthur Wolfman is an odd duck." He was indeed the person foremost in my mind. "I think a lot of that world weariness is an act. He likes to play the crusty curmudgeon."

"To cover his heart of gold?"

"No, to cover the fact that he's furious that people whom he considers totally lacking in talent are so much more successful than he is."

"I liked the housekeeper."

"Geneva? Yes, she's a treat. Apparently she's the only one who can keep Edison in line. Hillary told me that he called her and talked her into this little shindig before he even broached the subject to his nibs. That way she could prepare the groundwork and be prepared for any objections."

"Did you notice Mrs. Johnson and James Patrick?"

"She likes to flirt but he was uncomfortable."

"Since her husband was standing about six feet away, I think he had sufficient reason. But he already knew her. I heard her say something about having met on a movie set."

Dusty shook her head. "That's strange. A couple of his novels have been made for cable movies, but the Johnsons are above that sort of thing."

"Any idea why Naomi Winstead was sulking?"

"I noticed that too. Maybe she doesn't like it when she's not the center of attention. She apparently knows Edison better than the rest of us. She and Austin are the only ones staying at the house. The secretary is a nervous wreck as well.'

"Fannnon?"

Dusty nodded. "I was standing beside her when she poured a cup of coffee. Her hands were shaking."

"Maybe she just doesn't like crowds. She has a cute kid though."

"You're not supposed to notice the desirability of any woman except me."

"She's not a woman yet."

"Don't quibble."

We dressed up slightly at the motel. Austin insisted that it was all going to be very informal, but he had done so in that exaggerated way that suggests otherwise. Dusty had picked up a very handsome pants suit that made her look quite professional. I kept finding excuses not to leave right away but eventually submitted to the inevitable. We were technically the last to arrive but Naomi Winstead had gone up to her room "for a nap" and most of the others were standing near the bar. The photographers had requisitioned the cozy little den because it was the most photogenic place in the house – although almost any other room that I'd seen would have done as well. The downstairs bathroom was fancy enough that it could have hosted a poker game and everything was neat and clean. Either Edison had very high standards or more likely McCone did.

There was a bit of a scene a short while later. Winstead stormed downstairs insisting that someone had been in her room even though she had left strict instructions that her privacy be respected. Mrs. McCone showed up and soothed her down and it turned out that Tracy Fallon had gone in to make up the bed. Winstead did not seem completely mollified but admitted that no damage had been done and she even managed a sour apology for having over reacted. She had been on edge all day as far as I could tell and it obviously didn't require much of an excuse for her to fly into a rage. There was also some kind of flareup between Wolfman and Wright. They were out in the garden and I walked in on them as they stood glaring at each other, fists clenched, faces red. Wright turned on his heel and stalked off and Wolfman made some deprecating remarks about boys being boys. I found an excuse to move on quickly.

The rest of the press wasn't due to arrive for almost two hours and some of the guests had apparently grown tired of each other's company. A few had wandered off to explore the "nature trails" surrounding the house, either alone or with a companion. Mrs. McCone assured us that there was no chance of getting lost. "They're all well marked with colored crosses painted on rocks and trees. White cross is the easiest and red the hardest, but they're all petty safe except the blue dot trail. I wouldn't try that one for a casual walk. There are a couple of real bad spots thanks to all the rain we had last month. But I do suggest that everyone get back before dark."

Winstead denied having any interest in hiking. "I'm a city girl born and bred. The closest I get to nature is a window garden, and even then I need a native guide." Dusty was restless but I'd broken a toe a month earlier and wasn't up to a hike so she went by herself. I was as a consequence trying to escape from Winstead, who was regaling me with stories about the perfidy of publishers in the children's book business, when Damon Wright joined us, apparently having gotten over his tiff.

"Where is everybody?" We told him as much as we knew. "That's right. Hillary told me that the view from some of the trails is spectacular. I suspect this is my final visit up here so I suppose this might be my last chance. Anyone up for it?"

Edison appeared from nowhere, obviously having overheard us. "The red dot trail is the one you want. It's pretty buggy right now though. It stayed warm longer than usual this year and we had a lot of rain again last week. Normally we're almost bug free by now."

"That's all right. Apparently I don't taste good. I can walk unscathed through a cloud of mosquitoes."

"Can't get blood from a stone." Edison smiled and pushed on before Wright could take offense. "You won't want to wear that jacket. You'll snag it for sure." Wright was wearing an obviously expensive three piece suit. "Let me get to that closet." We shuffled aside and Edison opened a remarkably well organized storage space, foraged for a few seconds, then emerged with a light gray jacket equipped with a hood. "I'll swap you, but it's only a loan. This is my favorite." The silhouette of a cloaked wizard graced the back of the jacket.

Wright removed his tailored jacket and Edison hung it up. He looked a bit silly with linen pants and vest partly covered by the mildly disreputable hoodie, but it looked to be a lot more practical arrangement for scrambling around in the woods. "You can put the hood up if the bugs decide you're delectable after all. Sometimes they get desperate."

"You sure you don't want to come along?" Wright was looking at Winstead, who shook her head. "We haven't talked in ages."

"No way. In fact I think I might lie down again for a while. My allergies have been acting up and antihistamines always give me a headache."

I turned away as well but Edison took my elbow. "Actually, I wanted a chance to speak to you in private, Mr. Birch. Join me in my office for a minute, won't you?"

The fabric of the hood was stiff and in places stuck to the skin and hair beneath it. I tugged gently but decided that it didn't matter. It was too dark now to make out any details, particularly here in the shadows. The left cheek was covered with sticky, partially dried blood. My stomach turned a little but I told myself to view this objectively, as an object rather than a person. After all, it wasn't really a person any more.

But then I noticed the curvature of the right side of the skull, which was concave where it should have been convex. There was blood on that side as well but I didn't explore any further. I guessed that there had been at least two blows with a heavy object, possibly more. The entire right side of the face was deformed and the crown of the head – though still covered by the hood – seemed unnaturally flat. It was more than I really had wanted to know and I removed my hand, letting the hood fall back in place.

I was surprised to discover that I was breathing rapidly and that my heart was racing. It had felt as though I was a detached observer. I stood up and backed away, trying not to stray from my original path. Without looking up I called out, "He's gone. We'd better call the police."

Our mini-tour hadn't included Edison's office, so when he unlocked the door it was virgin territory. Two of the four walls were lined with bookshelves – reference books, a lot of mythology, some natural history, and odds and ends. There was an enormous walnut desk set under a many paned window, the top of which was very neat. To one side was a smaller one of glass and chrome with two computers set side by side. This area was considerably less organized. There were papers and books scattered apparently at random, at least two wine glasses, and a few paperweights, some of them makeshift. An empty brandy bottle sat on the floor under the table.

"Close the door, will you?"

I did so. Edison opened what I thought was a closet, but it was actually a bar, a smaller version of the one in the dining room. "I keep the really good stuff in here. Can I get you something?"

"I'm good."

He poured himself a small glass of Glenfiddich neat and gestured toward a leather covered couch. I sat, and so did he. He took a sip, closed his eyes, and sighed. "I understand that you're a private detective."

It was my turn to sigh. "My firm does security and related investigation work, mostly for small to medium businesses. I don't have a deer stalker cap, a gat, or a secretary with long, shapely legs."

"Different times call for a different kind of detective."

"True enough."

"As it happens, I'm in need of a bit of investigating myself. Since you're in that line of work, I thought you might at least be able to steer me in the right direction."

"It depends upon the nature of the problem. What is it that you need detected?"

"I need to find out who is trying to kill me."

I've had clients say some pretty provocative things, but this left me momentarily speechless. I rubbed my chin and tried to look thoughtful to cover my surprise, but Edison had turned away. "There have already been three attempts, but obviously none have succeeded."

"Have you notified the police?"

He made a pushing gesture with his free hand, as though the matter wasn't even worth discussing. "They're useless, of course, as I'm sure you already know, though I suppose it's not entirely their fault. Whoever is responsible is clever enough not to be too obvious, but not so clever that I'm not aware of the danger."

For want of anything better to say, I asked when the three attempts had taken place.

"The first was almost two years ago. It was a long shot but it could have killed me and Ronald as well since he was driving. The brake line was cut. Fortunately we weren't in a really dangerous place at the time so Ronald was able to bring us to a safe stop. Nothing damaged but my composure. I had been convinced for several weeks that there was danger in the air. I'm very sensitive to atmosphere, you see, which is one of the reasons I keep pretty much to myself. Crowds tend to bring tension to the forefront, as you may have noticed yourself earlier today."

I hadn't thought about it but he was right. Naomi Winstead was uptight and had made an absurd little scene, the Johnsons hadn't spoken a word to each other all day, Dusty was furious with Damon Wright, James Patrick and Meredith Fallon both seemed preoccupied and worried, and Wolfman was mad at the world in general and Wright in particular. Only Hillary Austin seemed actually to be enjoying himself, and perhaps Mrs. McCone.

"What did the police have to say?"

"Their investigation was perfunctory and inconclusive. Apparently the malfunction might not have been sabotage but simply a subtle defect. They almost had me convinced and I let the matter drop. Then, about six months later, there was another incident. I do a lot of hiking and occasionally camp out on one of the trails over on Mount Bluszco or down along Spitfire Notch. Not so much nowadays because I lack the stamina for a really prolonged hike, but three or four times a year I make the effort to get away by myself. Naturally I always tell Geneva where I'm going to be and I carry my cell phone for emergencies. Anyway, on this occasion I was on Bluszco at the north end of the state park. There's an excellent spot there just above a pretty little brook. I had just set up the tent when I heard a sort of buzzing sound and noticed a hole in the fabric. Two holes, in fact, one on each side. Someone had shot at me."

He gave me a belligerent look, challenging me to argue with him. "And what did the police say that time?"

"They suggested it was probably a stray hunter. They're allowed to hunt on the far side of the park, but there's a safety zone to protect hikers. The shot had to have been fired from inside that perimeter, which was clearly illegal. There have been incidents in the past where someone deliberately violated the rules because they were following a deer and weren't willing to give it up or simply became disoriented and strayed into the wrong area. The rangers looked around for a few hours but they didn't find anybody."

"There was only the one shot?"

"It was the only one I heard. I suppose there could have been others. I'm not ashamed to say that I ran back to the ranger station without investigating."

There was a long pause. "And the third time," I prompted.

"I almost caught him this time."

"Him?"

"Or her. I'm normally a sound sleeper but one night about three months back I found myself wide awake at three in the morning. I tried reading for a while, but that didn't work, so I came downstairs to make myself a cup of tea. We don't bother closing the curtains here while the weather is good. There are no neighbors within a mile and the property is posted. I was in the kitchen when I happened to glance down toward the road. Something moved. Someone actually, and whoever it was stood just outside the window. I called the police and turned on all the downstairs lights. Geneva and Ronald both came down and Ronald went out to look around. The police mistook him for the prowler in fact."

"But obviously whoever it was had disappeared."

"We're surrounded by forest. An elephant could have concealed itself quite easily. The police made a cursory search but even I could see that it was a wasted effort."

"Any physical evidence?"

"A couple of scuffed footprints. They made a cast, I think. No damage or anything."

"Do you keep your doors locked?"

"Of course. There was no obvious attempt at entry but I can't imagine someone going to all that effort just to take something from my garden."

"It might just have been a vagrant looking for something to steal, or a burglar checking the place out to see what kind of alarm system you have."

"The police were more inclined to believe that it was some demented fan trying to visit the great author's home undetected. It used to happen with some frequency although we've been undisturbed for some time now."

"I suppose that's possible." It didn't seem likely. What would be the point of coming in the dark and not seeing anything?

"The police contend that there is no evidence of any connection among the incidents and that all three might be perfectly innocuous. I prefer to think that it testifies to the cunning of my enemy."

Enemy or not, there was more than a slight touch of paranoia here. I decided to tread softly. "Well, it's not really my specialty and I'm not licensed in New Hampshire in any case. If you want, I can ask around and see who's in the area who might be able to help you."

"That would be very kind of you, Mr. Birch. I don't know if you have any idea what it feels like to be insecure in your own home."

Actually I had a very good idea, thanks to my somewhat
involuntary involvement in a murder case earlier in the year. Even if,
as I suspected, Edison's suspicions were without merit, I could
sympathize with his uneasiness. I glanced at my watch. "I suppose
we'd better show our faces. Aren't the press people supposed to be
arriving about now?"

"Not for a while yet, hopefully. I detest publicity, but I
suppose it's a necessary evil. And actually, I have a bit of a surprise
for them, so I'm almost looking forward to it."

"A movie sale? A new series?"

"Something like that. But you're right. I'm hardly being a
good host if I hide from my guests."

There weren't many guests around to hide from. Hillary
Austin was talking to the photographers and Arthur Wolfman was
sitting on the patio reading the latest Stephen King novel – although
he didn't appear to have made much progress. No one else was in
sight except Tracy Fallon, who was wiping down the picnic tables.
Edison went over and spoke to Wolfman, who appeared to be
uncomfortable, so I went out into the garden and tried to wrap my
mind around my conversation with Edison. It was possible that
someone did in fact intend him harm, but I found it hard to believe
that the local police would ignore a credible threat to a prominent
person. The potential negative blowback was too great. In fact, I
suspected they had gone out of their way to investigate and still
came up dry.

I did in fact know someone who was licensed for all of
northern New England who might like a referral, although I hadn't
spoken to her in a while. I decided to call her Monday and see if she
was interested and if she was I'd warn her that the whole thing might
well be pointless. On the other hand, Edison had lots of money and if
spending a little of it chasing windmills made him feel better, then it
was a win-win situation.

The hikers started straggling in half an hour later. Some of
them looked beat, notably the Johnsons who arrived separately –
apparently still not speaking. I was pretty sure Peggy Johnson was
the woman I had seen in the parking lot with Damon Wright and I
wondered if her husband had gotten wind of their little assignation.
Dusty looked as fresh as ever, but she manages to do that even when

she's dog tired. The press people arrived about that same time, two men and two women, not the crowd I had half expected.

Dusty came over and punched my arm. "Is there any cold beer around? My throat is full of pollen or dust or both."

I fetched her one with a glass, which she disdained except in polite company, which this sort of was. "Anything exciting happen while I was gone?"

"Edison wants me to track down a murderous stalker."

"You're making that up."

"Would that I were. I suspect it's paranoia overlaid on a foundation of coincidence, but I know better than to contradict someone's deeply held illusion. It would be like convincing your brother Scott that global warming was real."

Austin started bustling around, herding people into their places for the press conference. Since I was nobody, I was shunted to the rear where I was almost invisible, which was fine with me. Everyone looked excited except for the photographers and Edison, all of whom merely appeared to be bored. There were two shoulder held film cameras and one young woman taking still shots. None of the reporters had familiar looking faces so I assumed they weren't anyone I should know by name. I heard Austin ask a couple of people if they'd seen Wright, but no one had. Edison grumpily told Ronald to go look for him "out on the red dot." Wright was presumably still pursuing his nature walk, or maybe we were lucky and he'd gotten lost. Naomi Winstead had reappeared looking tired and dourer than ever. Her nose and eyes were red and she sneezed occasionally, although very daintily. Apparently her nap hadn't done much good.

Austin gave a signal and things started to roll. He performed some perfunctory introductions of the dignitaries – skipping over me. I wasn't bothered. I suspected that this part would be edited out in any case. Then he launched into an obviously prepared speech, a summary of the career of the "greatest fantasy writer of all time", which was a bit of hyperbole. Edison didn't look flattered; I don't think he was even listening and to be perfectly honest, after the first couple of sentences, neither was I. Apparently nor were the reporters, who began to clear their throats and move restlessly. Austin took the hint and wound down.

"So now I'd like to introduce our host, whose fifty novels have all become classics of the fantasy genre."

Dusty nudged me and whispered. "Well, about half of them anyway. And can a book written two years ago be called a classic?"

I missed the next sentence but then Edison stepped forward. For such a reclusive man, he certainly knew how to physically dominate a room. He paused and looked around as though he was about to address the multitudes from the Vatican balcony. Clearly he liked being the center of attention, if not routinely, at least on this occasion. Then he launched into what was probably also a prepared speech, although it felt spontaneous, explaining that he'd first been driven to write because he had been something of an outcast among his peers and had wanted to invent playfellows. "I was actually surprised to find out that I had a genuine talent for it and that other people would pay to visit my fantasy worlds." There was some more about people who had helped him along over the years – his first editor, his first agent, a few others – though I noticed that neither Hillary Austin nor Damon Wright qualified for beatification.

"*The Feldspar Diadem* brings the latest cycle of novels to an end in a manner which I hope will satisfy my readers. I particularly hope that I've done a good job this time because I am now officially retiring from writing. Fifty books in fifty years is enough. It's time for me to make room for some other lonely kid with a powerful imagination. From now on my personal fantasy worlds will be reserved for my own use."

Climbing back up to the trail was rather more difficult than the climb down and two pairs of helping hands reached out as I struggled toward the top. Then I was on firm ground again, brushing myself off while I caught my breath.

"He must have fallen."

I shook my head. "I'm afraid not. Someone bashed his head in."

I had intentionally been blunt and both of my companions took a step back. Neither of them tried to argue the point."

"We need to call the police right away. And someone needs to stay here and make sure no one disturbs the scene."

I glanced back and forth, but I had already assumed that was going to be my job. I wasn't superstitious and wasn't afraid of waiting in the dark with a dead body, but I wasn't looking forward to it.

There was a moment of silence, then a fusillade of questions from the reporters. I caught a glimpse of Austin's face and his expression made it clear that this was as much a surprise to him as it was to everyone else. He looked quite pale and I wondered just how much of his income was dependent upon his being the preferred editor for the works of Martin Edison. Austin might have to consider shopping at less pricey clothiers in the future.

But as if that wasn't excitement enough, Ronald returned at that precise moment. He was red faced and out of breath and he nearly stumbled as he entered the room. "He's dead! I found him up on the trail and he's dead!"

The double surprise caught everyone in mid-reaction so a few seconds passed before Martin Edison's clearly irritated voice – he evidently didn't like someone stealing his thunder – asked Ronald what he was talking about.

The younger man made a visible effort to control himself but only partially succeeded. "It's Mr. Wright! He's up on the red dot trail, down on the overlook. Someone bashed his head in and he's not breathing!"

The cameraman had swung reflexively to film the newcomer, so that's the clip that appeared on the evening news.

Ronald was hyperventilating and pale. Mrs. McCone appeared out of nowhere and spirited him away before anyone could object. Edison was the first to recover. "Ronald is excitable but not delusional. Obviously something has happened to Mr. Wright and we need to determine what it is. Mr. Birch, you're the closest we have to a policeman. Would you come with me, and perhaps you as well, Mr. Patrick?"

My foot throbbed in protest but I nodded and Patrick, after a brief hesitation, did the same. The reporters and photographers wanted to come as well, but Edison refused to allow it. "You will remain here or you will leave my property immediately. The police will decide what information gets released and what does not. Meredith, would you call Chief Tibbett and apprise him of the situation?" She nodded and walked briskly away.

It was still light out but the sun could drop out of sight quickly in the mountains. We made good time at first, though I was sweating and breathing heavily almost from the start and my bad toe complained a good deal, but then the path grew steeper and narrowed. After about ten minutes during which no one spoke, Edison cautioned us. "The overlook is just ahead. I think the authorities would prefer that we not disturb things any more than is absolutely necessary."

I was the one elected to climb down and examine the body. It didn't take an expert to know that Wright was dead and that it hadn't been an accident. I hadn't liked the man but I hoped he had died quickly.

After climbing back up to the trail, I suggested that someone should stay with the body while the rest went to get the police. To my surprise, Patrick spoke up.

"I'll do it." I must have looked surprised. "It's not the first time I've sat up with a dead body."

I found the remark a bit strange but Edison just shook his head. "All right. We shouldn't be long. The police will probably be there when we get back to the house."

And they were.

Chief Tibbett had come in person. He and Edison greeted each other as Hank and Marty and they were about the same age. I learned later that they'd gone to high school together although they had not been friends. Tibbett was a big man, broad and tall, with a bit of a paunch and some sags here and there, but I sensed that he was not a person one treated lightly. There was also a youngish detective named Thorndyke and two uniformed officers hovered in the background. Thorndyke was wire thin with dark hair and pencil thin moustache. His eyes seemed to be in constant movement. Edison provided a brief summary of what had happened insofar as we knew at that point, leaving nothing out that I could think of. Tibbett gave me a funny look when Edison identified me as a detective.

"Corporate security," I said hastily. "I'm not a gumshoe."

Tibbett frowned. "I thought you were satisfied with that new burglar alarm I recommended, Marty."

Edison shook his head. "Never had it installed. Hate those things. That's not why he's here. He's a guest. In fact, he was invited by accident." He gave me an apologetic look. "Sorry. I imagine this isn't the kind of weekend you were expecting."

An ambulance pulled up and two EMTs got out and began unloading a stretcher. "I guess we'd better attend to the body." Tibbett glanced over at the news people, who were positively panting with anticipation. "One photographer can come with us. No publication of the pictures until it's authorized. That's the deal. Take it or leave it."

They conferred briefly and a youngish man stepped forward.

"Leave the video camera. There's not going to be enough light for it anyway."

Edison glanced at me. "Would you mind playing guide? My legs are a bit unsteady."

He looked about as unsteady as Gibraltar but I nodded. By now the toe was numb and silent but I'd pay for it during the night.

It took longer this time because the light was almost gone. The sheriff and the detective both had flashlights and they examined the body for a while before allowing the photographer to join them and take flash pictures. Patrick was sitting on a fallen tree not far away when we arrived. He'd waved but hadn't spoken. I walked over and sat down beside him. "Anything happen while we were gone?"

He shrugged. "I asked a couple of questions but Wright wasn't talking." He was doing his tough guy act. I could tell because I'd seen people do it before. But even in the encroaching darkness I noticed his hands were shaking.

"I have a feeling it's going to be a long weekend."

"Yeah. Me too."

It took a while to get Wright's body back up to where it could be loaded onto the stretcher. I had told Tibbett about the bloody rock and they tagged and took that as well. The detective had some baggies but they weren't big enough. Tibbett came over to us as they were readying the stretcher for the trip back.

"Someone didn't like this fellow."

"He's a literary agent," said Patrick. "He probably didn't even like himself."

"And you are?" I introduced them. They didn't shake hands. "They'll take the body to the coroner. Meanwhile I imagine Thorndyke and I will have some questions for you folks."

"I imagine you will," I said, my last comment until we had completed the trudge back to the house.

They had asked everyone back at the house to remain together with one of the uniformed officers present, presumably so that no one could concoct a collaborative story unless they borrowed some of the magical talents found in Edison's novels. I went to sit with Dusty, who looked bored and fascinated at the same time. I'm not sure how she managed that. The rest of us joined the group and Tibbett asked Edison to sketch in an outline of the afternoon and evening's events. He did so, accurately as far as I could tell, although obviously he had no idea where most of his guests had been for much of that time. "The hikers pretty much went off by themselves although they might have seen one another. Most of the trails run pretty much parallel or intersect. Birch was with me though. I'm his alibi." Which also meant that I was Edison's.

There was a lot of talking all at once and it took a while for Tibbett to restore order. As far as I could gather in that first rush, we were the only two who were not obviously suspects except for Mrs. McCone and Tracy, who'd been working together in the kitchen together for most of the critical time. McCone had left exactly once. "I was down in the wine cellar for a few minutes. But it wasn't anywhere near long enough for Tracy or I to run to the overlook, bash Mr. Wright, and come back. And Tracy went out to pick some mint but that only didn't take long either."

After some semblance of order had been restored, Patrick said that he had noticed Peggy Johnson sitting under a tree while he was out, but they hadn't spoken and she didn't remember seeing him. Dusty was pretty sure she had spotted Arthur Wolfman from a distance, but he insisted he hadn't left the immediate vicinity of the house and she admitted that it had been more the shape and size that she'd noticed. Wolfman was quite tall, but then again, so were Wright and Austin.

Austin claimed not to have gone out into the woods at all. Wolfman was reading in the garden, so he said. Austin explained that he had spilled something on his shirt. "The photographers were all set so I went upstairs to change into a clean shirt and rehearsed my speech for a while. I'm not big on birds and trees anyway."

Naomi Winstead explained that she had been sleeping – or trying to - and hadn't heard or seen a thing. Almost everyone, by their own admission, had been alone for at least part of the critical time. The photographers and reporters left their names and contact information and were told they could leave. Some of the latter wanted to stay and were rebuffed.

Tibbett was clearly unhappy. I imagine he had hoped for a simple solution. "Martin, do you have a room we could use? We're going to have to interview everyone individually." I noticed that Edison wasn't "Marty" any longer.

The logical choice was Edison's office and he knew it and wasn't happy about it, but with poor grace he suggested that it might suit their purposes. "Are you all staying here tonight?" asked Tibbett.

"Only Mr. Austin and Ms Winstead. The rest are at the Culloden Inn as far as I know, except those who were planning to leave tonight." We all nodded.

"I suggest that each of you call and extend your stay if you were planning to leave today. You won't be going anywhere before tomorrow." There was a general wave of discontent but Tibbett waved it off. "We'll do this as quickly as possible and your cooperation will help us move things along, but this is a murder investigation, obviously, and that takes priority over your personal plans."

The murmuring died out, almost.

"Right. Just give us a few minutes to get organized and we'll get this started." He and Thorndyke followed Edison into the office while we all looked at one another. Mrs. McCone stood up. "It looks like we're going to be here a while, folks. I had planned something a little more formal but a cold platter and hors d'oeuvres ought to work."

One of the two uniforms looked as though he might object, but McCone gave him a look that silenced him. "I don't suppose they'll want any of you others hobnobbing with me in private but I imagine Tracy and I can manage."

I hadn't even noticed the girl was present; she was sitting in her mother's shadow. But the teenager was obviously playing close attention because she sprang to her feet with obvious relief. McCone gestured and the two went off to the kitchen. "Quiet kid," I whispered to Dusty. "I suppose this isn't the kind of house where kids are encouraged run around laughing and shouting."

"Probably not," she agreed. "She's mute."

So much for my trained powers of observation.

They brought people in to be interviewed one at a time. Each interview ran at least fifteen minutes and some went over half an hour. Those of us who remained dozed off while others returned to the motel or, in Naomi Winstead's case, went upstairs to bed. They called Dusty in toward the end – Patrick, Meredith Fallon, and I and the servants were all sitting close together, although there was no conversation. Ronald sat all by himself in a corner, looking shell shocked and not speaking. He had been the first one they interviewed but he'd rejoined the group and didn't seem to know what to do with himself. Mrs. McCone spoke to him softly and he nodded but didn't move. She patted his shoulder, then set about clearing away the remains of the food she'd brought out. Tracy was back curled up on the couch next to her mother and both of them appeared to have fallen asleep.

Dusty returned from her interview looking subdued and slightly angry, if I was reading her correctly. There was no chance to talk to her since I was next.

Thorndyke sat at the desk facing me while Tibbett was off to my left, just outside my immediate field of vision. The preliminaries were formulaic – name, address, occupation. They were obviously not impressed that I was an investigator but they did allude to it right away. "Do you have much experience with this sort of thing?"

I sighed. "None at all, actually. I deal with fraud, embezzlement, missing persons, security procedures, sometimes background screening. We don't normally get involved with crimes more violent than temper tantrums or the occasional outraged spouse."

Thorndyke pushed some paper around, pretending to be consulting his notes. "You're here with Ms Rhodes?"

"Yes."

"How long have you known her?"

"Almost two years. We've lived together for about half that time."

He nodded as though this was significant. "And why was Ms. Rhodes invited?"

I shrugged. "She's a writer. She wanted to come. Her agent – that would be the late Mr. Wright – arranged it somehow. Dusty is one of Edison's fans. She wanted to meet him."

"But you're not?"

"I've never read any of his stuff. Dusty says I lack the ability to suspend my disbelief long enough to enjoy fantasy. I got half way through the first Harry Potter book and quit."

"Yes, well, Mr. Edison tells us that she was not on the list of guests he approved in advance."

"Apparently Mr. Wright took it upon himself to revise the list."

"And why would he do that?"

"He didn't say, at least not while I was present." I didn't actually know that it was to soothe his conscience because he was going to drop Dusty the same weekend, though that's what I suspected, so I felt no obligation to say anything further.

Thorndyke asked me to run through the day's events, which I did fairly easily for the most part. My memory is good and I could have quoted several conversations if I'd tried. The ritual exchanges that I didn't recall wouldn't have interested them in any case. When I mentioned my discussion with Edison about the attempts on his life, if that's what they were, Thorndyke and Tibbett exchanged glances.

"He was convinced that you weren't taking his concerns seriously and wanted to know if I'd be willing to look into the situation. I declined. If the incidents had all occurred within a shorter period of time, I might have been more sympathetic, but spaced out over more than a year, they felt more like coincidence."

Tibbett cleared his throat. "We hadn't completely discounted the possibility that Edison was in danger. But he has a long history of seeing bogeymen under his bed and it wasn't his body that we just sent to the coroner."

"No, but it was someone close to him."

"That's a fact."

Tibbett settled back into his chair. Thorndyke asked if I'd noticed any tension among the attendees and I mentioned what I'd observed about the Johnsons, although I left out the late night encounter in the parking lot since I was speculating about that. "A

couple of people seemed to be a little on edge but that's about it."
There were a few more questions of no consequence after which I
was dismissed. "We'll have a stenographer over at the Inn tomorrow
afternoon to take formal statements. After they're done you'll be free
to go, but we may have more questions later."

I rose, nodded at Tibbett who appeared to have fallen asleep
– although I very much doubted that was the case – and went out to
collect Dusty. She was dozing lightly and stirred when I touched her
shoulder. We had started for the door when Mrs. McCone
intercepted us. "Mr. Edison would like to speak to you for a moment
before you leave, Mr. Birch."

"We're both very tired."

"He said it wouldn't take long. He's waiting in the breakfast
nook."

Dusty tapped my arm. "Give me the keys. I'll bring the car
around."

Edison was wearing a silk dressing gown, appropriately
decorated with wizards and unicorns and fairies. He was drinking
coffee and reading a collection of poems by Robert Frost, which he
set aside after carefully inserting a bookmark.

"Thank you for seeing me. I know you must be exhausted.
Can I offer you some coffee?"

I shook my head. "Dusty and I are going back to the Inn to
get some sleep." I allowed a little irritation to show in my voice but I
don't think Edison noticed. He had probably played lord of the
manor for so long that it came natural to him.

"You remember our earlier conversation?"

"Of course."

"Then you realize how much more grave my situation is
now."

"Not really. Wright was murdered, not you. My
understanding was that technically he wasn't even your agent any
more. He probably had his own set of enemies, or this might even be
a random killing. Your prowler may have returned for some reason."
I realized I was floundering, more tired than I had realized, and I
shut my mouth.

Edison shook his head vigorously. "You're rather missing the
point. Wright's death was obviously an accident. Oh, I don't mean
that it wasn't murder, but the killer was really after me not him. Don't

you remember? Wright was wearing my favorite jacket and he had the hood up. We're not the same height and weight, but we're close enough that from above the difference wouldn't be obvious. With the hood up, his hair was covered. I imagine he was sitting on the ledge to catch his breath and enjoy the view when the killer came up on the trail above him, saw his chance, and bashed Wright's head in. But I was the one who was supposed to die out there tonight."

I rubbed my forehead. It sounded plausible but I was so tired that I'd have believed in the tooth fairy on flimsier evidence. "Have you mentioned this to the police?"

He made a dismissive gesture. "Of course, but they'll discount my opinion just as they did in the past. Henry is a competent administrator but he's not Sherlock Holmes. He'll look for the simplest possible explanation and once he's found it, he won't budge unless forced to by circumstances. He's been that way all his life."

"I explained earlier that this isn't my area of expertise. Why are you telling me all this?"

"Because I'm not sure whom I can trust any more. I'm convinced that one of the people who attended our little get together is trying to kill me, and while I'm not impressed with the competence of my enemy to date my good luck won't last forever. I want someone investigating this who has my best interests in mind."

I shook my head. "I'll think about it. Tomorrow. After I've slept." And then I left.

It was too late for breakfast when we got up in the morning. We both ordered BLTs and coffee. The Johnsons were sitting in one corner, apparently still not talking to one another, and they didn't acknowledge us when we came in. Wolfman showed up a few minutes later, nodded in our direction, but made no effort to join us, walked over to an empty table in another corner.

"So are you going to take Edison's case or not?"

I sipped coffee. "Murders are not my turf, remember?"

"You solved the last one you were involved in."

"It was the only one I was involved in, we both almost got ourselves killed, and I didn't know who the killer was until after she kidnapped you. Hercule Poirot would throw me out of the club."

"You solve puzzles, Paul. Sometimes that means poking and prying to see if anything falls into place or looks out of place or whatever."

"Well this time I'll let the police do the poking and prying. I'm not licensed up here even if I was interested, which I'm not."

"You don't have to have a license to ask questions, do you? As a private citizen, I mean."

"The authorities generally frown on people who try to skirt the rules. They call it obstruction of justice or interfering with a police officer in the performance of his duties. It's generally not a smart move."

She sat back and pressed her coffee cup against her chest. "It doesn't bother you then that I'm probably their prime suspect."

"What makes you think that?" Dusty experienced an occasional lapse into the melodramatic so I didn't take her too seriously.

"I have an obvious motive. Damon had just dropped me as a client. My entire career could be in jeopardy. I might have been caught by surprise and without time to adjust to my new situation. I had the opportunity. No one saw me after I left the house – at least as far as I know. The murder seems to have been an impulsive act. I'm strong enough to have done it. Motive and opportunity. Aren't those the things they look for?"

"If everyone who was dropped by their literary agent resorted to murder, the jails would be full of highly literate people."

"I'm serious."

I thought about it. I knew that Dusty would never have done such a thing, but that might not be as evident to others. And she had been visibly angry when Wright broke the news at the restaurant. Some of Edison's other guests might well have known that and certainly our waitress aware of the tension. "There have to be others here with good motives. Maybe Wright wasn't getting along with Austin. Maybe Edison is right and the wrong person was killed. Maybe it was just some random crazy trespasser who gave in to impulse and hit Wright over the head."

"So you're positive I'm not a suspect?"

I wasn't sure and I said so. "Thorndyke and Tibbett aren't dummies and they have lots of information that we don't. It's possible that someone saw something that will suggest an alternate solution. There were half a dozen people wandering around those trails. Everything will sort itself out."

"I suppose." She didn't sound convinced.

Thorndyke showed up with a stenographer about noon. They used an empty room and took us one at a time. There were draft statements for us to read and the stenographer typed corrections into a laptop and then used a nifty little portable printer to provide revised copies for us to sign. When my turn came, I asked Thorndyke if he'd made any progress.

"Some." That was all I was going to get from him.

We drove back as soon as we were released, no longer interested in sightseeing. Dusty dozed in the car and I mentally reviewed everything that had happened the previous day. My brain was fuzzy because my sleep pattern had been disrupted and I had trouble arranging the facts in an orderly fashion, so eventually I stopped trying and concentrated on driving.

Dusty woke up just before we arrived, a mysterious ability that I suspected had something to do with the sounds of Providence and/or the smell from Narragansett Bay. She was clearly depressed and didn't even stoop to greet Darla, who had finally deigned to allow someone other than me to pet her. I checked the cat food and water, replenished the latter, and unloaded our stuff from the car. When I was done, I found Dusty in the den. She had poured two brandies.

"Who had a good reason to kill Damon Wright? Besides me, I mean."

So we were going to play detective. I drank some brandy. "We can speculate, but we don't have enough information to get very far. Austin is the only one who seemed to have known Wright well, and the other writers present all have different representation."

"He'd known Naomi Winstead for a while. You could tell there was tension between them, but also some familiarity."

"Did he ever represent her?"

"Not that I know of, but maybe he did at one time. They've both been in the business for over thirty years."

"Wolfman mentioned that he had met Wright previously but he didn't relate the circumstances."

"And we know Damon was trying to lure James Patrick away from his current agent so they obviously weren't strangers."

"Which gives Patrick's agent a motive, I suppose, but I didn't see any sign that Wright was having any success. Patrick seemed to be actively avoiding his company all day."

"Leaving aside motive for the moment, who had the opportunity?"

"Almost everyone except Edison and I. Naomi Winstead had gone up to her room, but I suppose she might have sneaked out. There's a rear staircase. I saw Mrs. McCone and Tracy in the kitchen and I could hear them off and on when I couldn't see them. I don't see how either could have gotten away without being noticed even if they'd been in collusion but I suppose it's possible. Wolfman claims not to have left the garden, but we only have his word for it. Some of the hikers might have spotted one another, but we don't know who or when. Presumably they told Thorndyke. Or lied to Thorndyke. I'd be very suspicious if the Johnsons gave each other alibis."

"We could ask them ourselves."

"Like I said, Chief Tibbett might take umbrage if it appears I'm impeding a police investigation, possibly by trying to coordinate witness accounts."

"All right then, what if Edison is right and he really was the intended target?"

"That opens up more possibilities. His surprise announcement would certainly have given Austin grounds for a grudge but Wright was already dead by then and Austin looked genuinely shocked when Edison gave his little speech so I doubt he had advance warning. Wolfman didn't like either man very much but I think it was contempt on the one hand and envy on the other rather than hatred. The Johnsons may have had the strongest motive."

Dusty raised an eyebrow. "Why is that?"

"Patrick told me that he was surprised that Edison had invited them. They were the ones who acquired the movie rights to one of his books on behalf of the European production company. It was supposed to be the first in a series of films, each based on another volume in the series, five altogether. They lost some of their funding for the project and cut a lot of corners, and as you mentioned they used the source material more as a guideline than a text. The end product may have been artistically flawed but according to Wolfman it made a lot of money."

"I've seen it. Edison tried to make them take his name off the credits but he'd signed a contract. Not bad of its type, but I can see why Edison would be pissed."

"According to Patrick, the movie did so well that the Johnsons got their funding back and then some. Unfortunately their option had lapsed and Edison was in no mood to renew it even when they sweetened the pot with more money and some kind of creative approval. They were losing a chance at some significant profit."

"Maybe he invited them because he was reconsidering. And in any case, killing him would have eliminated any chance of convincing him to change his mind.'

I shrugged. "They might have decided that the estate might be more amenable. And Edison himself is hard to figure. At times he seems self contained, confident, and even masterful. At other times he's impulsive, indecisive, and a bit paranoid."

"Do you think he's right about the earlier attempts on his life?"

"I couldn't tell you with any certainty. I hinted to Thorndyke that there might be some connection during my interview but neither he nor Tibbett reacted. If Edison told him his theory about mistaken identity they didn't share their thoughts with me."

"You'd think they'd want help wherever they could get it."

I laughed. "You've been reading the wrong mystery novels. Lestrade might have been dependent upon Sherlock Holmes to solve all those convoluted crimes, but I doubt he was ever happy about it."

When I left for the office the next morning, Dusty was still in bed. She'd been up before me most mornings for the past month, excited about her new novel, and this was very unlike her even when she wasn't caught up in something. I decided it was probably just a delayed reaction but I made a mental note to pay more attention to her for a while.

The office, needless to say, had survived without me on Friday, and we technically had been closed over the weekend although it was not uncommon to have one or more people come in for a few hours to work on a case in relative quiet. Steve was at the front desk doing something with his computer and he hardly glanced up when I came in. "How was your weekend, boss?"

"Interesting," I said shortly. "How are things here?"

"The ongoing crises are still ongoing. Mr. Shaw did something that crashed the network again and Ms Kirk is mad at him. Mrs. Brubaker interviewed interns at Roger Williams College Friday afternoon and she has some prospects."

"Any checks in the mail since I've been gone?"

"A couple. The ones we expected. Vandervalk still hasn't paid the balance on his account and the Cockrills are questioning some of the expenses we billed for."

I barely made it to my private office before Tina Kirk caught up to me, complaining about unauthorized software and how it compromised our network security. "I have a good mind to deactivate all the DVD drives in the building."

We'd been down this road before. I told her I'd speak to Barry, since he was the chronic offender, and she went away at least partly mollified. A quick check of my inbox and my calendar told me that I could probably have stayed away another day or two but I had a particular reason for wanting to come in promptly. I wasn't going to admit it to Dusty yet but my curiosity was piqued. I might not be licensed for New Hampshire, but that didn't mean I couldn't look into things from a distance and with delicacy. But first I called Susan Hawks, an operative I used from time to time when I needed a woman to go undercover.

"This is Susan Hawks. How can I help you?"

I identified myself and her formal tone disappeared. "You used to work up north, didn't you?"

"Bangor for six years. Couldn't take the winters longer than that."

"Do you know someone good up there who might be able to look into something for me in New Hampshire?" I gave her a brief description and she whistled.

"Since when do you get involved with murder investigations?"

"Since Dusty became a suspect."

"Is she? That'll probably show up in her next book. Look, I don't know anyone from back then who's particularly good, but didn't Cordelia Grayson move up to Brattleboro last year?"

Cordelia specialized in divorce cases, for which I didn't envy her one bit. But she was good. "I'd forgotten all about her. Do you have her number?"

She did. I copied it down, but I didn't call her immediately. Instead I went upstairs.

Merrilee Brubaker looks like a kindly grandmother but she runs a tight ship. She has been with me longer than anyone else in the firm, and I pretty much let her run the second floor as her private domain. Almost the entire area is given over to cubicles, each with a computer. We employ anywhere from four to twelve interns depending upon our workload and they generate better than half the company's income without ever leaving their desks. We do regular contract work for law firms, credit card companies, and others who have lost track of someone they want us to locate. Sometimes the lost ones have skipped out on a debt or bail, sometimes they are named in a will, sometimes they are wanted as witnesses or for other reasons. There is a vast quantity of information available via the internet – from online services for which we pay handsomely – that allow us to track down most of these people in less than half an hour each. All you need is two or three pieces of information – social security number, name, and date of birth in most cases – and you can find out a whole lot more.

Merrilee has a desk at the head of the stairs – she declined the office I offered to have built – and she was sitting there when I reached the top. "Have a nice weekend, boss?"

"Dusty lost her agent. Met some boring people. One of them got murdered. Dusty is a suspect."

"That good, huh? Aren't you glad you didn't go off for a whole week. Anything I can do to help?"

"As a matter of fact, there is. Can you have someone do a background check on these people for me?" I handed her a list.

"We have a pretty light load today. I'll have Jerry and Pam do it. How deep do you want to dig?"

"Just a quick look around unless they spot something interesting. I might want more later."

"Where do you want this charged?"

"A new client. Paul Birch. I'll have Tina send you an account number."

The rest of the morning was pretty dull, just the way I like it. We got a nice referral that should generate some new business and the Bobbsey Twins – Bob Wilson and Bob Goodman – finally got some pictures of a "disabled" man playing volleyball with his nephews. The insurance company would be delighted. I made a couple of calls about overdue payments, approved the two new hires Merrilee had proposed, and typed up everything I could remember from the weekend that seemed potentially significant. I was unhappy that it took so little time to do so. I know that I had had several conversations with various people other than those I summarized, but I couldn't recall anything that was said during them, despite my famously retentive memory. On the other hand, if they were that unmemorable, they probably would not have been helpful.

The most glaring omission from my notes was Meredith Fallon. I know that I had spoken to her for several minutes but the only thing I can recall is that she seemed more than slightly apprehensive. In retrospect, I realized that she must have known or at least suspected that Edison was hanging up his keyboard, so maybe she was worried about her job. I made a mental note to ask Dusty to jot down her own recollections, then put the thought on hold. She'd been uncharacteristically withdrawn ever since her interview with the police in Culloden. Maybe I should tread warily for the moment.

I almost managed to forget about Martin Edison and Damon Wright that afternoon. Two prospective clients showed up, one convinced that his wife was cheating, the other worried about petty theft at his garden shop. I referred the first to someone I knew who specialized in that kind of case – we don't do divorce work ourselves unless business is really off. There are too many risk factors and sometimes the clients refuse to accept the proof we find, in either direction, and balk at paying. The other was more promising and I made an appointment for one of our subcontractors to go out and do a preliminary site survey.

Dusty's car was in the driveway when I got home and I eventually found her in the attic rearranging mountains (blankets) without much enthusiasm. "So how did your day go?"

"Figure out who did it yet?"

"Figure out who did what?"

She stood up and stretched. "You didn't forget about this weekend any more than I did. I know you. Puzzles are like challenges. Or poison ivy. You have to keep scratching at it."

"Scratch too much and you get an infection. Okay, I have someone checking out a couple of things but I don't expect to find much. It might even have been a random killing, you know. Edison has had trespassers before."

"Trespassers don't usually sneak around when there's a party going on."

We went downstairs and I cooked supper. Dusty and I sort of alternate depending on which of us is in the mood. If neither of us are, we usually go out. Halfway through the meal, Dusty put down her fork and asked me who I thought was the killer. "I know there's not enough information to make an educated guess, but what's your gut feeling?"

"Peggy Johnson," I said almost instantly. "But it's probably because I just didn't like her. She was in a foul mood all day, I'm pretty sure she was cheating on her husband with Wright, and she's furious with Edison for not selling her movie rights. It's probably unfair but I got the impression she's superficially competent but actually not very bright."

"Wouldn't that make the husband the more likely suspect?"

I thought about it. "Logically, but you asked for my gut feeling. I don't think he's the type. He's too passive. I'd bet he knows about his wife's indiscretion but avoids confronting her."

"Do you still think it might have been a case of mistaken identity?"

I thought about it. "No, I don't it's likely. Unless it was one of the servants, the fact that he was wearing Edison's jacket is immaterial. The rest were relative strangers who wouldn't have recognized it as belonging to Edison."

"Doesn't that invalidate your hunch about the killer?"

I shrugged. "Do I contradict myself? Very well then, I contradict myself. Hunches don't follow logical patterns and my personal hunch batting average has never been very good anyway. So who do you think did it?"

"James Patrick. He was on edge since the moment we first saw him and always seemed to be on the fringe of the group. I think he spent more time talking to little Tracy than to any of the rest of us. He knows how to read sign by the way. Her hands were going a mile a minute and he seemed to have no trouble following."

"Maybe she's his co-conspirator. Then was he after Wright or Edison?"

"Wright. He had never met Edison before but Damon was trying to lure him away from his current agent. Maybe Damon knew some deep dark secret from the man's past and was trying to blackmail Patrick into making the switch."

"I always thought you liked Damon."

"I liked having him as my agent. He was very intelligent, a good negotiator, he actually read and provided useful feedback on manuscripts, he knew a lot of people and a lot of them owed him favors. But personally, he was a snake, ruthless, predatory, and unprincipled."

"Sounds pretty thin, but we just don't know enough to have an educated opinion. For all we know, Tracy committed the murder thinking it was her mother wearing the jacket. No, that doesn't work. We know she didn't leave the house long enough to go up the trail and back."

"Are we sure that Tracy was actually out in the kitchen all that time?" She waved her hands. "No, I don't think she's an under aged Moriarty but just as an exercise, is her alibi air tight?"

"I heard Mrs. McCone talking to her several times." I thought about it. "But obviously I never heard Tracy herself. Still, that's quite a reach and it requires a conspiracy between her and McCone."

We switched subjects but our hearts weren't in casual conversation that evening and we finally retreated into our own interests. I managed to read a chapter of *The Guns of August* before admitting to myself that I wasn't paying attention. Dusty disappeared into the attic and occasionally I heard banging, thumping, and dragging sounds. She was still there when I went to bed, banging, thumping, and dragging.

The next morning at work was crazy. One of my subcontractors had been investigating several incidents of vandalism at a nearby mall which appeared to be related, but she was afraid she'd been spotted by one of the three young men she'd been watching so we needed to arrange for substitute coverage. Adrian Jessop called from Eblis Manufacturing to tell me that his internal auditors had questions about our loss prevention analysis and wanted to meet. Barry called in sick. A middle aged woman arrived without an appointment and insisted that she needed someone to prove that her next door neighbors were practicing witchcraft. I directed her to her local priest and hoped she wouldn't tell him who had sent her.

I had just about gotten all of that straightened out when a call came in from Meredith Fallon asking if I'd given any consideration to Mr. Edison's business proposition. That reminded me that I'd promised to recommend someone to look into his near death experiences. "I've found an investigator who might be available but I haven't spoken to her yet. I promise to call her today."

The Bobbsey twins came in with their photographs and a written report and as usual they wanted to talk. I managed to cut the conversation reasonably short without offending them. Then Dusty called and I had to admit that I hadn't had time to look at whatever Merrilee and her minions had gathered for me. "If I don't get to it this afternoon, I'll bring everything home with me and we can read them together. In fact, that's probably even better than doing it here."

So that's what we ended up doing. Merrilee had quite a big packet for me and I made a point of thanking the two "kids" who did all the work. I brought it down to my office to read, but I didn't manage to do more than glance at the first page before the next interruption came. This wasn't a typical day at the office, but it wasn't entirely atypical either.

So I bundled everything up and took it with me when I quit for the day.

Dusty had supper simmering and a bottle of wine already uncorked. We had a quick meal during which we both pretended we weren't interested in the portfolio that I had dropped on the couch on my way in. We took the rest of the wine with us after clearing away the dirty dishes. "How do you want to do this?" I asked. "Split the stack in half and then swap?"

"No. Let's take turns reading them to each other."

"Sounds good to me."

The first file we pulled was Martin Edison and I read it aloud. In general it followed the summary Dusty had already provided and what I'd read on the internet. Orphaned in his early teens, he became introspective and studious, sold his first novel before he could vote, and was one of the key players in the emergence of fantasy as a genre separate from science fiction during the 1970s. There were rumors that he had suffered from bouts of deep depression during his youth, and it was clear that he was discharged from the army because of emotional rather than physical problems. His work during the 1970s was sometimes rough around the edges but was lively, inventive, and well received. The books published during the 1980s were generally considered inferior by critics although his fans had remained loyal. By the early 1990s, following a three year gap during which he produced no new material, he returned to his early form and produced the bulk of his best work. Every book during that period made the bestseller lists. The novels published during the 1980s were no longer in print, at his own request, and some titles were quite valuable. He rarely wrote short fiction, had forty-nine published books, and had won several awards. The awards were invariably accepted by proxy since Edison would not attend conventions.

Edison bought the property in New Hampshire in 1975 at a bargain price because the original house was in terrible condition. He spent five years tearing most of the house down and replacing it with the present structure. His first agent was Lurleen Glass, since deceased. His agent for the past six years had been Damon Wright. There had been several in-between. He hired Louise Bowman as his secretary and housekeeper in 1975 and married her in 1982. She died in early 1991 in an apparent hiking accident while Edison was on the West Coast for one of his rare book signings. Although he had done some minor promotional work during the 1980s, he continued to shun photographers and would not allow his likeness to appear in any of his books. By the end of the 1990s he could no longer be tempted out of his private retreat for any public event, although there were rumors that he occasionally traveled incognito.

His net worth was estimated at fifty million, but it could have been even more if he had been willing to sell movie rights to his books. There was a full paragraph about his tiff with the Johnsons. Apparently he had threatened to sue them for breach of contract as well as withholding further rights. Two other film companies had approached him with similar results. Fool me once, shame on you. His current staff had been with him since the early 1990s, starting with Geneva McCone, who arrived in 1991. He had no living relatives except for a cousin who lived in Europe; as far as was known they had not seen each other since childhood. It was all rather dull with one exception, and that exception took us both by surprise. Martin and Louise Edison had had a child, a son born in 1984, named Ronald Charles Edison. This was almost certainly the same

Ronald who had cooked our steaks on Saturday and who had found Wright's body. I had never heard his last name and, except for Tracy Fallon, he was the only one from the party whose name I hadn't given to Merrilee.

"You'd never have guessed," said Dusty. "Edison treated him like a servant."

"Well, he pretty much treats everyone that way, but you're right. He never even introduced us to Ronald. There's an interesting story buried there, although I don't know if it's relevant."

We played with our new bit of knowledge for awhile but neither of us could figure out how to connect it to the murder of Damon Wright, even if he'd been mistaken for Edison. Ronald would have recognized the jacket, of course, and I couldn't remember seeing him during the period when the hikers were out, but it was hard to imagine anyone so self effacing deciding to bash someone's head in with a rock. On the other hand, he wouldn't have been the first person to murder a father who treated him contemptuously, particularly a father worth fifty million dollars. I wondered who would inherit when Edison died. Ronald had "found" the body rather quickly. Might he already have known it was there?

Dusty picked up Meredith Fallon's report and read it to me. Meredith was a Katherine Gibbs graduate who had worked as a publisher's assistant for a few years, then freelanced doing secretarial and editorial work for a variety of magazines and authors. She settled down with Esther Browning for four years –Browning wrote time travel romances – then returned to freelancing following Browning's death in a plane crash. Martin Edison hired her in 1998 and she gave birth to a daughter Ellen that same year. She had refused to identify the father.

"Might be Edison," I suggested. "If she'd done some freelance work for him and they ended up in bed, he might have hired her in order to soothe his conscience."

"Or maybe they were still an item. For all we know, they might be even now."

"He doesn't seem to me the type who would hire a pregnant, single woman and move her into his home as an act of charity."

"Don't rule it out. The hero in *The Sapphire Dragon* becomes the patron of young woman who was raped by an evil fairy. That was published the same year or thereabouts. We authors always get told to write what we know."

I nodded. "He does tend to strike poses a lot. Maybe he sees himself as an exiled prince living in his mountain retreat, waiting for the world to call him back."

"I think it's more likely to be the misunderstood genius with a heart of gold that he keeps concealed from prying eyes. That's the sorcerer in *The Curse of Mist Valley*."

"I'll defer to your greater familiarity with his work. Anything else there on Fallon?"

There was one other interesting nugget. The folder contained only a partial list of her clients during Fallon's years as a freelancer, but one of them was Arthur Wolfman. "Why would a critic need a secretary?" I asked.

"Oh, didn't you know? Wolfman is also an author. He writes intricate stories of human interactions which invariably turn out badly and demonstrate the hostility of the universe to the creative spirit."

"Does anyone read that stuff nowadays?"

"No, and that's why he has to talk about other people's books in order to make a living."

Geneva McCone was next. She was born in Taunton, Massachusetts, finished high school and immediately married Jamiel Nash. The marriage lasted less than two years and produced a son, Malcolm, currently a staff sergeant serving in Afghanistan. McCone took back her maiden name and supported herself as a clerk at Eblis Manufacturing – one of my clients – where she eventually became office manager until her job was eliminated in 1985. There was a year's gap in her employment before she took a job as office manager at Granite Press, a small specialty publisher based in Burlington, Vermont. Edison hired her away from them in 1991 and she'd been with him ever since.

"Did Granite Press ever publish anything by Edison?"

"None of his novels, but I think they may have done some of his stories as chapbooks – fancy expensive editions of short stories usually in hardcover – and it's possible that's how they met. It's their kind of thing. Or was. They only do ebooks now."

Arthur Wolfman was next. Born and raised in Cambridge, Massachusetts, attended but did not graduate from Harvard. He was the author of four novels from four different publishers, two of them university presses. I had heard of neither of the other two imprints – Purple Porpoise and Thoughtworks. Wolfman reviewed for a variety of markets including everything from the *New York Times* to the *Kitchener College Newsletter*. He was known for his acerbic comments and an intense dislike of any form of speculative fiction, particularly fantasy which he deemed "stories designed for people who have neither the wit nor the courage to move beyond childhood." Wolfman had never held a steady job, however, his family was quite wealthy and he lived much better than his career would suggest.

Naomi Winstead's report was considerably longer. She was the youngest of three sisters born in a small town in upstate New York but had moved to Brooklyn following high school and was rumored to have been estranged from her family for reasons unknown. There she had worked as a waitress while taking classes in commercial design, although she never received a formal degree. She sold her first book for children – which she wrote and illustrated – in 1979. For the next decade she had produced an average of three books a year, none of them bestsellers although she was nominated once for a Caldecott Award. Her professional resume was solid but dull. Her personal life was more interesting.

Although she retained her maiden name, Winstead had been married to Damon Wright from 1980 to 1982. I stopped reading when I reached that point, trying to process the information. Dusty looked as surprised as I felt. "Why would they keep their relationship a secret?" she asked at last.

I thought about it. "I don't know that they did. The subject would hardly come up in casual conversation. I imagine she told Thorndyke. He would have found out in any case."

"It gives her a motive."

I shook my head. "Not really. The marriage ended over thirty years ago. If she was still holding a grudge, she would have done something about it sooner."

"But she did know that it was Wright in that jacket and not Edison."

"Yes, but she also went up to her room rather than outside. If she had come back down, there was a strong risk of her being seen." I saw the flaw in that argument right away. "On the other hand, she could have used the back staircase. With luck she could have slipped out past the kitchen when McCone and Tracy were looking elsewhere."

We decided that Winstead technically had had an opportunity, the same as almost everyone else, but neither of us could think of a plausible motive. Lingering resentment from the divorce seemed unlikely. Admittedly things had seemed cool between them, but then Winstead tended to be cool with everyone as far as I could tell.

The Johnsons had been combined into a single report. Peter was from London, Margaret from Sydney, Australia, and they had been business partners before they were married, initially making documentaries for Australian television. Peter directed and co-produced with his wife, but she was generally considered the brains behind the financing as well as having developed the connections that led to more ambitious projects. Apparently she was brighter than I had thought. They had moved up to low budget horror for a while, then a couple of moderately successful action films neither of which I had ever heard of. The Edison deal had looked like it might propel them into the big time but there had been some problems early on – apparently not the fault of the Johnsons – and their budget had been slashed. Since their option on the material was getting close to its expiration date, they rushed through what was generally acknowledged to be an inferior product. As usual, the critics felt insulted by the contrived plot and familiar tropes but viewers loved it despite its many flaws. Nevertheless, Edison refused to renew the options for the rest of the series and had threatened further legal action. The Johnsons were able to find more work and while they may have regretted losing Edison, they hadn't done badly for themselves. Their current project was based on the Kenneth Roberts novel *Arundel* and they would be scouting locations in Maine for the next few weeks.

There was a lot of gossipy stuff which was labeled "speculative" suggesting that neither of the Johnsons was particularly faithful. Several actors, actresses, and industry figures were named. If half of the rumors were true, I wondered when they found the time to actually produce their films. Peter had been convicted of assault back when they were still working in Australia, but it was a fight in a bar and he had not served any time in jail. His wife had been sued for slander the same year and had settled out of court. The aggrieved party, to my surprise, was Hillary Austin, whom she had accused repeatedly and publicly of having sabotaged the negotiations with Martin Edison.

"Why do you suppose Edison invited these particular people?" I asked. "He doesn't seem to have liked any of them. Wolfman panned his work, the Johnsons arguably debased it, he was dumping his agent and his editor, and as far as I can see he had never heard of Winstead, Patrick, or you, for that matter. This last is of course his loss."

"He didn't want me. He wanted Dusty Trails, or whatever the guy's real name is."

"Right. I didn't include him on the list but maybe I should have him checked out as well."

"I looked him up. He dedicated a couple of his books to Edison."

"Flattery will get you somewhere."

"And you're wrong, Edison did know Winstead before last weekend. She mentioned that was why she had been invited to stay at the house. She said she'd first met him a long time ago, although she didn't mention the context. But they couldn't have been close because she hadn't been to the house since before Mrs. McCone was hired."

There were no real surprises in James Patrick's report. He was born James Patrick Burkhardt, which was still his legal name. Although he had never married, his name had been linked with that of several minor league actresses and models during his younger days. He relocated from New York City to Boston in 1999 and had kept a fairly low profile from that point on. His novels did not make the bestseller lists, but they often came close and he turned out two per year as regular as clockwork, most of them featuring Griff Standish and the Payback Squad. One of them had been a made for television movie, but the Johnsons weren't involved.

Hillary Austin had led an even less exciting life, at least in public. He'd gone into publishing as an intern straight from college, changed firms three times, and was now senior editor at Pikestaff. He had been in a serious relationship with a lawyer, Edgar Northrup, from 1995 until 2008, when Northrup died of AIDs related causes. A list of authors with whom he had worked revealed no names on our list except for Dusty. "He did my first book, but he only handles the big names now."

Finally I read the report on Damon Wright, which added little to our small store of knowledge. His firm still represented Naomi Winstead, but one of his partners had handled her books since their divorce. He had accumulated two more ex-wives and had died unattached, officially at least. I hadn't noticed Peggy Johnson breaking up over his death so he might well be unmourned. None of his marriages had resulted in children. There was no report of tension between him and Edison. Wright had been regarded as one of the most sought after agents around and he was reportedly better off financially than many of his clients.

There was a stack of paper remaining but it was primarily lists of books by the various authors with samples of reviews and other material that did not seem presently relevant. Dusty looked disappointed, as though the solution should have leaped out of the stack of paper. "So what's next?"

I shrugged. "I could open a fresh bottle of wine."

"But shouldn't we draw up diagrams or a time line or something? You always do that."

"That's for Thorndyke and his minions. It's nothing for us to worry about at this point. We're discussing, not investigating. And even if we were, we don't have enough information."

"Easy for you to say," she said sulkily. "You're not a suspect."

The next morning I called Cordelia Grayson and gave her a brief summary of my conversation with Martin Edison and the subsequent murder. "Edison claims the police don't believe the earlier incidents were actually murder attempts and he's probably right that they don't and they're probably right that they aren't. On the other hand, Wright was wearing the old man's jacket when he was killed and it certainly could have been a case of mistaken identity. I should warn you the local police aren't likely to be happy about a private investigator showing up during an active murder investigation, but then again, they never are."

Cordelia was about my age but sometimes I thought she was experientially a lot older. There were few aspects of the business she hadn't been involvedwith, her technical knowledge was encyclopedic, and she seemed to have met everyone who mattered anywhere in New England. "Is Tibbett still the chief down there?"

"Yes. You know him?" I wasn't surprised.

"Henry and I are old acquaintances. He can be accommodating if you don't get in his face and if you promise to share information." She asked a few questions, which I answered as best I could, then agreed to talk to Edison. "Frankly I could use the business. Adultery seems to have gone out of fashion up this way, or maybe people just don't care any more."

We talked a little longer and then I tried with some success to set aside Martin Edison and his problems and concentrate on my own business and it wasn't until I was almost home that evening that I started turning over the puzzle pieces in my mind again. Dusty was right. It was like a sore tooth. I had to keep pushing on it even though it was making me crazy.

For her part, Dusty was sulking. "Thorndyke called today with more questions."

"He's just doing his job. Ask enough questions and the answer shows up somewhere along the line, most of the time. The trick is recognizing it when it does."

"Okay, Sherlock, but it's still not comfortable being the prime suspect."

"Did he say you were the prime suspect?"

"Not in so many words."

"In what words did he say it then?"

"Well, it wasn't so much what he said as what he implied."

"So what did he imply?"

"Oh, all right. He was actually very polite and assured me several times that he was just making routine follow ups. But then, that's what he would say, wouldn't he?"

Nothing I could possibly suggest was going to help. Dusty just didn't like having a cloud hanging over her head, for which I couldn't blame her, and Thorndyke's call had just been an excuse to talk about it. I reassured her as best I could but I knew that she would be on edge until they finally caught whoever had murdered Damon Wright. The possibility that they might not – there was still a remote chance that it had been a random act of violence by an unknown party – was not something that I could suggest to Dusty in her present state of mind.

She was restless all night, tossing and turning, and at least twice she got up and walked around for a few minutes.

The next morning I called the Culloden police department and asked for Detective Thorndyke. There was a brief wait and then the familiar voice. "Good morning, Mr. Birch. How can I help you?"

I had an excuse ready. I told him that I had been in touch with Cordelia Grayson and that she would likely be investigating the alleged attempts on Martin Edison's life. "I don't know if she and Edison have spoken yet."

"As a matter of fact, I have an appointment with Ms Grayson later today."

"I don't want you to think I lack confidence in your department," I fibbed. "I hope that she'll be able to put Mr. Edison's mind at ease. Sometimes it's more convincing coming from a disinterested third party."

"It's not a problem, Mr. Birch. We're familiar with Mr. Edison's idiosyncrasies and it's understandable that he's concerned about what might have happened in the past given last weekend's tragic events."

I decided to chance a probe. "But you think he's wasting his money."

"Not if it makes him feel safer." Thorndyke hesitated. "We did take his earlier reports seriously. We brought in the state police crime scene people to go over his vehicle. Their findings support the conclusion that it was a mechanical failure, not sabotage."

"Unless someone was very clever."

"They could not rule out that possibility. You can't prove a negative."

Thorndyke seemed inclined to talk so I pushed on. "How about the shooting incident?"

"It certainly happened the way he described it, but we never found the round or a casing. It was probably an irresponsible hunter who strayed out of bounds either accidentally or otherwise."

"And the prowler?"

"Even in Culloden we have prowlers. Nothing was taken or damaged and there was no sign of an attempted break in. Might have been a vagrant. Might have been kids. Might even have been an animal."

"Edison said there were tracks."

"They might have been there for a while."

The conversation was nearing its inevitable end and I hadn't figured out how to ask what I wanted to ask, so I just pushed forward. "Miss Rhodes is not happy about being a suspect."

"Understandably. I would be happy to eliminate her if I could, simply to narrow the focus of the investigation."

"But you can't."

I was pretty sure I heard a sigh. "No, I can't. She didn't have much of a motive to kill him, but neither did anyone else as far as I can tell."

"You don't think it was someone from outside our group then?"

"Do you, Mr. Birch?"

I had to confess that I did not. A random attacker would have taken Wright's wallet and watch. "Well, thank you for speaking to me. If there's anything I can do to help, let me know."

Thorndyke answered quickly. "You're going to poke around on your own, aren't you?"

I hesitated. "I might look into a couple of things, but I won't interfere with your investigation."

"And you'll let me know if you find anything?"

"Certainly." But with reservations. I certainly wouldn't share anything that I thought might mislead them into becoming more suspicious of Dusty, for example.

I went through the reports Merrilee's kids had compiled and wrote down addresses. Wolfman and Austin were in New York City, Winstead lived in Western Connecticut, and Patrick was a Bostonian. The Johnsons were presumably somewhere in Maine. I buzzed for Steve, then handed him the list. "I'd like to talk to these people as soon as possible. I'll take the train to New York but try to arrange the two of them there for the same day. The Johnsons are probably on the move a lot but do the best you can."

I didn't have a theory, a strong suspect, a plan of action, or even much hope that I could spot something the police had missed, even if the others were willing to speak to me in the first place, but like I told Dusty, sometimes you just have to keep asking questions until something shakes loose.

Barry was still out sick so I had to take over for him – leaning heavily on his notes and Tina Kirk's data – during an overly long meeting with Eblis Manufacturing's cost accountant and their production manager, who both insisted that our analysis of their repair operation was faulty. It never ceases to amaze me how many people will spend ten dollars to repair a five dollar part rather than just throw it in the scrap barrel and start over. They eventually accepted our figures, at least intellectually, but I would have bet an expensive lunch that six months from now their procedures would not have changed significantly. It also amazes me how many companies will pay big bucks for expert opinions, and then disregard those that don't conform to what they expected to hear. I once had a production manager named Lorenzo tell me that the company was wasting its money on my firm because if there was anything that could be done to improve security, he would already have thought of it.

When I got back to the office, a neatly typed itinerary was on my desk. Arthur Wolfman would be pleased to see me at his apartment at mid-morning. Hillary Austin could squeeze me in at three o'clock the same afternoon. James Patrick was in Chicago for a round of book signings and would not be back until the weekend. Naomi Winstead had not answered her telephone or called back. Steve had not yet located the Johnsons.

I called Dusty, who sounded tired although that might just have been my imagination, and told her I was going out of town early in the morning and might not be back until late evening. "That's okay. I have to go somewhere tomorrow and if things run late I might stay the night."

"Someplace interesting, I hope."

"Research."

"So you're going to Pullemia?"

"Something like that."

Supper that evening was uncharacteristically quiet. Dusty deflected any questions about her plans for the next day and I was sufficiently miffed that I reciprocated. Actually, I wasn't sure it was a good idea to tell her where I was going. Her inflated opinion of my sleuthing ability was flattering at times, but I didn't want to raise her expectations to a point I could not reasonably hope to reach. In fact, I was very doubtful that I would accomplish anything at all, but at least I would be doing something. I think that's the point where I realized that above and beyond my desire to relieve Dusty's anxiety,

I really wanted to know what had happened that evening in New Hampshire. I hate unsolved puzzles.

Dusty was up when I left in the morning, but we didn't talk much. I found an all day parking lot not too far from the train station, picked up the ticket Steve had arranged, killed some time at a newsstand, and spent most of the trip reading the first half of the latest J.D. Robb mystery novel. Wolfman lived on Pineapple Street in Brooklyn, not far from the bridge. and the taxi dropped me off almost an hour before my appointment, so I killed more time at a coffee shop.

I was buzzed in promptly and rode the elevator to the third floor. The building was clean, if a bit shabby, and I suspected it was rent controlled. Wolfman had left his door open but I knocked and waited until he called from somewhere out of sight to invite me in. I'm not sure what I expected, something outlandish I imagine. Wolfman struck me as the kind of man who would fashion his private world as a protest against the culture that surrounded him. Quite to the contrary, his apartment was furnished conservatively and tastefully with comfortable looking, practical furniture. The walls were lined with loaded bookshelves which I browsed while he brought out coffee. There was less fiction than I might have expected, more poetry and drama, and a great deal of history mixed with biographies and memoirs. There was one tiny shelf holding perhaps two dozen dvds. They all seemed to be opera or ballet.

"The young man who called didn't explain the purpose of your visit, but I suppose that would have been superfluous. You're here about the late, largely unlamented Mr. Wright, of course."

"This is purely unofficial, Mr. Wolfman, but it's obviously in everyone's best interest to get this cleared up as quickly as possible."

"Not quite everyone. I imagine the killer would prefer that the situation remain unresolved. But even he, or she, would have to pretend to be cooperative in order to avert suspicion. In fact, the villain of this piece might well initiate an informal investigation just to discover what the rest of us know."

"I didn't kill Damon Wright. but your point is valid."

Wolfman, who seemed overdressed in a white silk shirt and ascot, let his shoulders sink in mock resignation. "Alas, Martin Edison has given you an alibi. It might almost have been worth my while to have put up with his company long enough to accomplish the same. I never did find out why he spirited you away."

"It was a different matter entirely." I wondered if that were true.

"Perhaps. So how can I help you?"

"If you could just run through the events of the day for me, in as much detail as you can remember. I know this is a pain but I can't very well ask the police for a copy of your statement."

Wolfman looked unhappy and I thought he might balk. He poured himself a second cup of coffee and settled back into his chair. "Make yourself comfortable, Mr. Birch. This might take a while."

As it happened, Wolfman had a wonderfully retentive memory, better than mine in fact. He even recalled a brief exchange between the two of us that I'd completely forgotten. I think he was trying to be objective, but his contempt for several of those present - Winstead, Wright, and Austin in particular – was not very well concealed. His admiration for Edison was limited but seemed sincere. He expressed no interest in the Johnsons, whom he called simply the "movie people." Oddly enough, he rather liked James Patrick. "His books are trashy and formulaic, but they're honest. And he at least has the grace to learn from his mistakes."

"I imagine most writers improve with practice."

"That's a common fallacy. A great many burn out and descend into unintentional self parody. It was not his books I was referring to. They've remained adequate but uninspired throughout his career. Mr. Patrick led a somewhat dissolute and irresponsible life for many years. He drank a great deal, involved himself with a succession of women, generally tried to emulate the protagonist of his wearisome novels. Then, quite suddenly, he became a reformed character. He relocated to Boston and cleaned up his act. I'd like to say that his art improved at the same time but truthfully there was no real change. Perhaps a hint of self mockery but no more."

"When did this happen?"

Wolfman rubbed his chin. "Fifteen years ago, perhaps a bit more."

"Any idea what precipitated it?"

"Not the slightest. Perhaps he woke up one morning passed out beside a woman whose name he didn't know and experienced an epiphany."

He ran through several more conversations he'd either participated in or overheard, but none of them seemed significant. I asked about the crucial period during which the guests had scattered and the murder had taken place.

"Ah, had I been prescient, I would have overcome my dislike of the outdoors and accompanied someone who could provide me with an alibi. Or perhaps not. I rather enjoy being a suspect. In any case, I simply sat in the garden and read a Stephen King novel – it was less bloated than usual – until we were all summoned for the ceremony. I saw that young blonde girl carrying things about a couple of times but I doubt she noticed me. I did notice your young lady when she started up the path – she is quite attractive - and Winstead told me she was going upstairs to lie down, but I'm afraid I don't recall seeing anyone else until we were summoned inside. I may have dozed for a few minutes."

"Did you ever find out why Edison invited you?"

"Not in so many words, but I think that deep down somewhere the man believes that he is a fraud, that his writing is pedestrian, that he just happened to be at the right place at the right time, and that I'm one of the few critics who recognized the truth. It's not an entirely accurate description. Edison has the virtue of understanding the English language well enough to employ it correctly. If he had chosen more conventional subject matter, he might have produced more lasting work. But he would not, of course, have made nearly as much money. On the other hand perhaps my chronic dislike of his work irritated him enough that he wanted one last chance to display his superiority before retiring from the field of literary combat."

I asked a few more questions about the other guests but Edison provided no new insights except when I mentioned that I was meeting with Hillary Austin later that day.

"Count your fingers and toes when you leave. Underneath that charming veneer is a grasping, avaricious thief."

"I wouldn't think the publishing business would provide much opportunity for larceny."

"There are ambitious people who use disreputable methods when it is to their advantage in any human endeavor. There are others whose nature is so inextricably threaded with chicanery that it becomes their preferred modus operandi."

"I don't suppose you could be a little more specific?"

"I think not. But you have been warned."

I took another taxi back to Manhattan and ate lunch at a very busy deli. Since I had time to kill I walked uptown to the building where Austin had his office, not far from Central Park. It was an older building, well maintained, with an armed guard sitting in the lobby. The receptionist was a petite Asian woman whose welcoming smile was automatic and unconvincing.

"I hate an appointment with Hillary Austin. He works for Pikestaff."

She consulted a printed list – there was no computer terminal in sight – and pointed toward the elevators. "Pikestaff is on the eight floor."

The elevator made mildly disquieting noises as it rose but delivered me safely to my destination where another receptionist, this one a tall black woman with cornrows, made no effort to smile but nodded when she checked my claim. She did have a computer. "Someone will be out for you in a moment. Please take a seat."

It was more than a moment but not terribly so. A young man came for me eventually and led me through a maze of offices. Hillary Austin was ensconced as far as possible from the front. I suspected this was deliberate, that his guests were expected to be impressed by the size and complexity of Pikestaff Books by the time they were ushered into his presence. Although his space was not spacious – my own officer was slightly bigger – it was tastefully furnished. The oversized desk matched the small conference table and chairs, and the wall paneling looked to have been done by hand.

Austin wore a three piece suit and he made a point of moving some papers around before glancing up at me. "Ah, Mr. Birch. Please sit down. I'm afraid I'm rather disorganized this morning. We're approaching our busiest time of year."

"Then I won't take up any more of your time than necessary." This seemed to please him and I settled back into a chair. "I imagine you know why I'm here."

"Actually, I don't. My secretary indicated that it was a matter of some urgency but she said that the person who called insisted that it was personal and confidential."

"You do know that they still haven't made an arrest in the Wright murder?"

"Is that so? Well, I don't imagine that they have the kind of resources that we do in the city. Poor Damon probably surprised someone doing drugs or something of that sort. I don't suppose we'll ever know what really happened."

"So you don't think it was one of our party?"

Austin looked as though he'd just found something nauseating. "What possible reason could any of us have for killing Damon Wright? He wasn't the easiest person to work with but he was tactful and classy most of the time. It had to be an outsider, someone random."

"The police don't seem to think that's the case. And as long as the murder is unsolved, it's going to be hanging over all our heads."

"Nonsense." He didn't sound quite so certain though. "Do you have any idea how many unsolved murders take place in this city every year? Do you think anyone cares once the initial excitement dies down?"

"Murder is more memorable in a small town, particularly when it's at the home of someone as prominent as Martin Edison. They could keep the investigation open indefinitely and they almost certainly will start talking to people we know – friends, family, business contacts, employers." I emphasized the last word slightly and Austin flinched more than slightly.

"I think you're overstating the case, but you wouldn't have come to see me if you didn't have a suggestion to make."

"Nothing so concrete, actually, but I am taking a look at things. If I can help the police channel their investigation into more fruitful areas, those of us who are innocent might benefit."

He thought it over. "I don't see how I can help. I told the police everything I knew, which wasn't much."

"I'd like to go over it again if you don't mind. Sometimes a fresh set of eyes can find a pattern that the official investigation overlooked. And this is my business, after all." Okay, I fibbed a little. Murders were not something Birch Investigations normally tackled. Austin probably wouldn't realize that.

It was almost painful to listen to Austin's recitation of the critical day's events. He was possibly the most disorganized thinker I'd ever met. His narration jumped around in chronology and sometimes I had to stop him so that he could explain what period he was talking about. He confused Wolfman with Peter Johnson and seemed to have forgotten Ronald completely. He contradicted himself several times but I don't think he was trying to mislead me. At one point he said that he'd seen Winstead walking toward one of the paths, but when I pressed him he corrected himself and said that it was Meredith Fannon whom he'd seen. I couldn't recall if she'd been one of the hikers or not.

I lasted another hour before deciding that further conversation with Austin was more likely to muddy the issue than cast light upon it. I thanked him for his time, he asked me to keep him informed about my progress, and it was with a palpable sense of relief that I escaped to the street. I made some effort to organize what he'd told me into a coherent narrative while I was waiting for my train, but it was a hopeless task.

Dusty was not home when I arrived around suppertime and I ate alone. Despite her warning that she might be gone overnight, I waited up until nearly midnight before going to bed. It wasn't that I had a lot to tell her; it was too soon to decide whether or not my trip had been a complete waste of time. But I knew that Dusty was feeling perhaps disproportionate stress because of the cloud hanging overhead and I wanted to see her and be able to gauge how much it was bothering her. I had called her cell phone but she probably had it turned off. She hated them and only carried one when she travelled, and only then because I made her promise to do so. She hadn't promised to turn it on.

I had to go to the office the following morning but I left a note for her to call as soon as she got in. Barry Shaw was back at last; I could hear him arguing with Tina about something the moment I entered. I waved at Steve and walked to my office. He knocked a minute later and brought in my coffee.

"How was the trip?"

"Inconclusive. What's happening here?"

He shrugged. "No new crises. I still haven't tracked down Naomi Winstead. No reply to my messages. James Patrick is due back from his signing tour late Sunday, so I'll call Monday morning. I do have some good news. The Johnsons are going to be in Newport this weekend. Their publicity man is supposed to call me today to arrange a get together. Any preferences?"

"Saturday is better. I want to get it over with." I wasn't looking forward to talking to the couple. They generated a faint air of superiority that always tempted me to say something outrageous. Well, perhaps "outrageous" is too strong a word, but you get the idea.

"I'll let you know."

Dusty called about mid morning. She sounded tired. "How did everything go?" I asked, not knowing what everything was or how it should have gone.

"Disappointing. I'll tell you about it when you get home." She didn't ask me about my own trip, which bothered me a little.

I glanced at my watch. "How about lunchtime? I don't have anything pressing here."

"Okay. I'll make something."

"Don't knock yourself out. You sound beat."

"Yeah, well by 'make something' I actually meant I'd order some Chinese." There was a trace of life in her voice and I felt heartened.

"I want egg rolls."

We ate out on the back porch and since I was very curious about Dusty's mysterious trip, I made a point of telling her all about mine first, in great detail. "Not very much new, I'm afraid," I summarized.

"It wasn't as if you expected either of them to confess."

"No, but it would have pleased me immensely if one of them had. So what about you?"

Dusty bit her lip, a sure sign that she figured I wouldn't approve. "I went back to New Hampshire."

I'm not sure what I expected, but it had never occurred to me that Dusty might investigate on her own. The only previous time she'd tried to help out with one of my investigations, she had nearly gotten both of us killed. That wasn't entirely fair since I'd been just as far off the mark as she was, but even so.

"That might not have been such a great idea." Thorndyke seemed to me an intelligent man, but he would have to be wary of a suspect who poked around unofficially. She might be trying to cover her tracks, or find out what the police knew, or if the murder had in fact been a case of mistaken identity, she might be looking for a way to correct her mistake.

"You'd better tell me about it."

There hadn't been a real plan. Dusty had decided to drive up to Culloden and just talk to the local people on the off chance that she might learn something useful. It actually wasn't a bad idea, but I should have gone instead of Dusty since I was not a suspect. Better yet, I could have asked Cordelia Grayson to do it. Dusty had made no effort to talk to anyone from Edison's household and she had not told Thorndyke that she was in town. "I didn't really expect to find out anything, but I just had to do something."

I told her I understood, which was mostly the truth. "So what did you find out?"

"Nothing we didn't already know. Edison is not popular with the locals, who consider him standoffish, a snob. They don't think much of Meredith Fallon either. She has a boyfriend who comes up to see her occasionally but they always went off someplace together and no one I talked to knew who he was, or at least they wouldn't tell me. It must have been fairly serious because Tracy usually went with them."

I had been assuming all along that the woman I glimpsed in the parking lot at the motel with Damon Wright was Margery Johnson, but it might have been Meredith Fallon. They were both the same size, both had long hair. Fallon's was much lighter but in the dark I probably wouldn't have noticed a difference. I was quite sure that the man had been Damon Wright because he had turned his face toward me, but the woman had remained mostly in shadow.

"They really like Mrs. McCone, though. She does charity work at the local church whenever she can, and sometimes Tracy and Ronald come along to help."

"Did you ask about the other guests? Had any of them been there before?"

"A couple of people knew Damon. He always stayed at the Inn when he came out and he wasn't the kind of person you forget easily."

That was pretty much it. Dusty spent the day visiting every local business, asking lots of questions, getting rebuffed politely several times and not so politely a couple more. She split the evening between the two local bars where she learned absolutely nothing except that somebody who might have been Damon Wright might have been in there a time or two in the past and might even have picked up one of the local girls but even though she had a photograph of Wright with her, no one could – or at least would – make a positive identification. One waitress said she was pretty sure he was the one who had asked her who in town would know the most gossip.

She had considered driving back but she'd had a few drinks, thought better of it, and went to the Inn. "I even had the same room."

"You know it wasn't a great idea to go back there?"

She nodded. "I realized that on the drive up, but I had to try."

We finished our Chinese, Dusty decided she was going to take a nap, and I went back to the office.

Since I had promised to keep Thorndyke informed, I called him. It took a lot longer to track him down this time and he sounded harried when he answered. I explained the reason for my call and provided a quick summary of what I had learned – more precisely hadn't learned - from Wolfman and Austin. I didn't mention Dusty's trip because she hadn't discovered anything worth repeating and I didn't want Thorndyke to be thinking about her any more than he was already.

He listened quietly, asked no questions. When I was done, he told me that he'd been about to call me in any case. Something in his tone set off my personal alarm system but I kept my voice level. "Has something new turned up?"

"In a manner of speaking. We don't know yet whether there is any connection to Mr. Wright's death, but if not it would be quite a coincidence."

I decided not to prompt him. He'd either tell me or he wouldn't.

"Tracy Fannon is dead. It happene sometime late in the afternoon or early evening yesterday. The coroner doesn't have a time of death yet."

I had to try twice before my voice would work. "What happened?"

"It appears that she fell from one of the trails above Edison's place."

"Accident?"

"Maybe. There was no sign of a struggle but there were no witnesses either. Could be a coincidence."

"I don't like coincidences."

"Neither do I."

I thought about it. "If someone killed her, Wolfman and Austin both have alibis. They were both in New York that day. I might have been talking to Austin when the girl died."

"Doesn't mean they didn't kill Wright."

"No, it doesn't. I think you have a mess on your hands, Detective Thorndyke." And that's when I realized that Dusty probably didn't have an alibi. She had in fact been in close proximity to the crime, if it was a crime. "And so do I. I need to tell you something." He'd find out about Dusty's trip sooner or later and it would be worse if I concealed what I knew now, would look as though I was covering for her, or thought she was guilty. I told him about her misguided excursion and its inconsequential results.

"Her timing could have been better," he said quietly.

"I know."

"I'm going to have to talk to her."

"We could drive up in the morning." I hoped Steve hadn't scheduled a meeting with the Johnsons.

"There's no hurry. We won't have the autopsy results until tomorrow. They might tell us something more. How about Sunday, around one?"

"We'll be there. Should we bring a lawyer?"

"You'll have to do what you think is best, but it's probably premature. I don't like her for Wright's murder and I can't see any reason why she'd kill the Fannon girl, but it wouldn't be the first time I've been wrong."

I asked Steve to bring me a fresh cup of coffee and drank it slowly, then picked up the phone again and called Dusty. I would rather have told her about Tracy Fannon's death face to face but I had a client coming in and I didn't want to chance her hearing it on the news. Her voice was under control when I told her what had happened but I could tell she was upset.

"Do they know who did it?"

"They don't even know how it happened yet. It might have been an accident."

"Awfully big coincidence."

"Awfully big."

"You don't like coincidences."

"No, I don't."

She was quiet for a few seconds. "I was up there when it happened."

"So were lots of other people."

"How many of them were also suspects in Damon Wright's murder?"

"It's all right. People saw you there. You probably have an alibi. If it makes you feel better, write up a time line of where you were and who you spoke to."

"That won't make me feel better, Paul. That little girl is dead."

"Yeah. She is."

"I have to go. We'll talk when you get home."

"I told Thorndyke we'd drive up on Sunday."

"Okay. Maybe we should rent a room up there for the season." It wasn't funny.

I left as soon as my meeting was over, but it ran long so I wasn't particularly early. Dusty was in the dining room. I had made her a copy of the profiles and they were scattered across the table. She sat with a pen in her hand, staring down at a yellow lined pad covered with her unmistakable calligraphy grade handwriting. She seemed surprised to see me. "Is it that late already?"

"Almost. Can I get you a drink?" She shook her head so I poured one for myself. "Any new insights?"

She sighed and put the pen down. "If it was an accident, then nothing is changed. But I doubt that anyone believes that it was. But I can't figure out how this connects to Damon Wright. I don't think she ever even spoke to him, signed to him, whatever. If his death was a mistake and Edison was the real target, then there are plenty of connections but none of them make any sense. Why not just kill the old man?"

"Maybe someone with a grudge against Edison is taking it out on people close to him."

Dusty nodded. "Or maybe she saw something when Damon was killed that could identify the killer."

"Then why didn't she tell the police?"

"Maybe she didn't know it was significant."

I drew up a chair and sat down. "You've been reading too many mystery novels. If that was the case, why did the killer wait so long? And what could she have seen? Remember, she was in the kitchen with Mrs. McCone during the critical time. Or most of it anyway."

"I know that. Why didn't you make me a drink?"

"You said you didn't want one."

"Well I do." She got up and mixed one for herself. "Something else occurred to me."

"What's that?"

"If the killer is capable of two murders, there's no reason for him to stop."

"Or her."

Dusty nodded. "So we have to stop him, or her, don't we?"

"Maybe this was the last one."

"What are the odds?"

My appointment with the Johnsons was for Saturday brunch at the Seacoaster in Newport. I thought things might go better if Dusty wasn't along, but I invited her anyway. She declined. "I'd just be in the way." So I drove down alone. There hadn't been much in the news about Tracy Fannon's death. I'd searched the internet and couldn't find anything except a brief notice about an apparent accident which the police were investigating. Thorndyke had apparently told me – or at least implied - more than he had said to the local reporters, or they'd agreed to play it down for the time being. There was no suggestion that it was tied to Damon Wright's murder, but then again, the police probably requested that as well.

I was early but the Johnsons were already seated on the patio when I arrived. Both of them were on cell phones. He waved; she ignored me. I sat down and accepted a menu from the waiter who promised to bring me coffee. I tried to look as though I wasn't paying attention to what my hosts were saying but it was hard to miss. Peter Johnson was berating someone because he hadn't found them the kind of location they wanted. Peggy was complaining about money. "This isn't going to be direct to video, you know. We need more than the contents of your piggy bank."

He finished first, smiled and shook my hand. She talked a little longer, frowned, and complained that the waiter hadn't taken their orders yet.

"So how can we help you, Mr. Birch?" The waiter appeared and Peggy ordered an omelet.

"I was hoping we could talk about last weekend. It's obviously in all our interests if this gets cleared up as quickly as possible."

Peter ordered a skipperjack, whatever that was. His wife looked at me for the first time. "There's no such thing as bad publicity, Mr. Birch."

I asked for a BLT and fries. 'That might be true, but I would imagine that your busy schedule doesn't leave much room for return trips to New Hampshire to speak to the police."

"That's not likely, is it?" She lit a cigarette, ignoring the fact that there were no ashtrays because smoking in a public place is against the law.

I shrugged. "Now that there's been a second death, all bets are off."

They both looked startled. I thought it was genuine, but these people were in the movie industry. Pretense was their business.

"What are you talking about?" asked Peggy with a glare designed to turn me to jelly. It didn't work.

"Tracy Fannon was killed on Friday."

They exchanged looks. "Who is Tracy Fannon?" asked Peter.

"Meredith Fannon's daughter. You met her at Edison's place."

"The little dumb girl?" Peggy looked amused. "Why would anyone want to kill her?"

"I don't know. Do you?"

She ignored me and puffed energetically. A man at the adjacent table gave her a dirty look which she couldn't have missed but completely ignored. Her husband at least pretended to be sympathetic. "How did it happen?"

"Fell to her death, or was pushed. The exact circumstances have yet to be determined."

"At the same place where they found Wright?"

"No, but nearby. The coroner hasn't officially called it homicide yet, but the odds against it being an accident seem pretty high to me."

"It may well be but I don't see that this concerns us. We were nowhere near the Edison place on Friday." She said it was a level voice but I saw something in her husband's face. She was lying.

"I wasn't accusing you of anything," I said mildly. "I'm just trying to get an understanding of what happened last weekend."

"Isn't that Detective Thornton's job?" She clearly didn't want to talk to me, which made me curious. People who don't want to talk often have the most worth saying.

"His name's Thorndyke. Yes, it is. He's aware that I'm looking into matters on my own."

"That's right. You're the private eye, aren't you?"

Obviously she didn't like me, or didn't want to answer questions about Damon Wright's murder, or most likely both. Her husband hastily tried to play peacemaker. "I understand your desire to put all of this to rest, but we barely knew Mr. Wright and I don't think either of us even spoke to the young girl. I don't see that we can be of any help."

Normally I'd have let him think he'd smoothed things over but he irritated me almost as much as his wife did. "That's odd. I've been told that you knew Wright quite well. Wasn't he working on Edison to get movie rights for you? I understood that to be a pretty big deal for you if it happened." I was guessing about this. Wolfman had raised the possibility but had admitted it was sheer conjecture. It had the ring of authenticity though and the looks on their faces told me there was at least some truth to it.

Peter looked as though he'd been slapped. Peggy pretty clearly wanted to slap me. "We've spoken about the possibility in passing, but Edison is an odd duck. We told Damon that we were leaving the offer open in case Edison changed his mind but it was never a major part of our plans. Damon never called back so we assumed that Edison wasn't budging from his original position."

Our food came. Mine was pretty good but Peggy seemed to have lost her appetite. She pushed the omelet around the plate and drank coffee instead. Peter ate heartily but I sensed it was so that he didn't have to talk to me. I decided to run through the questions I had before the atmosphere grew any worse.

Peter replied to everything I asked, but only after thinking about each of them. I didn't know if he was lying to me but he was obviously taking care not to say anything he thought might reflect badly on one or both of them. Peggy didn't answer directly at all, just nodded to confirm what her husband had already said. Their story was bland and uninformative. They had talked to various people, they couldn't remember much about what was said, they hadn't seen anything suspicious or unusual. Each admitted that they'd gone to walk on the mountain. He claimed to enjoy being outdoors. She had wanted to clear her head. They had not been together at any point and neither of them had seen anyone else while they were out and about. Nor could they suggest any reason why someone would want to bash in Damon Wright's brains.

It was almost like talking to myself.

They had invited me but I picked up the tab as a subtle gesture of my contempt. If they noticed, they didn't show it. I thanked them profusely for their help, but they didn't notice the sarcasm either. I wondered how people who spent their lives bringing stories about people to life on the screen could be so lacking in empathy or good manners, but then I remembered some of the movies I'd seen lately.

I stopped by the office on the way back. Tina was there alone. I tried to get her to go home but she just had one little thing that she needed to deal with, which is the same thing she told me every time I caught her working extra hours. I had belatedly asked Merrilee to run up a profile on Ronald Edison and sure enough, it was in my inbox. It was pretty short.

Ronald had been born in 1984, which made him older than I'd expected. He graduated from Culloden Region High School, spent one year at the University of New Hampshire before dropping out. No police record, not even traffic violations. He worked in the Culloden Inn as a waiter for a year and then for two years in Brattleboro, Vermont, at a fast food restaurant. No other work history after that. He was the only one on my list who had a Facebook profile, but he hadn't posted there for two years. His mother was Louise Bowman Edison who died accidentally in 1991 in a hiking accident. I had forgotten that last item which was now somewhat more interesting, although perhaps irrelevant. Still, there were a few too many hiking deaths on Mount Brandoch as far as I was concerned. I wondered if I should mention the manner of her death to Thorndyke but decided Tibbett would already have known that.

With a final, probably futile demand that Tina finish up whatever she was doing and go home, I left the office.

Dusty's spirits seemed to have improved. She wanted to know everything about my meeting with the Johnsons and pretended to think that I'd accomplished a lot instead of virtually nothing. She confirmed my low opinion of Peggy Johnson. "She's a bitch. Did you notice that she wouldn't speak to Mrs. McCone or even meet her eyes? I think she's a racist."

"She's from Australia," I said. "Not many people of color there. Maybe she was just uneasy because she didn't know how to act." Why was I apologizing for Peggy Johnson? Dusty put her hands on her hips and cocked her head to one side with that look that meant I was talking nonsense, that both of us knew it, and that I should stop wasting our time. "But yeah, she's not a nice person. Neither is her husband, probably, but at least he makes an effort to hide his indifference."

I reminded her about the way in which Martin Edison's wife had died.

"Yeah, I made a note about that and I googled some stuff. She was at the house alone when it happened. Edison was in San Francisco signing at one of the big chain bookstores. They had a cleaning woman and a cook who both lived in the house at the time, but it was the weekend and they were both off. There was no suspicion of foul play, at least not officially."

"Still might be connected."

"Can't prove a negative, but none of our suspects even knew the Edisons at that time, except Ronald and he was seven years old. And maybe Naomi Winstead. I don't know if she ever met the wife." She smiled. "Ronalld has an alibi for his mother's death, if you care. He was attending school when she fell to her death. Or was pushed."

"Wasn't Edison already with Pikestaff even back then?"

"Yes, but Hillary Austin wasn't. Edison hadn't hired Mrs. McCone yet, although I suppose he might have met her. Arthur Wolfman still hadn't reviewed any of his books, the Johnsons and the movie business were in the far future, he had a different agent – since deceased, and he didn't hire Meredith Fannon until sometime in the late 1990s."

"Still, I wouldn't rule out a connection we just can't see."

"I defer to your superior experience and training."

"As well you might."

She kissed me then. "Thank you for doing all this." And then she thanked me some more and the details are none of your business.

We were both pretty quiet on the ride up to New Hampshire the following morning. Dusty had written up a timeline of her last visit but when I looked it over I noticed several long gaps and some of the listings would be hard to confirm. We still didn't know exactly when Tracy Fannon had died, but the odds weren't greatly in Dusty's favor. I felt a little better about things because Thorndyke had sounded as though he was only including Dusty to be thorough, but I knew that wouldn't last if something turned up that seemed to implicate her more strongly. Since we were planning to drive back home after the interview, we didn't reserve a room after all. The Culloden Inn looked completely deserted when we drove past and turned down the short side street that led to the police station.

Thorndyke didn't keep us waiting long. He even smiled as he shook our hands and led us inside. I thought he looked tired and decided he was somewhat younger than I had thought originally, probably barely into his thirties. I was relieved when he brought us to his office, a somewhat cramped space, rather than an interrogation room. He even offered us coffee which we both declined.

"I appreciate your taking the time to drive up here. We could have done this over the telephone, but it would probably be a good idea if we got a written statement from you." He pointed to a small tape recorder on his desk. "I'll record this if you're agreeable."

"We hadn't planned on spending the night," I said cautiously.

"As soon as we're done I'll give it to Ethel to type up. It shouldn't take much more than an hour and I imagine you'll want lunch before you start back."

"How is the mother doing?"

"Not very well. They were very close."

Thorndyke started the recorder, gave the date and time and named us both, then summarized the reason why he'd asked her to come in. He provided no details about the death of Tracy Fannon other than the simple fact. Then he asked her if she could account for her time on the day in question.

"I typed up everything I could remember, where I was, who I talked to. Most of them will probably remember me."

She handed him the printout and he glanced over it quickly. "May I keep this?"

"Yes, of course."

"I'm going to read it into the statement." And he did. It only took a few seconds and then he set it aside. "I'm particularly interested in the time between three and five in the afternoon."

Dusty bit her lip. Her morning's activities were easy to confirm, her afternoon and evening less so. Both were disasters in terms of establishing an alibi. She had visited the convenience store, the butcher shop, and a couple of small businesses, but it was unlikely that the people she'd spoken with would be able to pinpoint the times and in any case she hadn't been in any one spot long enough to matter other than half an hour with the Methodist minister starting at two o'clock.

"You didn't visit the Edison house at any time during the day?"

"No. I called late in the morning because I wanted to take Mrs. McCone to lunch but no one answered."

"Mr. Edison and Miss Fannon were the only ones home that day. He usually doesn't answer the telephone and for obvious reasons she didn't either. There was no message on the answering machine."

"No, I didn't leave one."

"You talked to several people during the course of the day."

"Yes, I did."

"And for the record, your purpose was to investigate matters related to the death of Damon Wright?"

"Yes, I thought I might be able to help. It probably wasn't a good idea."

"I don't suppose it did any harm." He actually smiled at her and I liked him better. "It's not pleasant being a murder suspect, is it?"

"No, it certainly isn't."

He asked a few more questions, but they were more form than substance. When he clicked off the recorder, he sat back and folded his arms. "Technically I should chastise both of you for potentially interfering in a police investigation."

I started to say something and he waved his hand. "I'm not going to do that. I understand your concerns. If our situations were reversed, I'd probably do the same." He raised both hands and smoothed his hair back. "We're not certain how the Fannon girl died. It might have been an accident. Despite what you see on television, we can't get a professional tracker to look the scene over and tell us she was pushed to her death by a left handed man wearing cowboy boots who has a slight limp. We don't know what happened and we might never know for sure. Personally I think she was murdered, but my thoughts and opinions are not admissible as evidence. There is nothing to suggest that anyone else was on Edison's property at the time."

I decided to see how forthcoming he would be. "I assume she died sometime in the middle of the afternoon." He'd already as much as told us that much.

"We know when she left school and how long it would have taken her to get home. The body was found by Mrs. McCone at half past six. There's a blueberry patch nearby that they both were in the habit of visiting."

"I just don't see how her death could be connected to Damon," said Dusty. "I don't think they ever even spoke to one another." She flushed. "You know what I mean."

"There may be a connection we don't know of." Thorndyke leaned forward and rested his arms on his desk. "Meredith Fallon has never identified the father, for example, Or she may have seen something that she shouldn't have."

Dusty nodded. "We wondered about that. But why wouldn't she have told you?"

"Sometimes teenagers like to keep secrets. More likely, she didn't realize that what she'd seen was significant. This is all theoretical, of course."

"Is there anything else you can tell us about the manner of her death?" I didn't really expect him to answer but it was worth a try.

He was quiet for an unnaturally long time. "Unofficially, I don't think either of you had anything to do with either death. I do appreciate the information you provided about your meeting with the two New Yorkers, little as it seems to be."

"I got even less from the Johnsons. They've been making movies for so long they turn everything around them into drama."

Thorndyke smiled more broadly this time. "The Chief and I made that very same observation."

"I still have to track down Patrick and Winstead. They've both been out of touch."

"When you see Miss Winstead, would you ask her a question for me?"

"Sure."

"Ask her why she never mentioned that she owns a little cottage over in Jaffrey?"

"Jaffrey?" Dusty and I exchanged glances. "Over near Monadnock?"

"That's right. About half an hour away. She bought it just over a year ago."

I searched my memory. "I thought she said she was a city girl, hated the outdoors."

"That's what she said."

"Could it have been an investment?" asked Dusty.

"Possibly. But she hasn't made any effort to rent it out. And she bought it from another non-resident. The property formerly belonged to Damon Wright."

'Interesting," I said. "You do know that they were formerly man and wife?"

"That was a long time ago. Centuries, according to Ms Winstead."

"They may have remained friends."

"They didn't act very friendly while we were around."

"It's probably nothing, but it does draw another line between two of the characters."

"I'll ask her about it, if I ever track her down," I agreed. "I don't suppose you could give me the address?"

"I don't see why not. It's a matter of public record." He consulted a file on his desk, wrote down the address on an index card, and handed it to me.

"Are we finished?" asked Dusty.

"I don't have any more questions." Thorndyke stood up and we followed suit. "I'll get the transcription going right away. It'll be waiting at the front desk."

We were almost out the door when Dusty stopped. "I don't suppose Tracy kept a diary."

Thorndyke gave her a speculative look. "Yes, in fact, she did."

"Then you've read it?"

"I have. There's nothing there that helps us, although there are some things I don't understand. She apparently had her own personal shorthand. And there are references to her father."

"Does she know his name?"

Thorndyke shrugged. "She doesn't mention it. But some entries imply that she's talked with him. A lot of it is obscure."

"Would her mother know what she was referring to?"

"We haven't been able to ask her yet." He hesitated. "The girl also had a pad of paper she kept on her person, so she could communicate with people who don't sign. It was with her when she died. She wrote some things there as well that we haven't deciphered, but I'm not at liberty to divulge just what they were but we think one of them was very recent."

"Maybe Tracy knew more than we realized. She was so quiet, people might have talked in front of her without realizing that she could hear them," I suggested.

"The thought had occurred to me."

For want of a better idea, we ate at the Culloden Inn, taking our time over the food. We were back at the police station early but the statement – actually a transcript of the conversation – was ready and Dusty signed it in front of the desk sergeant. When we got back into the car, I made a turn that took Dusty by surprise.

"Where are we going?"

"Jaffrey."

It only took her a second. "Naomi Winstead's place."

I nodded. "If she's there, it would explain why we haven't been able to reach her in Connecticut."

Thorndyke's estimate of the travel time was a little low. It took forty minutes, but to be fair, we dithered a bit trying to find the right address. The cottage was even more remote than I had expected – Jaffrey is pretty well settled after all. It was on the outskirts of town at the end of a dirt road and the grounds were so overgrown that we passed it twice before spotting the building.

There was no driveway, just a bare patch of ground, and no vehicles in sight. The cottage was small and in good repair, but there were no signs of occupation. The drapes were drawn and some of the windows were actually shuttered. There was no mail in the mailbox except a circular so old that it had curled into a tube. I tried the doorbell and knocked, but the house felt empty. It would not have surprised me to learn that no one had been here since the day Winstead bought the place.

It was Dusty who spotted evidence of more recent habitation. She had walked around to the rear while I was at the door and she called to me. I joined her at a small stone fireplace about ten feet from the back door. Someone had been burning papers there and hadn't done a very good job of it. I used a stick to push the charred remains around and found a fragment of a newspaper less than a week old. I showed it to Dusty. There was also the corner of a road map, piece of cardboard that was probably part of a pistol target, and an almost untouched Boston bus schedule.

"She's been here."

"Someone has," I answered. "But there's no one here now."

"Maybe she came up for a few days of solitude and headed back to Connecticut."

"She lives alone. Why would she drive all the way up here for solitude?"

Dusty punched my arm. "You're a very suspicious person."

"Comes with the job."

I looked around some more, found a garbage can but it was empty and had been for a long time. Dusty tried looking through the unshuttered windows but without any luck. There was a stone lined firepit in the back with some fairly recent ashes. I poked around a bit and turned up part of the skeleton of a small animal, probably a rabbit, but nothing else. We had made a long diversion for nothing but it had been worth a try.

Dusty walked around the far side of the house and I started across the back yard toward the remains of a gazebo. The white paint was peeling off the fragments. Just beyond was a towering spruce tree whose bark was pockmarked by jagged holes. A single nail protruded at about eye level. This, I concluded, was where the target had been mounted, but the scarring didn't look much like bullet holes. If I'd had to guess, I would have said arrows.

"Find anything," called Dusty.

"Not really." I took another quick look around and walked back to the house.

"At least we're not any worse off," said Dusty.

"Wasted a quarter tank of gas. Any useful suggestions or observations?".

"Let's go home." And we did

Steve brought me some interesting news with my coffee on Monday morning. "You won't have to drive up to Boston to speak to James Patrick."

I glanced at my wristwatch. "You must have gotten him out of bed if you've talked to him this early."

"Actually, he called us. He wanted an appointment to see you. He'll be here at ten."

That was interesting. "Did he say why?"

"No, and when I asked him if he'd received any of my messages he said not. I asked what it was in reference to and he said private. He's a man of few words."

"Not common in a writer. Or maybe he just saves them up to put them on paper. Everyone must have a maximum number of words they can produce and writers can't afford to waste resources."

Steve ignored my attempt at humor. "I'll try the Winstead woman later this morning. I assume you still want to see her."

"Yes I do. And find out if there' a listing for her in Jaffrey, New Hampshire."

Patrick was on time, early in fact, and he was clearly upset about something. My first thought was that Thorndyke had spoken to him and that he was convinced that he was a serious suspect. I pondered the ethics of letting him hire me to prove him innocent, given that I was already trying to do the same for Dusty, even if that was pro bono. I hadn't decided yet when I let Steve send him in.

We shook hands and he sat down, although he was so restless I expected him to jump up and start pacing at any moment. "I assume that you know I've been trying to reach you."

"Yes. Your young man mentioned that. I'm sorry that I didn't get your messages but I live alone and I was away on a book tour."

"So I understand."

"I don't know if you've heard but Tracy Fannon was killed a few days ago."

"Thorndyke called. All indications are that it was an accident."

"You don't believe that, do you?"

I was hesitant to commit myself until I had a better idea of where this was all leading. "I'm not in a position to make that call."

"It has to be related to the Wright case. You must see that." I had never seen Patrick so animated.

"There's a very good chance that it could be. It might help if you told me just why you're here."

He stood up and began to pace, just as I'd expected. "I want to hire you, Mr. Birch."

"I already have a client involved with this case." I didn't think of Dusty as a client exactly, but it was too complicated to explain to him, and none of his business.

Patrick spun around. "Are you telling me they have a suspect in Tracy's death?"

I thought that one over. "My client is a potential suspect in the death of Damon Wright. There is as yet no reason that I'm aware of to suppose that anyone is suspected of killing Miss Fannon."

"Well that's what I want you to do for me. Find out who killed her. I don't care a rat's ass who offed Wright. He was a prick at the best of times."

"I don't understand your sudden interest, Mr. Patrick. If you're not a suspect, then why do you care what happened to Tracy Fannon? You'll have to pardon my frankness, but you don't seem the type who would be so outraged by the death of a young girl you'd just met to spend money trying to find out who, if anyone, was responsible."

Patrick's face ran through a gamut of reactions, shock, anger, unhappiness, and then slid toward some amalgamation of them all. "Tracy Fannon was my daughter, Mr. Birch. Until today she and her mother and I were the only ones who knew that."

I struggled to keep a neutral expression and probably failed. "I'm very sorry, Mr. Patrick."

The confession seemed to have deflated him. He walked back to his chair like a very old man and dropped into it rather than taking a seat. "I met her mother at a publisher's party years ago. We both had a lot to drink and in those days I thought I had a macho image to live up to. I considered Meredith just another fan to be bedded and forgotten. I was wrong about that. It wasn't her first time, but she wasn't very experienced and I don't think she's been with anyone else since. It's not love, don't get me wrong. Neither of us ever pretended that it was. But we liked each other right from the start and we still do."

"So why didn't you acknowledge Tracy as your daughter? I don't see that it would have hurt your reputation."

"Meredith insisted. She was very insecure back then. Hell, she's not much better now. Her family was still alive when Tracy was born and she didn't want them to think of her as someone who slept around. They were very religious."

"So how did she explain Tracy?"

"Said she was raped. They were the kind of people who wouldn't want to report something like that. They'd have been ashamed. They were ashamed, as a matter of fact. When we found out that Tracy couldn't speak, they claimed it was a judgment of some kind."

"That must have been very difficult."

'Yeah, it was. Meredith and I were just friends, you know, but I loved that little girl. I want whoever did it caught and I don't care how much it costs, Mr. Birch."

I was still trying to fit this new information in with everything else I knew, or didn't know. "Are you sure no one else was aware that you were her father?'

Patrick shrugged. "We were pretty careful. When Meredith went on vacation, I arranged to pick them up, but never at the house. No one in town knew who I was, but I kept a low profile just in case. We always went places where there weren't a lot of people – rented a cabin, flew to Bermuda once. It's possible that someone saw us together, but they wouldn't necessarily make the connection even if they did recognize me. Tracy looks…looked like her mother. And I was always careful not to let people know I could read sign. So I don't think anyone could have guessed and I doubt very much that Meredith ever told anyone, not even Edison although he probably suspected something when she asked him to invite me to that party."

"Does Detective Thorndyke know?"

"Not yet."

"Have you spoken to him at all about Tracy?"

Patrick shook his head. "I was thinking of going up there tomorrow, but I wanted to talk to you first. The guys in my books solve things by sticking their nose in places where they don't belong, pushing people around when necessary. They're scary and confident and they have the author on their side. I don't have any of those advantages. I wouldn't know where to start."

"Real life detectives don't have a lot of those advantages either. Have you talked to her mother?"

"I called as soon as I heard. She broke up on the phone and hung up. They were close. She's going to stay in town for a few days. Says she can't stand looking at the house and not seeing Tracy there."

"It still might have been an accident."

Patrick shook his head. "I don't believe it. She was more at home on a mountain trail than anyone I know. Can you help me?"

I sighed. "I don't know. I can look around, ask a few questions. I'm doing that already. Thorndyke and I get along. He might tell me something that he wouldn't tell you if he thought it might lead to closing the case. I think you need to tell him about the relationship as soon as possible. He'll keep it quiet unless it's germane."

"I'll drive up first thing. So how much do you want for a retainer?" He took out a checkbook.

"Like I said, I already have a client. I'll bill you for expenses and round it up a little. Are you going to see her mother tomorrow?"

"Yes. I don't know how much good I can do but I have to try."

"I'll need to talk to her myself at some point. It would help if you told her I was working for you and why."

"Yeah, I see that. I'll take care of it."

"So what can you tell me that I don't already know?"

Patrick looked surprised. "About what?"

"Let's assume for the moment that it wasn't an accident and had nothing to do with Damon Wright. Do you have any enemies who might have suspected the relationship and used it to get at you?"

He looked as though the possibility had never even occurred to him. "I have some old girlfriends who weren't too happy with me, but that all stopped almost twenty years ago."

"Someone in the publishing business with a grudge?"

"Sure. Damon Wright. He'd been after me for a couple of years to change agents. I blew my stack at him the day before he died. I told Thornydyke all about it. We were alone but someone might have heard the shouting. I didn't want him to think I was hiding anything."

"No one else?"

He shrugged. "I live alone, I don't have many friends, and I'm not ever going to beat someone out for a coveted literary prize. I complained about one of my neighbors who has a dog that won't stop barking. Some guy used to stalk me – he always dressed up like the hero in my books – but he got hit by a utility truck and died. That's about it. I've led a pretty dull life the last few years."

"How about Meredith Fannon? Do you know if she had any enemies?"

"Outside of her lousy family, no, and they're all dead or in convalescent homes. She was always really shy. Doesn't like crowds. Not a party animal. Meredith was destined to be private secretary to a recluse like Edison. I've probably got more relatives than she had acquaintances."

"What about connections to Damon Wright?"

"Well, she obviously knew who he was and vice versa. He's been to the house several times over the last few years. He was Edison's agent, after all. Meredith handled all of the old man's correspondence and a lot of his other business stuff, so they would have spoken more than occasionally, but I don't imagine he had much time for a kid. He couldn't read sign in any case."

Tracy Fannon had progressed beyond the kid stage but I didn't think it would be a good idea to mention that. "What do you know about Wright? Did he have enemies?"

Patrick made a sound denoting disgust. "The question is whether or not he had any friends. I was always amazed that someone so transparently obnoxious could get himself in a position where people entrusted their careers to him." He shifted uncomfortably. "Though I have to admit that he was good at his job. I sometimes thought he must be blackmailing all the publishers because I never met an editor who claimed to like him."

"Seriously?"

"Not the blackmail part. He was just a born negotiator."

"So why didn't you switch?"

"If I was younger and hungrier, I might have. But I've been with the same guy right from the start, he's done well by me and I feel some loyalty. And I don't spend the money I earn now. Why would I put up with an asshole in order to put more money away for my heirs." This last seemed to remind him that his only apparent heir had recently died. He looked as though he was on the verge of tears.

"It's possible that Wright was killed by mistake and that Edison was supposed to be the victim."

Patrick had not considered this possibility before and I had to explain about the borrowed coat. "That explains some of the questions Thorndyke asked that night. I wondered what he was getting at."

"Edison doesn't seem to have been the easiest person in the world to get along with."

"A lot of people envied him, but I don't see how he could make enemies living up on his mountain. He probably went for months without seeing anyone not part of the household." Patrick shook his head. "Maybe some fan went nuts. No, I just can't see it."

"But obviously Edison was connected to both Tracy and Damon Wright. He's just about the only common factor."

He thought that over. "I don't see how that helps us."

I shifted the topic slightly. "I know how everyone else at that party was linked to Edison, and I have a good idea why they were invited. But why were you on the list? As far as I can tell, he'd never met you before. So why did Fallon want you there that particular day?"

"No, we hadn't met. Meredith told Edison earlier this year that we were friends, but not that I was Tracy's father. He probably thought we were sleeping together during her vacations."

"Weren't you?"

"Only the one time. We had separate rooms when we went away. But I suppose Edison might have jumped to the same conclusion you did."

"There must have been a particular reason why she wanted you there."

"Yes. We'd talked about it. I was going to stay over an extra day and we were going to tell Edison the whole truth, that I was Tracy's father. Meredith wasn't comfortable about letting the secret out after all these years, but she knew Edison was planning to quit writing and that she'd probably be out of a job before long. He'd been good to her and promised her a hefty severance pay – enough that she'd never have to work again – and even offered to let her stay on at the house. She thought she owed him the truth about whose daughter he had been supporting all these years. I think the old man rather liked Tracy. Treated her better than his own son, anyway."

"He and Ronald don't seem to be close."

"They're not. Edison mostly ignores him, but he supports him as well. Merry never could figure out what was wrong between them."

"I think you should call Thorndyke right away and let him know you're coming." I stood up to indicate our conversation was over. "I'll be in touch as soon as I know anything."

I repeated everything that Patrick had told me to Dusty as soon as I got home that evening. She was startled a bit when I told her Tracy was Patrick's daughter, but for the most part she seemed preoccupied. It wasn't that she wasn't paying attention, but she wasn't paying FULL attention, and that seemed odd. When I was done, she asked me if I wanted a drink and I said yes. She made two of them silently, then handed me one.

"I need to talk to you."

"Okay."

"I never told you the whole reason why I drove up to New Hampshire on my own."

"There's no reason why you should have."

'Yes there is. We're supposed to be partners. The thing is, I know I can lean on you when I want to. I mean, here you are running off to New York City and everything just to help me feel better."

"I actually didn't accomplish very much."

"That's not the point. Look, my father is a little old fashioned about gender roles."

"I've met him, remember?" Ed Rhodes was suave and self confident and overbearing. He doesn't approve of our living together without benefit of marriage, nor does he approve of women with careers. Oddly enough, I think he'd be happy to see us married, which sometimes makes me wonder about myself.

"He's used to making decisions for other people. He pre-approved everyone I dated in high school, told me what electives to take then and in college, threw out record albums and books he didn't think were appropriate for me, and so on. You know all this.

The worst part is that for the longest time I didn't object. It was just the way things were."

"Some fathers are overly protective." And obsessive.

"He's a control freak, Paul. But that's not the point. I worked through that after I dropped out of college. But buried down somewhere I'm afraid that I might fall into the same trap again, that I might allow myself to become so dependent on someone else that I was abdicating responsibility for my own life."

"I try not to infringe on your space."

"You're not the problem. It's just that I realized I was thinking that you might be able to figure out what really happened and my name would be cleared and everything would be great. Except that if I did nothing, it would be like slipping back into old bad habits, expecting some man to come to my rescue, make the decisions for me. One of the reasons I like living with you is that when I have a problem you listen and make sympathetic noises but you don't tell me how to fix things unless I ask you. That's rare in a guy, frankly."

"I didn't realize I was such a paragon of sensitivity. Would it make you feel better if I was a little less perfect?"

She laughed and hit me on the arm. "You can rescue me any time you want. I just need to feel that it's my decision at least as much as yours. But I don't want you to think that just because I'm trying to help myself as well it's because I don't trust you."

"The thought never crossed my mind."

"See that it doesn't." She looked greatly relieved. I had sensed something of this ambivalence about taking care of herself in the past but never with this much intensity. "So how does this affect our analysis of Damon's murder?"

It was an obvious change of subject. "Well, if Tracy's death was an accident, it has no effect at all."

"But we don't think it was an accident, do we?"

"Is the bear Catholic?"

"So why would someone kill her?"

"Two scenarios come immediately to mind. First, the killer might have intended to eliminate her all along for reasons we can't yet know. Wright might have been a case of mistaken identity but there's no chance of a similar error with Tracy. That suggests there was some connection to either Wright or Edison that meant that both of them had to die. I can't figure out how she could be significantly linked to Wright. I mean, if it had turned out that he was her father rather than Patrick, there might have been a hook there that we could tug on. As it is, it's quite possible that they'd never even spoken to one another. He apparently didn't know sign and frankly he wasn't the kind who would interact with children or even teenagers very successfully."

"It would never have occurred to him to try because they weren't in a position to help his career. The world accommodated itself to Damon rather than the other way around."

"So my guess is that in this version of events, there exists some relationship between her and Edison beyond the obvious. If so and if Wright did die by mistake, then Edison is still in danger."

"I assume that he has taken steps to protect himself."

I shrugged. "I don't know. I suppose he might have hired a bodyguard and/or beefed up his security system. There was talk about an updated burglar alarm he was supposed to have installed but I don't know if it ever happened. The one he had when we were there is antiquated. I do know that he's spoken to a private investigator." I automatically glanced at my watch but it was too late to call Cordelia Grayson at her office and I didn't know her home number. "She's not acting as bodyguard though."

"He seems awfully vulnerable up on that hill."

"They'd have to get past Mrs. McCone."

Dusty laughed. "I assume the other possibility is that she was collateral damage. She saw or might have seen something that day, or at another time I suppose, which the killer considered a potential threat."

"Unfortunately, Thorndyke doesn't know or at least didn't tell us much about the circumstances surrounding her death. He did say that Tracy visited that area frequently to collect blueberries – though I think we're past that time now - and that Edison was unaware of anyone coming to the house that afternoon. No one else was home. Not that Edison's testimony eliminates the possibility. If he was shut up in his office, he might not have heard anything even if a brass band had paraded through the garden."

"If he's not writing any more, why would he shut himself away like that?"

"Habit maybe. Or to conceal the fact that he's drinking rather more than he should."

"You think so?"

"I saw his private bar. Very well stocked and most of the bottles were half empty. There were two dirty wine glasses on his desk and a recently used shot glass on one of the shelves. There was also a set of four brandy snifters that must have been recently washed because they weren't as dusty as their surroundings and an empty bottle on the floor."

"Ooh, detective stuff."

"You got it, baby," I drawled. "So the killer either convinced her to go for a walk or was waiting for her somewhere up on the mountain, followed her maybe, watched for an opportunity, then pushed her over the edge. I can't see anyone sitting up there on the off chance that Tracy would choose that particular day to visit that particular spot, so the killer either came to the house or contacted her at some point and arranged a rendezvous."

"I think that's a lot more likely than your first scenario."

I agreed.

"So who had the opportunity?" She flushed. "Besides me, I mean."

"Austin and Wolfman are both eliminated this time. Steve showed me the itinerary for the Johnsons. They were within fifty miles of Culloden that day. I don't know if they were together all day, and I wouldn't trust either of them to tell me the truth about it, but either or both of them could easily have made the trip to Culloden. I imagine Thorndyke will be talking to them. I think we could eliminate the mother out of hand, but since she was with Mrs. McCone that afternoon she's out of contention anyway. Winstead's location is unknown but it's possible she was at her little hideaway in Jaffrey. Patrick was signing books that morning in Bangor, but he was on the road that afternoon and there is plenty of flexibility in his schedule. He could have done it."

"Surely not his own daughter?" I looked at her and after a second she nodded. "All right. It's possible."

"He was about to be outed as her father. There could be something there. Maybe he was afraid it would spoil his tough guy image. We only have his version of what happened. It's possible that he raped Meredith Fallon."

"Another scenario just occurred to me," said Dusty. "Maybe Tracy was murdered but her death had nothing to do with Damon's. There might really be a nutcase hiding up there throwing people off the mountain. Or she might have been targeted by persons who happen to be suspects in Wright's murder but for reasons completely unrelated."

I had thought about that but had dismissed it because if either variation was true, it was unlikely that anything we could do would turn up the solution. "If there's a madman he isn't going to get caught by talking to the others. He'll make a mistake eventually and the police will have him, or he'll stop or move on and he becomes someone else's problem. Your second suggestion gives us at least two more suspects. We only have Martin Edison's word that he was alone in his office that afternoon. He could have accompanied or followed Tracy up the trail and done the deed."

"I don't see a motive."

"Doesn't mean there isn't one. Edison has his peculiarities. Don't forget why he was tossed out of the army."

"That was a long time ago."

"Sometimes things fester."

Dusty digested that but it clearly left a bad taste. "Who's the other?"

I'd lost my train of thought and it took a few seconds to find it again. "Ronald might have been suffering from sibling rivalry. It looks like Edison treated her better than his own son. Theoretically he wasn't home that day but he could have arranged to meet her in the woods. Thorndyke didn't say anything about an alibi for him."

"Ronald wasn't treated badly though. He had a roof over his head, an allowance, and I don't think Mrs. McCone would have stood for any actual mistreatment. She seems to be the boss in the house."

"Perception is everything. For that matter, we haven't serious discussed the possibility that Ronald also killed Wright. Maybe he decided that his father was being treated unfairly by Wright and wanted to curry favor."

"Wouldn't that have required him to tell Edison what he'd done?"

"Not necessarily. And he might also have killed Wright believing that he was killing his father."

"I could see him having a grudge against Tracy and his father, but wouldn't he have known that the man he attacked wasn't Edison? You or I might have mistaken one for the other but surely his own son wouldn't have been fooled."

I shook my head. "So it would seem, but I wasn't there. Circumstances might have misled him. It was getting dark. As far as I know, Ronald never saw Edison drag me off to talk about the alleged previous attempts on his life and he almost certainly did not know about the borrowed jacket."

"Do you think someone's really been trying to kill Edison all along?"

"The three incidents happened. He didn't imagine them. But I'm not prepared to say that they were attempts on his life or that they were all the work of the same person who killed Wright and presumably Tracy Fannon. We still don't know enough to eliminate any possibilities. Hell, we probably don't know enough to establish all the possibilities."

"Wouldn't that mean that all of our work so far is just a waste of time?" She sounded discouraged.

"Might be. Welcome to the romantic world of private investigation."

The following morning I rang Cordelia Grayson and left a message on her answering machine. She called back about an hour later.

"How did things go with Martin Edison?"

"I'm not sure whether to thank you or abuse you. He's an odd duck."

"I did warn you. I assume you've heard there was a second death."

"The young girl. Yes, a real shame. I saw her for a couple of seconds when I went out to talk to him. Seemed quiet."

"She was mute."

"Oh, I didn't know that. ."

"Did you take the case?"

"Yes I did, despite some sizable reservations. I have a mortgage and a cat to support. I let him talk me into it and force me to take a sizable retainer."

"Which means that you're subject to client confidentiality considerations."

"Yes it does. Are you looking for something specific, Paul?"

"No. But he's not my client so there's no reason why I can't tell you what I know." And I did, including events on the fatal weekend, my interviews with Wolfman, Austin, and the Johnsons, as well as what little I had gleaned from Thorndyke.

Cordelia listened without interruption until I was done. "I don' know if any of that helps."

"But it doesn't hurt."

"No, it doesn't. I don't have anything substantial to trade back, confidential or otherwise, but I will pass along an interesting tidbit because it's mostly part of the public record."

"Whatever you're comfortable with."

"You knew that Edison was in the army, right?"

"For about five minutes. Psychological discharge."

"I asked him for background and he talked quite freely about his childhood and early writing career. He never even referred to the military during our interview, which might have been simply that he was embarrassed or didn't think it was worth mentioning, but it did make me curious. I have a contact at Fort Leonard Wood who looked up his file for me. There was nothing very specific but it sounds like some kind of attention deficit disorder with a hint of paranoia. My friend says the doctor who examined him recommended further evaluation, but that was in the middle of the Vietnam War and once someone was moved from wheat to chaff, they just processed you out and moved on to the next case."

I thought about it. "Given his career, I'd say he probably turned any disconnect from reality into a profitable resource."

"He wouldn't be the first, but that's not what I found interesting. Edison did his basic training at Fort Sill, New Jersey and then went to Fort Lee, Virginia, where he was eventually discharged. One of the other houseguests at your little murder party was at Fort Lee at the very same time. In fact, he was in the same training company."

My mind raced. Patrick was too young, Johnson was British. Wright might have been old enough and both Wolfman and Austin certainly were. "Austin," I guessed. Wolfman was too effete to have been a grunt.

"Afraid not. It was Arthur James Wolfman."

"Damn. I'll have to send back my Sherlock Holmes merit badge."

"They might not have known each other. Training companies don't get to spend a lot of social time together."

"They shared a barracks, mess hall, class rooms. Hard to imagine them not having run into each other." I thought about it. "Lots of time has passed since then. Both of them have changed a lot. Even if they were acquainted fifty years ago, they might not have recognized each other after so many years. I'm not sure that Wolfman and Edison were ever in the same room again until that weekend."

"Still, it's an interesting coincidence."

"I hate coincidences."

"Me too. But they ignore me and keep on happening anyway."

I thanked her, told her I'd keep in touch. She invited me to bring Dusty up for a weekend some time. "You could leaf peak. It'll gorgeous up here in a couple of weeks. I like it so much better than Hartford."

"Gets pretty cold in the winter though."

"There's that. Everything is a trade off."

"Doesn't seem fair."

"Give my best to Dusty."

The following morning Steve finally tracked down Naomi Winstead. She was at home in Connecticut and would be there for the next three days. "I asked when it might be convenient for you to stop by and she said 'never' but I pretended she was joking."

"Obtuseness can sometimes be a virtue."

"She said tomorrow would be the least intrusive and inconvenient. She's in between two legs of her latest book tour."

And so it was that I drove out to Snowden, Connecticut, which was close enough to New York that one could drive or travel by rail and work or shop in the city without actually having to live there, but far enough away to look impressively rural. Once again I had some difficulty finding the right address. Winstead's house was on a long winding road with few driveways or houses. There was a mailbox but it had neither name nor number and the house itself was invisible from the street thanks to a screen of poplars. I couldn't imagine that Naomi Winstead cultivated obscurity to stave off legions of Poppy White fans but clearly she liked her privacy.

In contrast to the cottage in New Hampshire, this was obviously a place well lived in. There was a wide, wraparound porch with rocking chairs and wind chimes, well tended flowers on either side of the driveway and at strategic spots around the yard. There was a small swimming pool just visible in the back and a good sized greenhouse with a tiny field of what I took to be corn adjacent. A white satellite dish spoiled the lines of the house. There was a late model Honda parked in front of a two car garage designed to look like a small barn, complete with cupola.

I didn't have to ring the bell. Winstead opened the door just as I reached it. She was wearing a brightly colored day dress and a frown. "Come in, Mr. Birch. You're late."

Less than ten minutes but I didn't argue. "Sorry, I drove by without spotting the driveway the first time. You have a very nice place here."

"Can I offer you something to drink? Tea? Lemonade? I think I have some instant coffee somewhere." Her tone was perfunctory. She was performing a duty rather than welcoming a guest.

"Tea would be great, thanks." I didn't want tea but I did want a chance to look around a little before we talked. Sometimes you can get a good gauge of someone by seeing how they keep their home.

She had led me into a pleasantly arranged front room. There was a small television facing an overstuffed living room set. Two very good landscapes were on facing walls and neither of them appeared to be a print. There was a fireplace but either Winstead was a fanatically clean housekeeper or it had never been used, and a thin film of dust suggested the latter. The rug looked to be expensive. There was one bookshelf but all of the books were by Winstead herself. I saw no CDS or DVDS, very little to provide any clues to her interests.

I was sitting on the couch when she brought me my tea, which I politely sipped.

"Now what exactly can I do for you, Mr. Birch? The rather irritating young man who called wasn't very specific but he implied that it was important."

"I'm looking into the death of Damon Wright and more recently Tracy Fannon."

"Yes, I heard about the little girl. Tragic. But I understood it was an accident."

"The police aren't so sure, given the murder a week earlier in almost the same location."

"I suppose they have to keep an open mind. Which leads me to ask why you're involved. Are you working for the police now?" Her tone implied that I most certainly was not.

I shook my head. "This is a separate inquiry."

"Then I'm not obligated to answer your questions, am I?"

"Not legally, no. But it's to our mutual advantage to have things cleared up."

"I don't see that that's the case at all. I'm not a suspect in Damon Wright's murder and the girl might well have died accidentally. I don't seem to have any irons in this particular fire."

"She might have fallen," I admitted. If Winstead wouldn't talk to me, this trip would have been a bigger waste of time than the one to Newport to see the Johnsons. I searched for leverage but there didn't seem to be any. I decided not to appeal to her sense of public duty. I don't like being laughed at.

Winstead took a sip of her own tea. "All right, ask what you want. I may or may not answer. I warn you that I'm a very private person and if I refuse to respond to a question, I probably won't tell you why."

"Fair enough."

I went over the events on the day that Damon Wright died. She confirmed what I remembered of her activities, added a couple of irrelevant conversations she'd had at non crucial times that I listened to patiently only because I wanted to keep her talking. Once that was out of the way, I asked her about her marriage to Damon Wright.

For a few seconds, I didn't think she was going to answer. "That was a long time ago and it didn't last very long. We married in 1980 and divorced two years later. It wasn't amicable but it wasn't bitter. I requested that one of Damon's partners represent me from that point on but I didn't leave the firm and indeed, I'm still with them today. We managed to be civil when we met at public events, which wasn't often, but we no longer had anything meaningful to say to one another. I was probably emotionally unprepared for marriage and Damon had no time for anything but his career."

"You had no children?"

"God no! Neither of us wanted them."

"But you write children's books."

"Martin Edison doesn't have any wizards in his household that I know of, and your girlfriend isn't living with a dashing spy with a license to kill, is she?"

"Point taken. How did you meet?"

"Some publicity event. I think it was one my publisher co-sponsored to coincide with the National Book Awards. We ended up drunk and in bed, much to my surprise. I wasn't a virgin but I was pretty straight laced back then. Hell, I still am."

"Was Wright already an agent?"

She shook her head. "Editorial assistant somewhere, but he was busily making connections. I suspect he made a pass at me hoping to pick me up as a client. He started his own agency the first year we were married. Got me a damned good contract with Weinbaum and Lincoln. I never had any complaints about his work ethic. He got results."

"I don't mean to pry," I said without meaning a word of it. "But what actually caused the break?"

She laughed unpleasantly. "You can't break what was never whole. I was never sure why either of us decided it was a good idea. He hated my family – my sister detested him as well – and I never even met his relatives. Damon wasn't sentimental."

"Was it a messy breakup?"

"No, like I said it was actually quite civilized. One day we were talking – shouting really - and we discovered that neither of us knew exactly why we had gotten together. By the end of the day we had decided who got to keep what – and neither of us had much anyway – and we started the proceedings the next morning. We even shared the same apartment for a few weeks afterward while I was looking for a place."

"And there were no hard feelings?"

She considered that. "I don't think so. They were more firm than hard. Not on my part anyway. We were a little uncomfortable for a while afterward but we were both living in New York at the time and we kept running into one another. We even went out to dinner a couple of times, working out finances. I never took alimony but I had a share in the agency for a few years before he bought me out. I hadn't seen Damon much since I moved out here, but we certainly weren't on bad terms."

"You don't know why anyone would have had a grudge against him?"

"Not specifically. Damon wasn't a bad man in the sense that he wouldn't hurt anyone just for the fun of it, and he could even be generous at times. But he was very much focused on himself, his career, on turning things to his advantage. I know he used dirty tricks a couple of times to get what he wanted. Not blackmail, exactly, but maybe its next door neighbor. Sometimes there were ruffled feelings. I suppose it's possible that he offended someone enough to provoke violence, but it would have been through clumsiness rather than malice. Damon didn't like taking chances unless there was no alternative."

I figured she was going to be upset enough when I asked about Jaffrey. Since she hadn't even mentioned it to Thornton, it was clearly something she wanted to keep to herself. But I had no other gambits to play.

She reacted just as I had expected. "What right do you have to intrude into my personal affairs?" She was standing now, glowering at me.

"The purchase is a matter of public record, and the information wasn't something I discovered because I was investigating you." Not for want of trying, but she didn't need to know that. "The Culloden police asked Dusty and I to come up to be interviewed about Tracy Fannon's death and it was mentioned during the course of that conversation. Thorndyke didn't seem to think it was a big deal. He's probably going to ask you about it and I thought you'd like a heads up." I didn't tell her that Dusty and I had been out to the property.

She didn't appear particularly mollified but she did sit back down. "It was an investment property. I originally expected to turn it over almost immediately but the market has been soft and my advisor recommended that I hang onto it for a while. I'm not an outdoors person. I like cities."

I wondered why then she was living in such a quasi-remote setting but I didn't ask. "Have you been out to the property recently?"

I could tell that she was trying to decide whether or not to answer, but it went my way. "I spent a few days there this last week. The cottage has been empty and I don't have a caretaker so I stop by if I'm in the area and sometimes I spend a night or two, particularly if I'm doing signings up in that general area."

"Do you visit New Hampshire often?"

"My books sell particularly well in the Northeast and the West Coast so I go on tours there fairly often. Not otherwise."

"Where were you signing this past week?"

She stood up and rummaged in a drawer, then showed me fliers for a bookstore in Montpelier, Vermont, and a library in Concord, New Hampshire. Both had taken place within the past four days and both mentioned Winstead by name. "They were both pretty minor events but sometimes I just want to get away."

I glanced around. "From all this noise and activity?"

She smiled for the first time, tentatively. "What's your favorite cocktail, Mr. Birch?"

"Bloody Mary," I said instinctively.

"So when you go out, is that what you always order?"

"Not always. Occasionally I like a change."

"Exactly. And a cottage I'm already paying for is cheaper and quieter than a hotel."

"Point taken. How long were you there?"

She thought for a moment. "I drove up on Sunday night and stayed until this Sunday morning, but I was gone all day for the bookstore and almost all day for the library talk. And I drove over to Concord one day as well."

"So you were in the general area when Tracy Fannon died."

Her smile had turned upside down. "I suppose that's true although I don't actually recall which day she died. Are you trying to imply something, Mr. Birch?"

"No. I'm just suggesting that you might want to write down anything that might confirm where you were and what you were doing. Like I said, Detective Thorndyke knows that you own the cottage and it's only a matter of time until he asks you about it and where you were at the time of her death."

"I would never hurt a child."

"Someone did."

"It might have been an accident."

"I don't believe it was an accident and neither do the police."

I thought she might argue the point but instead she shook her head. "I don't suppose that I do either. It would be too much of a coincidence."

"There's that word again."

"What?"

"Never mind. Just thinking out loud." I stood up and handed her one of my cards. "Thank you for seeing me. I know it hasn't been pleasant. If you think of anything you've forgotten, feel free to call me at any time."

The next week passed uneventfully, at least with regard to Martin Edison and his acquaintances, living and dead. There were no arrests and we didn't hear from Thorndyke. Dusty seemed to have reverted to her normal cheerful industriousness, but every once in a while I caught her reading through the printouts or staring out a window with her face twisted into its serious version. I had intended to call Cordelia Grayson again but things got very busy at work and I forgot. We picked up three new clients and one of the jobs involved round the clock surveillance on at least six people, which meant that in addition to the usual people I used for such matters, I had to borrow manpower from another agency. Tina Kirk spent almost an hour explaining her ambivalence about upgrading the OS on our network, and I followed about ten percent of what she said and then nodded knowingly and told her that I trusted her judgment, which is what I would have told her if she hadn't attempted to explain it at all. Barry Shaw hinted that he'd been offered a partnership in another firm and I told him that I would regret to see him go but that I was glad he had the opportunity to better himself. His unhappy expression confirmed my suspicion that this had just been a bluff. He has been angling for a partnership since the day after I hired him.

Merrilee caught two of her "kids" smoking pot behind the building during their break and promptly fired them. "I don't care what they do on their own time but their asses are mine when they're on this property." The timing belt on my car broke while I was on my way to visit a client in Lincoln and we had a break in the sewage line at our house, which meant hiring someone to dig up half the yard. By the weekend I was frustrated and tired. Dusty was in full writing mode and often spent fourteen hours a day at the computer. We were both too tired for sex. Monday went a little more smoothly but I still had to deal with a recalcitrant client who refused to believe his employees would steal from him, one of the surveillance people I'd hired fell off a ladder and broke a leg, and by mid-afternoon I was wondering just what had convinced me to give up a promising career as a chain store manager in favor of spending my time looking into other people's business.

And then I found out that Martin Edison was dead.

Dusty had just heard it on cable news and had called me immediately. "They aren't saying much yet but it definitely wasn't natural causes."

"When did it happen?"

"I don't know. Apparently he'd been reported missing yesterday and they found him today."

"Found him where?"

"Outdoors some place. They kept the cameras away from the crime scene but there are lots of trees."

"Any official statements or just rumors?"

"Just 'no comment' and 'an investigation is underway' but nothing specific. The consensus has it that he was shot, but there's a rumor that he was killed with a sword. "

Fans. I'll never understand them. "Okay, let me know if they release anything new before I get home."

I almost gave in to impulse and called Thorndyke, but I was sure he had his hands full at the moment and I didn't have much information to trade with. I had never gotten around to telling him about Winstead's quiet visit to her retreat because I knew he'd find out without my help and had probably already spoken to her. Then I realized what the silver lining to this particular cloud might be. Dusty had been at home working for the last several days. I suppose that technically she could have driven to New Hampshire and back without my knowing it while I was at work, but three hours up and the same coming back didn't leave much time for any hanky panky. I could confirm her alibi each night, although I suppose that Thorndyke would have to take into consideration the possibility that

I was lying to protect her. Still, I was hopeful that Dusty was finally off the hook.

I still didn't know how Tracy Fannon tied into things, but it now looked more certain than ever that Damon Wright had died simply because he'd borrowed the wrong jacket.

There was national news coverage that evening and Dusty and I watched it together. Edison's body had been found in a grove of trees not far from the scouting camp on the opposite side of the mountain from his house. The police spokesman was a captain from the state police and he acknowledged that it was being considered a homicide and that the investigation was ongoing, but provided little other information. The reporter told us that sources reported Edison had been shot multiple times and had been discovered partly concealed in a thicket where a pair of unidentified hikers spotted him while answering the call of nature. There was no sign of Thorndyke or Chief Tibbett among the congregation of police and public officials.

The newscast had just ended when the phone rang. I answered it and a gruff voice greeted me by name. It was Tibbett.

"I assume you've heard the latest."

"We were just watching it on television." I was tempted to say more but held my tongue.

"They patted us on the head and told us the grownups were going to take over the investigation."

"The state people?"

"Governor called the mayor, mayor called me. Full cooperation. Give them everything we've got and get out of the way. Did you see the suit standing beside Captain Uptight during the press conference?"

Actually his name was Upjohn, but I decided not to be a stickler for detail. "I remember him vaguely."

"Special Agent Downer. Courtesy loan from the FBI which can't be involved officially. Did you ever notice that they don't have any regular agents? Everyone is a special agent. Makes you think they don't know what the word means."

I wasn't sure why Tibbett would call me just to sound off about a jurisdictional squabble. "How can I help you, Chief?"

I could almost feel his hesitation. Tibbett didn't want to say what he was going to say. "I called someone I know down in

Providence. He used to be chief of detectives before he retired. He says you're good at what you do."

Now I was the wary one. "I do mostly audits and security evaluations."

"He also said you were discreet."

"It's part of the job description."

"The thing is, I'd like to hire you to conduct a little side investigation. Keep the state boys honest. They're stumbling around like a wounded moose."

"Homicide is a bit outside my area of expertise."

"My friend says you've dabbled a bit, and successfully."

"It was one case, I stumbled on the answer, and Dusty and I almost got killed. Not the kind of stuff you want to put on your resume."

"But I'll bet it gave you a taste for that kind of work."

I denied it but I wasn't being entirely honest. It had been exhilarating, once I was done being terrified. Tibbett let me think about that a few seconds. "Why don't you come up and we'll talk about it? I'll pay for your time and expenses."

I argued a bit and told him that I'd have to bring Dusty along. "She'd never forgive me if I didn't include her."

"That's fine. The more eyes we have on this thing the better, and we've pretty well eliminated her as a suspect. Can't speak for Captain Uptight though. He advised us that the big leaguers are taking over the field."

"She might not have a strong alibi this time either. We don't know when Edison was killed."

"Between six and eight, evening before last. You didn't hear that from me."

I thought back. "We were having dinner at a fancy Chinese restaurant here in Providence. They'll remember us." The waitress was Dusty's sister-in-law.

"So when can you come up?"

I thought about it. "Tomorrow morning."

We didn't talk about Edison's murder much at all on the drive up. For one thing, we didn't have enough information to even speculate usefully. It was heavily overcast and we went through three local downpours on the way, one of which started inconveniently while we were inside a restaurant having coffee. It wasn't raining when we reached Culloden but the general gloom made the town look even more rundown and depressing than it did when the sun was shining. We checked in at the Inn, then drove over to the police station where we only had to wait for a minute or two before we were ushered into Tibbett's office.

Cordelia Grayson was sitting there.

Tibbett made an effort to smile as he rose from behind his desk to shake hands. "Sit down, both of you. Thorndyke is on his way up." We all introduced ourselves – Dusty and Cordelia had never met – and filled all but one of the available chairs. There was coffee and donuts and I nibbled a cruller while Dusty declined. The detective showed up a moment later carrying a stack of file folders. His expression was friendly but guarded.

"Since the powers that be have decided this case is too important to be entrusted to people so lacking in experience as Detective Thorndyke and I, we can't be sure that they don't know something they haven't shared with us. But everything we have is at your disposal, although I have to ask you to use it with discretion."

I swallowed my bite of cruller. "I understand your frustration, but aren't you likely to get into trouble initiating a separate investigation?"

"I've been in trouble before. Can't do this job if you don't want trouble." Tibbett glanced at Cordelia. "Ms Grayson here was working for Martin Edison at the time of his death."

Cordelia nodded. "Technically I was investigating what Mr. Edison believed were previous attempts on his life rather than trying to prevent a new one, but I still feel some obligation to the estate. And I received a generous advance which I have not nearly exhausted."

"Did you find anything interesting since we talked?" I asked.

She shrugged. "The incident with the failed brakes was almost certainly an accident, mechanical failure. The prowler never came back, as far as anyone knows, and there was nothing which might have helped with identification. Nor is there evidence that he or she meant to do any harm to Edison or anyone else. The house was secure, although the burglar alarm was not armed. Apparently Edison hated the thing and could never remember the disarming code. The shooting incident is more problematic. I've been to the site and Edison was out in the open when it happened, so it's hard to believe anyone mistook him for a deer. The area is nowhere near the game trails and well away from the posted hunting areas. It's very hard to see how a hunter could have strayed that far or, having done so, could have misidentified Edison as an animal. On the other hand, stranger things have happened. The shot might have been fired at some other target, a squirrel perhaps, by someone too inexperienced or inattentive to recognize the hazard."

I was still dubious about the idea of a parallel, slightly underground investigation, but I did want to share what little information I had. With Dusty's help, I described our trip to Winstead's cottage and my subsequent interview with her. "She might have come up again the night Edison was killed. Her lifestyle doesn't provide many opportunities for alibis. On the other hand, she had to eat while she was here. Somebody might remember seeing her."

Thorndyke didn't look hopeful. "There's nothing about her to make her stand out and we have lots of early leaf peepers all over the place, but I'll have someone ask around."

"You could take her picture from the dustjacket of one of her books," Dusty suggested.

"I tried calling Ms Winstead several times," said Thorndyke, "before they pulled the rug out from under us. No answer at her house in Connecticut and there's no phone installed in Jaffrey."

"Cell phone?" asked Cordelia.

"Apparently not, unless she carries a disposable."

"What about the others?" asked Dusty. "Do we know where they all were?"

"Patrick was up here, staying at the Inn. He's been looking after Meredith Fannon, who is not doing well. She's checked into a small nursing home just west of town. Fits of hysterics, trouble breathing. They don't have a locked ward and there have been at least two incidents where she's gotten up at night and started driving around. Says she's searching for her daughter, who's lost. They tried sedatives but she refuses to take them."

We were all quiet for a moment before Thorndyke continued. "Austin was on vacation and his office says he's been working on a novel he always wanted to write. He has a place near Bennington College, which is an easy commute to here. No one has seen any signs of activity at his house though. Wolfman is missing, or at least no one knows where he is at the moment. The New York police are looking around. Apparently he hasn't been in his apartment since Monday morning, but the super says he takes off once in a while without saying anything. He doesn't have a car although he does keep a license so it's hard to see how he could have rushed up here without leaving a trail, but it may take a while to uncover it."

"How about the Johnsons?" I asked.

"They're back in Maine. They could have driven down but they would both have to be in on it. We also checked on the son, Ronald, who was out running errands at the time. Nothing definitive either way. Same with Mrs. McCone, although she didn't have a vehicle at her disposal."

"Maybe you should give us the chronology leading up to Edison's death," said Dusty. "I'm getting confused."

Tibbett nodded to Thorndyke who summarized what had so far been determined. On Tuesday evening, Edison had sent Ronald and the car to run a number of errands which would leave him and Mrs. McCone alone and without transportation for the afternoon and possibly early evening. At about half past three, Edison had received a telephone call. McCone was outside so he picked it up himself which means we don't know if it was a man or a woman. He immediately called the local cab company, then told Mrs. McCone that he had to go out and that he might not be back until late. She described him as under control but visibly upset. She asked him if there was anything wrong and he said something vague about having to deal with an old ghost.

McCone decided to stay up reading in bed until Edison came home, but she hadn't been feeling well and fell asleep, so it wasn't until morning that she discovered he hadn't returned. She called the police, who promised to look around, but it wasn't until early that evening that two hikers stumbled upon the body. "He'd been shot three times the chest with a .38. Two of the three wounds would have killed him."

"I assume you tracked down the cab," I said when Thorndyke was done.

"That was easy. We only have one company servicing this area and they only have three drivers. Edison got out at the corner of Peaksview and Endicott. He didn't say anything to the driver accept that he was being picked up by a friend. There was no one waiting for him but he told the cabbie not to wait."

"I don't suppose anyone saw him get into another vehicle."

"That intersection is off a back road. Not even a street light."

Edison had been lying on his back about twenty yards from the nearest street. There was no obvious physical evidence other than the wounds. "The staties are looking for tire tracks but it's been dry for the last few days. They're not likely to find anything useful."

Cordelia asked a couple of questions that hadn't occurred to me, but elicited nothing new. "What about the first two deaths?" I glanced back and forth between Tibbett and Thorndyke. "Anything we're not likely to know that might suggest a pattern?"

Thorndyke glanced at Tibbett again, who frowned for a second or two before telling him to go ahead. Thorndyke consulted his memory. "There's nothing of consequence about the first death. The stories you heard were essentially the same as the original testimony. Everyone had the opportunity but no one had a motive."

"Someone did," suggested Cordelia.

"Unless it was mistaken identity," said Dusty.

"How about the blow itself? Did it require significant strength?"

"No. It might even have been dropped on him from above although the coroner thinks that's unlikely."

"So it really doesn't help," I said and he nodded agreement.

"We know a little more about the Fallon girl," continued Thorndyke. "But it's not all that helpful either. You do know that she routinely carried a small pad and pen with her, to write things when she couldn't use sign?" Dusty and I nodded; Cordelia did not. "She didn't die immediately when she fell, or was pushed, although she probably was unconscious within two or three minutes at most. Her back was broken and she tore an artery in her leg. We think that during the brief period before she died she took out the pad and wrote something, although it's possible that she'd done it earlier."

We all leaned forward.

"It was just the letter 'M' and it was almost illegible."

"Murder," I said automatically.

"Mother," suggested Dusty. ' Meredith or Martin."

"Or McCone or Margery or something else entirely."

Thorndyke shook his head. "It doesn't tell us anything."

"What about the diary? You said there were some passages you didn't completely understand."

Thorndyke shook his head. "That was before we knew who her father was. She had a code she used when referring to him. We even thought it might be a boyfriend that she nicknamed 'Dad' but one of them refers pretty clearly to a trip to Cleveland where we now know the Fallons were with Patrick."

""No references to anyone else on our list of suspects?"

"Well, her mother naturally, and the rest of the household."

"Any strain indicated?"

"She didn't like one of her teachers but otherwise she seemed happy with everyone she knew. She was a sweet kid. I knew her myself."

"Someone didn't like her," said Cordelia.

"There was one more thing we turned up in the Wright case, and it's suggestive. Wright had been having an affair with Mrs. Johnson and it ended the night before he died. Her story is that it was her idea to break it off but we only have her word for it. Her husband confirms her story, says they have an understanding and that he knew about it all along, but they could be covering for each other."

I nodded. "I think I saw her with Wright in the parking lot at the Inn that evening. I never saw the woman's face."

"What about the will?" asked Cordelia. "Who gets all the money?"

"Captain Uptight told Edison's lawyer not to talk about that," said Tibbett, grinning. "But Ted's my brother-in-law so we sort of postdated our conversation on the subject. Other than some institutional and other minor behests, the estate is split evenly among all the heirs. There are five of them named. Meredith and Tracy Fannon each would have received a full share, as does Ronald Edison and Mrs. McCone. The final share goes to Donald Mason, who is also the executor."

"Who's Donald Mason?" I had never heard the name before.

"Donald Mason is Martin Edison's cousin and, other than his son, apparently his sole living relative. Mason has been living in France since the 1970s, first as an employee at the American embassy and now as a retiree."

Old mystery plots unraveled themselves in my mind. "I don't suppose there's any proof that he hasn't been back to the States from time to time recently?"

"I imagine Uptight will look into the matter. Even he is bright enough to check the obvious."

The conversation turned general for a few minutes before Tibbett called us to order. "Ms Grayson has already agreed to help, at least until her advance runs out. How about you, Mr. Birch, and your associate of course?"

"I'm not sure your departmental budget could afford my normal rates…" I started.

"Don't concern yourself. The town's not paying for this. I've got more tucked away for my retirement than I'll ever spend. It wasn't my civic duty that made me call you. It was wounded pride. I don't like the way this case was taken away and I don't have any confidence that Uptight and his minions will do any better. Nothing would please be better than to have you show them up for the fools they are."

I nodded. "What I was going to say was that under the circumstances I'd be willing to wave my fee as long as our expenses are covered."

"I'm part owner of the Inn so consider your room, meals, and bar bills paid. Anything else that you consider necessary, you just let me know what it cost. But I want to be kept in the loop, understand? I'm not hiring you to do your own thing. I've already got Uptight doing that."

"Done then." I felt a momentary misgiving. Someone who had presumably killed three times already was not going to balk if it seemed necessary to eliminate one nosy private investigator and/or his girlfriend. But it was too late to reconsider.

We held a strategy meeting after that. Thorndyke would be the spider at the center of our web, making sure anything we found out was passed on to the rest. He was also positioned so that he could find out if the official investigation turned up anything interesting. "They're too interested in bragging about how much better trained they are to keep a secret for very long." Initially Cordelia would look into the activities of the Johnsons and Hillary Austin. Dusty and I would talk to James Patrick and Naomi

Winstead. Thorndyke was still "unofficially" tracing Ronald Edison's movements but doubted that he could find anything definitive. "He drove over to Keene and then up to Henniker. Spent some time at the Old Depot book store, he says, and ate supper at a Burger King. There's plenty of time for him to have gotten back to Culloden." Wolfman was still missing and there was nothing that any of us could do about that. Meredith Fallon was only lucid some of the time and we deferred talking to her for the time being.

We were about to wind our meeting up when the phone rang and Tibbett spoke into it briefly. When he was done up he sat back in his chair and clasped his hands in his lap. "That was Ted, the lawyer. He spoke to Edison's cousin last night and he'll be flying in to Boston later today. Ted reserved a room for him at the Inn. One or more of you might just happen to make his acquaintance. The reading of the will hasn't been scheduled yet but it will most likely be either Sunday afternoon or more likely following the funeral on Monday. Actually, since Edison is being cremated, I guess it's not really a funeral."

We all went back to the Inn and Dusty and I treated Cordelia to lunch. She and Dusty might not have known each other before but they were jabbering like sisters by the time the food arrived. I had used Cordelia as a subcontractor a few times when she was working out of Hartford and she was very good. I had been sorry to see her move out of the area but happy that she now had a successful agency of her own. "I could stand being a little busier but I'm getting there."

After lunch I called the office and confirmed that an earthquake hadn't swallowed the building and that Tina and Barry had refrained from tearing each other's hearts out. I asked Steve to see if he could track down Naomi Winstead again. "I don't want her to now I'm looking for her. I just want to know where she is. Leave a message on my voice mail and I'll check it tonight."

Dusty and I walked down to Patrick's room but there was no answer when we knocked. A passing maid told us that "Mr. Patrick goes out every afternoon. Sometimes he doesn't come back until late." Fortunately she was wrong this time because we spotted him getting out of his car a few minutes later.

"Let's go to the bar. I need something." He looked disheveled and tired and his clothes were visibly rumpled.

He ordered scotch, Dusty had iced tea, and I had coffee. The scotch disappeared quickly, but when the refill came, he let it sit on the table. "I've been over to see Meredith."

"How is she doing?" asked Dusty.

"Actually, a little better the last couple of days. She's stopped insisting that Tracy is still alive and she's calm most of the time. Doesn't cry as much as before. I think she's moved from denial to anger. She snapped at me a couple of times today but the nurse told me that's a good sign."

"Does she know about Edison?"

"Oh yes. We were watching television together when they broke in with the news. I was afraid she was going to have a relapse but she accepted it pretty calmly."

"I can't imagine what she's going through."

"She'll be all right. She's a pretty tough cookie underneath."

I took advantage of a momentary pause. "The police are going to be looking at alibis again."

Patrick nodded. "A rather supercilious Captain Upjohn interviewed me last night. I can't say that he inspired me with confidence."

"Were you able to satisfy him?"

Patrick looked at me oddly. "Are you working for me or the police now?"

"We're assisting Captain Tibbett, but it's very unofficial. He wants the same thing you do. Answers. And he's not sure Captain Upjohn is up to the task."

Laughing rather unpleasantly, Patrick sipped at his drink. "I'll bet he isn't. There's no love lost there. The captain made it quite obvious that he thinks Tibbett and his crew are a bunch of amateurs."

"The feeling is reciprocated."

"Yeah, well I don't have any confidence in any of them, so I hope you're good enough to make up the difference. I didn't like the old man very much, but I'm guessing he was killed by the same person that pushed Tracy off that mountain."

"There might be more than one killer involved." I cautioned.

"What are the odds?"

I had to admit they weren't good. "So where were you the night Edison was killed?"

He sat back and deliberately finished his drink, then signaled the waitress for another. "I quit at three," he assured us. "The truth is, I don't have an alibi. Meredith was going through a bad stretch. She'd wake up convinced that Tracy was lost somewhere. I'd taken her car keys and given them to one of the nurses but she left them at the desk and Meredith didn't need to be a master thief to get them back. She took off sometime early in the afternoon without telling anyone she was leaving. When I came to visit she was gone, so I spent the rest of the day driving around looking for her. When I checked back at the nursing home around ten, she had just returned and was safely in her room."

So he didn't have an alibi, and presumably neither did Meredith Fallon, although I couldn't imagine her killing her own daughter. On the other hand, if she thought Edison was responsible for Tracy's death, directly or indirectly, she might have wanted revenge. She could have called, lured Edison to the rendezvous, and killed him, although I wondered how she had dragged him so far from the road. Or had she led him out there at gunpoint or by means of some ruse and shot him where he lay? But if that was the case, how would she have gotten a gun? Did she own one? If she was in a nursing facility suffering from depression, they certainly wouldn't have let her keep one there. If she'd gone back to the house, Mrs.McCone would have seen her. Was it possible that there were three different killers? I made a mental note to ask Thorndyke which of our suspects had guns registered in their names.

We asked a few more questions but Patrick withdrew into himself and started answering with monosyllables and we really didn't have a good line of questioning to pursue in any case. I had just thanked him and was starting to get up when he waved a hand. "I do know one thing that you might find interesting, something I don't think the cops know."

"What's that?"

At first I didn't think he was going to answer, but he did. "Meredith says that Wright had been asking her questions the last couple of times he came up here, and he called her a couple of times."

"What kind of questions?"

"She said she couldn't have helped him even if she'd wanted to. He wanted to know family history, stuff that happened before

Edison hired her. He kept insisting that there must be something like a scrapbook or old papers or that Edison must have said something."

Patrick lapsed into a prolonged silence and I wanted to shake him. "About what in particular?"

"About his wife. Edison's wife." Patrick was starting to slur his words. "He wanted to know if Edison ever talked about her."

"Any idea why he was interested?"

"Maybe he wanted to write a biography."

"Doesn't seem like his kind of thing, does it?"

But Patrick was through being communicative for the night and we left him there, staring into an empty glass to watch the last of the ice melt.

I checked my voicemail. Steve had not located Winstead. "No answer at her home. I can't find anything indicating that she's on a signing tour. I called her publisher and pretended to be a reporter interested in an interview but they had no idea where she was. I'll try again tomorrow."

Dusty went to bed early but I was restless. I went looking for Cordelia but her car wasn't in the lot even though it was after ten. I felt disappointment rather than alarm. Cordelia could take care of herself. I I was drifting back toward the room when I noticed that the bar was still open and decided a glass of wine might help me relax. Patrick was gone but two locals sat at a table and another leaned over the bar and appeared to be asleep. One of the three booths was occupied and I was walking past it with my wine when I noticed who was sitting there.

It was Geneva McCone.

"Good evening, Mrs. McCone."

She looked up blankly, then belatedly recognized me. There was a flash of smile, so quick that I almost thought I'd imagined it. "Mr. Birch, isn't it? I wasn't expecting to see you back here."

"Please accept my sincere condolences. I know you'd been with Mr. Edison for a long time."

She smiled again, but it wasn't for me. "Yes, I was. Would you like to sit down?"

I'd been trying to figure out how to invite myself so I agreed readily and slid into the booth opposite her. "Any idea what you'll be doing now?"

She shrugged. "I'm sure Martin made provisions for me. I'll help tidy up the estate. I know where some of the skeletons are buried. He was getting on and his health wasn't as good as it could have been. His drinking didn't help. I've been preparing myself for this for quite awhile."

"It's just you and Ronald alone up there now, I guess."

"Just the two of us. I'm not sure what to do about him. He was more attached to me than he was to Martin. He'll have plenty of money, I imagine, but he's not very good about things like that. Someone will probably take it away from him."

"There didn't seem to be much of a father son relationship between them."

McCone laughed and I realized she'd had quite a bit to drink. "Not all that surprising considering that they weren't related."

I choked on my wine. Very poor manners, but I wasn't at all prepared for that. "I thought he was the son of Martin Edison and Louise Bowman."

"Oh, Louise was his mother all right, but Martin wasn't the father. Martin had some physical problems. He couldn't have children. I don't think he'd have wanted them if he'd been able. Too messy and undisciplined. I was amazed at how well he adjusted to poor little Tracy. She was a real hellion when she was younger. She'd turn her head away so she couldn't see you signing 'no' and do exactly as she liked."

"Was Edison impotent?"

She laughed a bit too loudly this time and covered her mouth. "Sorry, I'm not used to drinking so much. But tonight seemed like a good night to make an exception. No, Martin wasn't impotent, and I have good reason to know that. Quite the opposite if anything. But he was sterile. They told him that when he was in the army. I give him credit though. He treated Ronald like a son. Well, like a son he didn't particularly like I suppose. There was never any love lost between the two of them, but he provided a home, education, spending money, helped him get a job, took him back into the house when that didn't work out. I know Ronald is mentioned in the will as well. Martin didn't hold anything against him, but he didn't hold anything for him either."

My mind was racing. Damon Wright had been poking around in Martin Edison's past and now it appeared that there had in fact been something to uncover. Was he looking for some leverage he could use to force Edison to retain him as agent or was there another motive? Could Edison himself have arranged Wright's murder to shut him up? Hand him an identifiable piece of clothing so that a hired assassin would pick the right victim? But he couldn't have known that Wright would decide to use one of the trails so he couldn't have planned it in advance. And then Edison had himself been killed. Were there two killers after all? And why would Tracy Fannon have been a threat? Or was her death actually an accident?

I realized that I hadn't been paying attention and covered by asking McCone if she wanted another drink. "Thank you but no. I'm just sitting here until my head clears a little and then I'll call a cab."

I glanced at the time. "Do they run this late?"

McCone consulted her own watch. "Well that's not good. I seem to have lost an hour or so. Serves me right for feeling sorry for myself."

"Why don't you let me drive you home?"

She started to rise. "I couldn't ask you to do that. I'll just take a room for the night."

I stood up. "I'm here because I can't sleep. The drive will do me good. It's only a few minutes." It took a little more conversation before she was convinced but eventually she was in my car and we were headed back to Edison's house.

I drove slowly, partly because the road was poorly lit and wound rather sharply in a few spots, partly because I'd had two drinks, and partly because I was trying to think of a way to elicit more information from my companion.

"Edison's wife died on the mountain, didn't she?" I knew she had, and McCone knew that I knew.

"Fell to her death, not far from where Tracy died. Poor girl." I wasn't sure which of the dead women she was referring to.

"He was away when it happened?"

"That was before my time. We met a couple of years later when I worked for a small press that did limited editions of his work. You know, fancy binding, tipped in color illustrations, numbered copies all signed and sold out before they're even printed. It didn't pay much but I was out of work and desperate. But yeah, he was in Los Angeles or maybe San Francisco signing books for fans. The police asked him some questions but I suppose they were just going through the motions. It was pretty obvious he hadn't pushed her."

"Where was Ronald when this all happened?"

"There was a nanny. Critchens or Crutchens or something like that."

"Is she still around?"

"No, died before I came. Cancer I think."

"I'll bet she could have told stories."

McCone laughed. "Probably not. Martin lived a pretty quiet life until you people showed up."

"It's still a shame there's no one around who spent much time with Edison back then."

"Well, you could try talking to Mickey."

That was another name I hadn't heard before. "Who is Mickey?"

"Mickey Ross was Martin's handyman and chauffeur for many years. Martin never learned to drive on his own. Said his nerves weren't up to it, but I think he just liked having someone else take him places. For someone who didn't care to have many people near him, he sure was interested in his image. Anyway, Mickey got fired right after Martin's wife died."

"You don't suppose Edison thought he was responsible?"

"No. Mickey was drinking over in a bar in Keene that evening. He only worked at the house a few days a week. Martin said that when Louise died he just wanted to sweep away all the memories of their time together. There's not a picture of her in the house, he almost never mentioned her name, and he discouraged visits from people who had known them. I don't think he ever left the property during the first two years I was here. It was as if her death hit him so hard that he couldn't think about her anymore. Given that she was unfaithful to him, I find that quite amazing. The first time my husband stepped out on me, I threw all of his stuff out onto the sidewalk."

The house was just ahead and I slowed so I wouldn't overshoot the narrow driveway. "Where would I find Mickey if I wanted to talk to him?"

"He's got a cabin on the other side of town somewhere. I've never been there but I bet the post office could steer you in the right direction."

Or the police, I told myself, pulling to a stop. McCone thanked me, invited Dusty and I to stop by for lunch if we were staying long, and disappeared into the darkness. I sat in the driveway long enough to be sure she was safely inside, then turned around and went back to the Inn.

I knocked on Cordelia's door in the morning to invite her to breakfast but there was no answer. I had gotten in pretty late and she wasn't back when I finally went to bed, so I assumed she hadn't returned at all during the night. Her car wasn't in the lot. This made me slightly uneasy – too many people had already died in or around Culloden. But there wasn't a lot that we could accomplish locally and in fact right after breakfast Dusty and I drove to Naomi Winstead's cottage. Dusty hadn't slept well so she dozed and I got to wrestle some more with my thoughts.

This time we found the house occupie. Winstead's car was pulled up close to the front door and the curtains were open. I parked behind her and she came around the side of the house just as we were getting out. She was carrying a shotgun but she let the barrel fall as soon as she recognized us. We were not, however, greeted with a smile or a wave.

"We wondered if we might find you here," said Dusty cheerily, apparently oblivious to the lack of welcome although I was quite sure she was at least as aware of the tension as I was. "We're going up to sightsee in Concord and this was right on our way."

Sort of, if you define our way as way out of it. But I played along. "Turned out to be a longer side trip than we'd expected, but we got stubborn and decided to see it through."

"I'm really not in the mood for visitors," she said sulkily, but then relented. "I can offer you tea and scones if you'd like."

We followed her inside. She set the shotgun down inside a tiny hall closet. "I don't really like firearms, but this place is pretty remote and there have been some home invasions in the area."

The cottage was sparsely and plainly furnished and the contrast to the house in Connecticut was obvious. It looked like a hotel room. The bookshelves were more plentiful but just as empty and there were no paintings, print or otherwise, or other personal items. The rug was faded and cheap looking. Several newspapers sat on the coffee table but no magazines; there wasn't even an ashtray.

Everything looked generic. But if Winstead had indeed bought it as an investment, she wouldn't have had any reason to do much interior decorating. "I imagine you've heard about Martin Edison."

"Yes. I have a radio. Is that why you're up this way?"

"No, we're just taking a short vacation to look at the foliage. But since we happened to be nearby we did stop and talk to the local police. Apparently the state has taken over the investigation. I imagine they've been here looking for you."

"If so, they wouldn't have found me. I just drove up last night. You wouldn't be in the market for a getaway cottage would you? I've decided to take the loss and sell this place. It's just sitting here empty and it's too remote for me. Every time an animal runs through the yard at night, my heart goes on overdrive."

"It's a little too far off the beaten track. I'd be afraid to go outside and risk being shot by someone who thought I was a deer."

Winstead laughed politely. "You have a point. I know someone has been having target practice out back while I wasn't around. And I found the back door open when I got here."

"Burglars?"

She shrugged. "If so they didn't find anything worth taking. Maybe some homeless person was sleeping here and cleaned up when they left. Maybe I just forgot to lock it last time I was here."

She excused herself to put the kettle on. Dusty asked to use the bathroom. I sat down, glanced through the newspapers, and tried to think of something to say that would induce Winstead to say something useful, if she had anything useful to say.

Dusty reappeared and whispered to me. "She's been here longer than a day. Bathrooms never lie."

Or someone else has been here, I thought to myself.

The tea and scones arrived and were duly appreciated and consumed. Dusty and Winstead made small talk and the older woman actually seemed to relax and enjoy herself. I produced an appropriate monosyllable when prompted and tried to look for clues without looking like I was looking for clues. This assumed that there were clues to be found which, I eventually decided, was probably not the case.

We left amidst insincere mutual promises to stay in touch.

"So what do you think?" asked Dusty the moment we were out of sight of the house.

"I think she's a lonely woman who would be better served if she spent more time with people. She has rudimentary social skills but no real feel for it."

"I meant about her as a suspect."

"Of killing Edison? She's as good as any I suppose."

"She has a gun."

"It's a shotgun. Edison was killed with a handgun."

"Someone took a shot at Edison earlier, remember? That wasn't a handgun."

"You're reaching. I'll bet you that James Patrick has a handgun." Actually, I was cheating. I already knew that he had at least two registered in his name because the photograph on the dust jacket of his latest book showed him sitting in his den and there was a glass fronted gun cabinet mounted on one wall. "She'd hardly be likely to keep the murder weapon in her front closet when she's already a suspect."

"I guess." She was silent for a while. "Do you think Patrick might have done it?"

"It's possible, but he seems genuinely despondent over Tracy's death."

"Maybe he didn't kill her but he thinks that Edison was responsible and this was his way of getting revenge."

I sighed. "That would put us back to having multiple murderers." I did wonder, however, if Edison could have killed the girl. There wasn't anything resembling a motive that I could see, but there were emerging undercurrents that suggested life at Edison's house had not been as placid as it might have been.

"Or Tracy could have been an accident."

I agreed. "If we're going to go that route, then Meredith Fannon could have killed Edison. She was out that night by herself and apparently no one knows where she was for most of that time."

"Or she and Patrick could have planned it together."

"You're giving me a headache."

"Just making sure we're covering all the bases. So now what?"

"Off to Concord."

She looked momentarily confused. "Are we really?"

"No. We're going back to Culloden to see if we can track down someone named Mickey." I summarized what Mrs. McCone had told me the night before.

"You think some dark secret from his past has risen from its murky depths?"

"I'd put it a little less literarily, but I think it's a possibility. Someone disliked Martin Edison enough to kill him and, for whatever reason, two people close to him. That implies that Edison pissed someone off. But as far as I can see, Edison's recent sins were all minor. So it stands to reason that something happened in his past that we don't know about, or at least we don't recognize its significance."

"His wife had an affair and later died. It was ruled an accident but might not have been. Edison had an iron clad alibi so he didn't do it. But I suppose he could have paid someone else to do the deed."

"It has been known to happen."

"Revenge?"

"Or a falling out between thieves. Or Edison found out who killed his wife and was threatening to expose him, or her. Or someone was blackmailing Edison and things got out of control. It might have been your friend Damon Wright."

"Edison kills, or arranges for someone else to kill, Wright but Wright has a partner who gets even by shooting Edison. Too many conspirators and how does Tracy fit in?"

"Maybe she overheard a conversation between Edison and Wright or his partner and had to be killed to keep her quiet."

"I see why you draw charts and tables. This is worse than a wiring diagram."

When we got back to Culloden, I checked with the desk clerk. Donald Mason had indeed arrived but he wasn't allowed to give us the room number. I asked to leave a message, which the clerk accepted, and we were barely back to our room when the phone rang. A male voice with a very slight, unrecognizable accent asked if I was Paul Birch. "My name is Donald Mason. I understand that you wish to speak to me."

"Yes, very much." I gave him a quick summary of my involvement in the case and the informal relationship between myself and the local police.

"I'm a bit jet lagged but I would be happy to meet you for lunch in, say, half an hour here at the Inn?"

"That would do very nicely."

Donald Mason was a cadaverously tall, thin man with a ring of hair around a shining dome. He was slightly older than his late cousin but looked considerably younger despite his pallor. He greeted us politely, his voice deep and so precise he could have been a television announcer. We asked him about his trip, he replied politely, and we ordered our lunches.

"As I mentioned, we're trying to find out who had reason to kill your cousin, plus probably two other people whose connection we have yet to establish."

"A Captain Upjohn has assured me that everything possible is being done to bring the guilty party to justice. Actually, he said 'the perp'. He did not inspire confidence."

I made a noncommittal sound. "The local authorities have asked us to look into things from a slightly different perspective, just to make sure nothing is overlooked."

"You are detectives then?"

"I run a private security firm that has been involved with capital crimes in the past." Well, once anyway. "Dusty occasionally helps out." Well, once anyway.

"I certainly wish you well, but I must tell you that Martin and I were not close. In fact, the last time I spoke to him was in 1983."

"We have reason to believe that his death might be linked to something that happened a long time back, possibly involving his wife."

"Ah, Louise. A formidable woman. There was no question who made the decisions in that marriage."

"You met her then?"

"That one time, yes. I hadn't seen my cousin since we were children. I was still spending part of each year in Washington at the time. I had business up this way and called to see if we might have a drink together. I didn't even know that he had married. At first he put me off, but then he had an abrupt change of heart and told me that he altering his will and would tell me about it when I arrived."

"And did he?"

"Oh yes. Neither of us had any other family at the time so we had each assigned the other as executor of our respective estates. Martin explained that since he was now married and a father, he was replacing me with Louise. It all struck me as perfectly straightforward and I wasn't at all perturbed, although Martin seemed to expect resistance."

"But you ARE the executor of his estate."

"Yes, I am. I assume that he changed things back to the way they were following Louise's death. The boy was too young at the time. He never bothered to tell me, but as I said, we hadn't spoken since that afternoon."

"Did either of you write?"

"Not even Christmas cards. We didn't care for one another as children actually."

"How much do you know about Louise?"

"Almost nothing. As I said, I hadn't even known he was married .He did mention that she'd been a former employee – his housekeeper I believe. She was polite but not cordial. They were both rather reclusive. Martin had been an odd child, always the outsider, but highly imaginative. I suppose that was the genesis of his talent. At the time it was just unsettling."

"Did you see the boy, Ronald?"

"No, he hadn't been born yet. Louise was obviously pregnant. Martin seemed very happy about it."

Edison must have been a good actor since he must have known the child wasn't his. I had run out of questions. Dusty tried for awhile and learned only that Louise had been uncomfortable and irritable because of the pregnancy. "I'm anxious to meet the boy," he told us. "I imagine that as Martin's only son he'll be inheriting the bulk of the estate."

We didn't disabuse of him of the notion. We weren't supposed to know the provisions of the will, and it wasn't up to us to reveal Ronald's secret.

Thorndyke gave us the address for Mickey Ross along with detailed directions. There were no street signs at some of the intersections but we managed to find our way to his cabin – I would have called it a shack – which was stuck on a little dirt road all by itself, as though the town had discarded it years earlier. The yard was full of rusting machinery – two pickup trucks, a tractor, a couple of plows, bedsprings, rusting tools, corroded pipes, and a lot of things I couldn't identify. Thorndyke had told us that Mickey had spent years doing odd jobs and selling scrap metal and spare parts until his arthritis got too bad. Once he was old enough for social security to kick in, he had dropped all of his other sources of income.

The cabin had a slight lean and looked more precarious than it probably was. It had been built into the side of a hill, with a wide open porch. The roof needed to be replaced, at least one window had duct tape running along a crack, and there were many shingles damaged or missing. A good sized dog of indeterminate breed was sleeping on the porch but it didn't even look at us when we walked up and knocked.

For a few seconds I thought that no one was home, but then there was a rustling and a voice called out something indistinct. Dusty and I exchanged glances and I knew she was revisiting scenes from one of the direct to video horror movies she liked but when Mickey Ross finally reached the door, it was something of an anticlimax. He was thin as a rail and almost completely bald, with a short unruly beard inexpertly trimmed. He was wearing jeans and a white sleeveless shirt, but he seemed to be clean and alert and he smiled pleasantly.

"What can I do for you folks? Looking for directions?"

"Are you Mickey Ross?" I asked. He nodded. "Then we're not lost. We'd like to ask you a few questions if that's all right."

"About Martin Edison?" It was my turn to nod. I must have looked surprised because he laughed. "Whenever strangers show up at my door, it's always to ask questions about Edison. And I heard he died so I was half expecting you. Come on in. I have lemonade."

The cabin was much nicer on the inside. It was neat and orderly and as far as I could tell, reasonably clean. The furniture was old and some of it should have been thrown out long ago, but the front room and what we could see of the kitchen looked functional and almost welcoming. We sat at an oval shaped table whose top was cut from a single slab of wood on chairs which didn't match while Ross retrieved lemonade and glasses. I noticed a stack of library books – a history of Europe, a political memoir, and a

William Faulkner omnibus. Mickey had wide ranging interests, it appeared.

"So what do you want to know?"

Dusty spoke up first. "We understand you worked for Edison for several years."

"From 1981 to January 1991, ten years plus a few months."

"What did you do for him exactly?"

Ross scratched his head. "There wasn't much exactly about it. I did whatever needed doing that he didn't want to do himself. Kept up the gardens, ran errands, did some maintenance work, poisoned rats, chased away sightseers, stuff like that. Mrs. Bentley did the cooking and most of the housework. Mrs. Edison wasn't no help at all. She liked being waited on. They both did."

I took over smoothly. "You left his employ in 1991?"

"That's one way of putting it. He fired me and Edith both a few days after the funeral."

"That was his wife's funeral?"

"Yes it was."

"Who was Edith?"

"Edith Claire Bentley. Nice woman but ugly as sin. She passed away not long after."

"We're a little bit curious about Louise Edison's death."

"Not much mystery to it. She fell off the blue dot trail, at the Buckle. It's a long way down from there and the trail narrows out. She wasn't much for hiking anyway, but she went out from time to time. Should have known to take one of the easier trails. I'd have told her if she'd asked, but she didn't take advice to readily either."

"Edison wasn't home?"

"Nope. I drove him to the airport myself the day before."

"Was there ever any talk that it might not be an accident?"

Ross gave me a long look. "Not that I ever heard. She was too mean a woman to kill herself if that's what you mean."

"I was thinking more that she might have been pushed."

He thought that one over. "She and Edison got along pretty well. They both had kind of inflated opinions of themselves but they hardly ever argued. Mrs. Bentley had a bad hip and couldn't have made it to the first junction above the house and anyway, she was taking care of the baby, young Ronald, because the nanny had just given notice and was sleeping late."

"Where were you?"

He chuckled. "Edison gave me the week off since he was going to be away. I was up to Bangor drinking and fishing with some friends. Mostly drinking. They're all dead now. It's hard being the last musketeer."

I prodded him a little but as far as he knew, no one had ever suspected that Louise Edison's death was anything more than it appeared..

"Did Edison ever explain why he fired you?"

"Said he wanted a clean start with nothing to remind him of the past. Like I said, he let Mrs. Bentley go the same time, and the nanny was already gone by then. I came out like I always do and there was a Mrs. Wilson there to meet us and say my services were no longer required. He did send each of us a nice little severance check. I lived off mine for more than a year. And Mrs. Bentley was thinking of retiring anyway. Not that it did her much good. She was dead a year later. Heart trouble."

"So who raised Ronald?"

"There were a couple of nannies at first but neither of them lasted more than a few months. Not local people. Then Edison hired Mrs. McCone and Mrs. Wilson up and died right after. The boy was old enough that he didn't have to be watched every minute. He must have been ten by then. Edison let Mrs. McCone run things whatever way she wanted. She did all the hiring and firing when they needed work done and she kept people away from him that he didn't want to see, which was pretty much everyone."

"What did people around here think of the arrangements?"

"Well, to be honest with you, she was the first black person we had living in Culloden and there was some unhappiness at first, and people here don't like strangers on general principle. But she has a way about her and except for a few die hards, she's won people over."

"Was Edison popular?"

"Not so much, but we saw so little of him after his wife died that it didn't matter. Not much of him before that either as a matter of fact."

"What can you tell me about Louise Edison?"

"Not a whole lot. She was originally his housekeeper, you know? That was before I worked there."

"Her maiden name was Bowman. Was she local?"

"No, she wasn't local, and you're wrong about her name."

Dusty and I exchanged looks. "What do you mean?" I asked.

"Bowman was her married name. She was a widow. Edison hired her sometime in the early 1970s, before my time. Married her just before I started working for him. But people called her the widow when she first arrived and some people still did even after they were husband and wife."

"What about visitors? Did she have any family or friends?"

"No family that I know of, but then she'd never have reason to speak of them when I was around. To be honest, I never liked her much. She had a kind of superior air, nothing you could point to and take offense at but more like she was in on some wonderful secret that no one else knew and that made her better than the rest of us."

"Visitors?" I prompted.

"Not many that I can remember, but I wasn't there every day. The ones I do recall came to see Edison, not his wife."

"Did they ever have parties? Overnight guests?"

"Nope and nope. To my recollection anyway. He got better about it later on but when I first started working there, Edison didn't want to see anybody unless he absolutely had to. They had extra rooms enough to sleep maybe a dozen guests but I don't remember ever seeing one of them beds made up."

"It must have been lonely for his wife."

"Oh, she went away a couple of times by herself, never for very long. And I guess she didn't like company much either."

"Any idea where she might have gone?"

"Not the slightest."

We stayed a little longer but didn't learn anything else. Ross offered to make up another pitcher of lemonade – we'd drained the first one - but we declined. "We've taken up enough of your time, Mr. Ross." I shook his hand.

"Not a problem. I go so long without seeing anyone out here that my talking talents get rusty." We had both started toward the door when he spoke again. "Say, I never did ask why you're so interested. Are you writing a book or something?"

"No, not exactly," I replied.

"Because if you are, then I think some other fellow is going to beat you to it."

"Who might that be?" asked Dusty.

"City type. Three piece suit. Polite enough but I could tell he didn't want to stay here any longer than he had to. Told me he was writing a book about Martin Edison's life and wanted stuff that wasn't generally known. Offered to pay me for anything I could think of that might be interesting. Smarmy type. If I'd known any juicy scandals, I wouldn't have told him even for the money. Not that there were, mind you."

"Was he asking about anything in particular?"

"He seemed more interested in the wife than he was in Edison. And he asked a couple of times about some other man, but I'd never heard of him."

"Do you remember what this other man's name was?"

"Nope. That was months ago. My memory's not what it used to be. But I wrote it down on the back of the business card."

"He left his card?"

"Sure did. Hang on and I'll see if I can turn it up."

It took a few minutes but then Ross came back, beaming from ear to ear. "Don't know why I hung onto this." He handed it to me. The name written on the back was "William Grant". Printed on the front of the card was "Damon Wright, Literary Agent" with an address and email.

I handed it to Dusty who whistled when she read the front, then turned it over and read the handwritten name. "Who is William Grant?"

Ross and I both shook our heads.

Damon Wright's interest in Martin Edison's early life was interesting but with him dead, I didn't see it leading anywhere obvious. I wondered if Thorndyke had access to Wright's papers. There might be something there. And we now had the name William Grant to add to our list. But who was he? The name was so common that I doubted even Merrilee's kids could track down the right man without something else to identify him. As it was, we didn't know his age, whether he was alive or dead, where he was from, what he did for a living, or how he connected to anyone else.

Dusty and I headed back to the Inn where I called Thorndyke and told him what we'd learned.

"Who the hell is William Grant and what does he have to do with anything?"

I admitted that I had no idea and that it might be irrelevant. "I did wonder if anyone went through Wright's papers."

"We didn't find anything of interests, but we weren't looking for this Grant person. And now that you mention it, there was something I forgot to mention. We never located Wright's laptop."

"Did he have it with him at Edison's that day?"

"No one saw him with it, or remembers anyway. It wasn't with the effects from his room and it wasn't at his apartment in New York City, but the publisher insists that he had one."

"Stolen or lost?"

"Seems to be one or the other."

"I'd sure like to know what was on that laptop."

"So would I but by the time we found out that it existed, everyone was back home and had had ample time to dispose of it. There was no sign that anyone broke into his room at the Inn, but you can get past the locks there with a credit card. If he brought it to Edison's house that day, someone could have taken it after he died. It might have been tossed down the well or more likely just carried away when everyone left."

"You might want to look in that well."

"Already did." He paused and I was about to end the conversation when he started up again. "Your friend stopped by a little while ago."

"Cordelia?"

"I think she just had a taste of the frustration this case generates. I had the privilege of telling her that it appears Arthur Wolfman took a taxi to Grand Central on Monday morning. No one seems to know where he's been since then."

"He might have used a credit card to buy a ticket." I felt like an idiot. The police would certainly have thought of that. But he didn't seem to take offense.

"We're checking, but he could have paid cash, or he might have just walked away. He's a bachelor and a freelancer, so we can't ask his wife or employer. Ms Grayson did enjoy some success, however. She managed to locate Mr. Austin who is not where we thought he might be."

"Does he have an alibi?"

"Well, yes and no at this point. Initially he was supposed to have been in Boston all week to discuss the acquisition of a smaller publisher, something called Possum Books. Except that on Monday afternoon the owners of Possum Books decided they didn't want to sell after all and broke things off. The rest of Austin's contingent went back to New York, but he decided to take some vacation time. He told his associates that he was going to take a few days at his vacation house but instead he spent the balance of the week in Boston looking up an old friend, or so he says. He kept his room at the hotel and hadn't checked out when Ms. Grayson found out he was still registered and called, although he wasn't in. She left a message and he got back to her earlier today."

"I hope she had better luck with him than I did. Austin didn't strike me as particularly forthcoming."

"He gave her some attitude, but when she said she was cooperating with the Culloden police, he deigned to tell her he'd spent the day Edison was killed sight-seeing. He didn't actually hook up with his friend until Wednesday morning and they've been together pretty much ever since."

"A woman?"

"Yes. He wouldn't give her name and says he won't unless he's arrested. It doesn't matter anyway since he acknowledges they hadn't connected when Edison was shot. Austin, incidentally, has a permit for a .38. He claims he hasn't used the weapon in ten years and doesn't even know where it is. Anyway, on Tuesday Austin states that he had supper at Durgin Park, then went to a night club whose name he doesn't remember. Says he paid for supper with his credit card."

"If so, that would seem to let him out."

"Depends on the timing. Coroner puts time of death between ten and midnight. He could theoretically have eaten, rented a car, come up here for a quick kill, then returned to his hotel before morning. Or someone else could have used the credit card for him."

"It's hard to rent a car without a card."

"Might have borrowed one. Maybe from the same theoretical person who used the card."

"So where's Cordelia going next?"

"Boston, to check out his story. Not much she can do to find Wolfman at this point."

"He has to turn up eventually."

Dusty and I stopped to say goodbye to Donald Mason before leaving on Sunday afternoon. There wasn't much of anything we could do in Culloden that Thorndyke hadn't already covered. James Patrick stopped by to tell us that Meredith Fannon was going to stay with him in Boston for a while. "We'll leave right after the will is read tomorrow."

I spotted Donald Mason in the parking lot while I was loading our bags into the trunk and a question occurred to me. "Did you ever hear of someone named William Grant?"

He massaged his upper lip for a few seconds before shaking his head. "Not off hand. Do you have any context?"

I shrugged. "All I know is that someone of that name was connected somehow to your cousin and/or his wife."

"There was a handyman working in the garden the day I was there."

I shook my head. "That's Mickey Ross. I've spoken to him."

"A neighbor?"

Thorndyke had come up dry. "The police can't find any record of someone with that name living in Culloden. As far as we can tell, the Edisons didn't have any local friends at all."

"Well, they had at least one because they talked about visiting him. That was the excuse they gave for giving me the bum's rush. I was only in the house for about two hours."

"As you say, it might just have been an excuse."

"Possibly, but they were arguing about whether Louise would drive or whether they would ask the handyman to act as chauffeur. It was the only time I didn't see them in perfect harmony. And there was something about a check she was supposed to deliver."

"A check?"

"I think so. I was a long time ago. And it might have referred to another subject, I suppose."

"Well, thank you again."

I called Thorndyke who duly noted my vague report. I had the feeling that I was missing something obvious. It was so strong that I considered staying on another day. After all, we might find something out at the reading of the will, although I couldn't imagine what. Thorndyke and Cordelia were both attending though and it would look like overkill, or that I didn't trust them. Thorndyke was also going to visit Mickey Ross and see if he remembered anything about a sick friend, but neither of us expected anything to come of it.

So we went home.

Even two cups of coffee didn't get me in the mood for work Monday morning. I stopped by to see Merrilee and asked her to see if they could find anything on a William Grant, associated with Martin Edison, Louise Bowman Edison, or the town of Culloden. She gave me one of her rare skeptical looks but said she'd put someone on it.

Dusty had announced that she was going to put the whole thing out of her mind and concentrate on her novel so I hadn't brought up the subject over breakfast, but it simmered in my subconscious all morning. I was waiting for the phone to ring with details of the reading of the will, even though I knew it wasn't even scheduled until early afternoon. I snapped at Barry and Tina had to explain a fairly simple upgrade to one of the databases we subscribed to before I could understand what she was saying.

Cordelia called about two o'clock. She sounded excited.

"Just about everyone was surprised by the terms of the will, except for Mrs. McCone, who either already knew, didn't care, or is very good at hiding her feelings. Ronald looked elated rather than disappointed, which surprised me a little since under ordinary circumstances I would have expected him to be the prime beneficiary. I wonder if he knows that he's not really Edison's son. Fannon looked a bit dazed, but she looked that way even before the reading. It was all very orderly and only took a few minutes."

Nothing there justified the tension in her voice. "What aren't you telling me?"

"Well, everyone seemed at least satisfied after the reading was done. But then the lawyer brought out a batch of personal papers that he'd been keeping for Edison."

"What kind of papers?"

"The kind of stuff you usually find in a safety deposit box. Edison didn't like banks so he had his lawyer look after them. You know, birth certificate, army discharge papers, marriage license, deeds to the house and land, title papers for his car, a handful of bearer bonds, lists of all his assets and where they were kept and who to talk to. Oh, and a durable power of attorney and a bunch of family photos."

"Who was the designee on the power of attorney?"

"Mrs. McCone."

"Interesting but not surprising. So what are you holding back, Cordelia? You're teasing me."

"I so rarely get the opportunity." I swear she giggled. "Most of the photographs were from Edison's childhood. The more recent were mostly Tracy Fannon including one where she's just a baby and her mother is holding her. That was the interesting one."

I metaphorically scratched my head. What could possibly be interesting about a picture of Tracy Fannon as an infant?

"You know that Edison avoided photographers. There's not even a photo on the dust jackets of his books."

"Yes, I knew that."

"Well, in this particular picture, he's standing to one side watching Meredith and the baby. I don't think he realized that he was in the shot."

"And..."

"And when we looked at it, his cousin asked who the man was. Said you'd asked him about someone named Grant and this might be the man. So we told him that this was his cousin and he laughed at us and told us it most certainly was not Martin Edison."

"They hadn't seen each other in thirty years. He might just have been mistaken."

"He's pretty insistent. Says it looks a little like him but that it's definitely not his cousin."

"A lot of time has passed. People change."

"They do."

"But it's something we should probably look into."

"Someone probably should."

"You feel like poking around up there?"

"I'll give it a shot."

"How long is Mason staying around?"

"He wasn't sure. It will take at least a couple of weeks to clear up the estate. McCone gets the house as part of her share, on the condition that Ronald is allowed to live there for as long as he likes. Mason will be staying with them. I assume you know Michelle Fannon is moving in with James Patrick."

"They claim just to be friends."

"Tragedy changes people, but they act like they've been lovers for a long time. Any sign of Wolfman yet?"

"Not to my knowledge. The police are looking into Austin's alibi, so that leaves me with Winstead. I suppose I could drive out to Connecticut again."

"Don't bother. She's up here. Thorndyke told me she called to let him know she'd be staying in Jaffrey for a while, straightening out her cottage and getting it sold."

"I might drive to Connecticut anyway."

"Don't do anything I wouldn't do, and don't get caught at it either."

"I'll be careful."

Thorndyke called an hour later. "Talked to Mickey Ross."

"He makes good lemonade."

"He was drinking a mint julep when I stopped by. I asked him if he knew anything about a sick friend of the Edisons."

"And did he?"

"He says they knew someone in a rest home somewhere but the couple times when they went to visit, Louise insisted on driving herself.. Thought it was a little strange, but then again, he thought Louise was always a little strange."

"Might be worth checking with any nursing homes within a reasonable distance."

"We're making calls."

And they did, but nobody within fifty miles had anyone named William Grant as a current patient or as a resident during the 1980s.

I didn't have a chance to skip work until Wednesday. Thorndyke told me that Austin's credit card had been used at the time he said he'd been eating in Boston and one of the waiters remembered him because he gave an unusually large tip. Says he came in alone but might not have left that way. He still could have managed to drive up here in time to kill Edison, but it's a pretty tight fit."

"The large tip might have been to ensure that he was remembered."

"That occurred to us as well.'

"Nothing on Wolfman?"

"He has a cell phone, but it doesn't seem to be turned on. He did draw out an unusually large amount of cash the day before he disappeared."

"How large?"

"Two thousand. It stands out. He never withdraws more than a couple of hundred at one time. He does have credit cards but he doesn't use them very often."

"I understand Winstead called."

"That she did. Complained that her privacy was being invaded because I was giving her address to people of questionable ethics. She didn't name you specifically but she implied she was selling off her little hideaway because nosy people kept interrupting her when she was just trying to get away from it all."

"We each have a cross to bear."

"She has a theory about the murders."

"That's more than I have."

"She thinks that Edison set up Wright by giving him the jacket so that a third party, who didn't know Wright by sight, would kill the right person. Then there was a falling out between the conspirators and the third party killed his employer."

"We talked about that. Then how do we account for Tracy Fallon?"

"Collateral damage. She may have overheard something related to the plot so Edison took her for a walk and pushed her over the edge."

"It might have happened that way."

"Why would Edison have it in for Wright?"

"Well, we do know that he had just given Wright notice so there probably was some sort of tension between the two. On the other hand, Edison had a habit of cleaning house. He fired his entire staff and his agent in 1979 and again in 1991. In those cases there was no sign of animosity. All of the servants were given sizable severance checks and good recommendations. Edison might have known that Wright was looking into his late wife's activities and it's possible that this William Grant person is Ronald's real father. Edison might not have wanted that to come out. We know Edison couldn't have killed Wright himself, but he might have hired someone to do it for him."

"If it really is a third party, we're probably not going to catch them."

"Not unless there's still something holding them here."

"How is the official investigation going?"

Thorndyke chuckled. "Captain Upjohn's almost as bad as Chief Tibbett says he is. They haven't even asked us about the alleged earlier attempts on Edison's life, and they've concluded that Tracy Fannon died accidentally. The leading theory is that a crazed fan heard that Edison was retiring and has been lurking in the woods waiting for the chance to punish him for abandoning his readers."

"Might work for Wright, but how did this alleged maniac lure Edison out of the house the night he was killed?"

"Doesn't really pass the smell test, does it?"

I had no difficulty finding Winstead's Connecticut house this time. There were no cars around and no other residences in line of sight, so I turned into her driveway confident that I was unobserved. There were no vehicles parked at the house but just in case Winstead used a house sitter, I tried the doorbell, knocked at the front and then again at the back. During my previous visit I had noticed that she had no alarm system and the lock in the back proved to be no serious deterrent. My cover story if discovered was that I had stopped by to ask some more questions, had heard furtive movements in the house, and that someone had burst out of the back door and disappeared into the nearby woods. I was even prepared to provide an unhelpful description. Since I had forgotten to bring my cell phone – it was in the glove compartment in my car – I would naturally go inside to use the telephone to summon the police. If anyone turned up, I would be doing that very thing when they found me.

As soon as I was inside, I made a quick run through the house just to make sure that I was indeed alone. Everything was neat and orderly including the bedroom and a small den/office, neither of which I'd seen on my first visit. There was also a pantry off the kitchen that struck me as obsessively neat even before I noticed that the canned goods were arranged in alphabetical order. It was possible to find dust but only because I was a trained investigator.

Once assured that I was alone, I started a closer search, including looking behind everything hung on a wall to see if it concealed a safe – which I wouldn't have been able to open even if I had found one, which I didn't. Winstead's office contained a very practical desk with a docking station for a laptop that wasn't there. A fancy laser printer sat at the edge of the desk. There were two filing cabinets, an overstuffed easy chair, a handful of reference books, an air conditioner in the one window, a table with a single drawer full of pens, index cards, and other office supplies, and some spiral bound pads. A narrow closet held an umbrella, a couple of sweaters, and a substantial stock of artist's supplies.

The bedroom was almost gender neutral. There was nothing frilly, the colors were all earth tones and subdued, and there was no mirror. I found nothing hidden under the very conventional clothing in the dresser and closet, there wasn't even a dust bunny under the bed, and the closest thing to a decoration was a framed picture on the dresser of a younger version of Naomi Winstead standing with another woman of about the same age who looked vaguely like her. I removed the backing of the frame so that I could read what had been written on the back. "Me and Sis, May 14, 1975." I put it back as it was.

There was the usual array of cosmetics in the bathroom, though perhaps fewer than I might have expected. Aspirin and some antihistamine in the medicine cabinet but no prescription medicines. Of course, she would have taken those with her. The front room was as I remembered it but I took another walk around, discovering nothing I hadn't seen before. There was no sign of an attic but there was a door to the basement off the kitchen.

The basement wasn't as clean as the house proper but it was just as orderly. Almost everything in storage here had been boxed and sealed, with the contents noted on the outside in black magic marker. I passed spare dishes, extra copies of various Poppy White books, old correspondence – which would have been tempting if I had been willing to go through a rather large and heavy box full, extra blankets, and a few other household goods. A metal utility rack held cleaning supplies, boxes of light bulbs, more artist's supplies, and bug spray. Near the bulkhead door, securely locked from the inside, were rakes, hoes, shovels, trowels, and other gardening equipment along with jars of seeds, neatly labeled and alphabetized, a couple of bags of fertilizer, and similar items.

I was starting back toward the stairs when I spotted a small box I had missed earlier, marked "photographs." Unlike the others, it wasn't taped shut, and I took it down, sat on the basement steps, and started looking through them. I found quite a few of Winstead, mostly at book signings and other public events, and a couple more of her sister, but none of them were informative. Then I found a whole bunch of pictures of Winstead and Wright, all gathered together with a pair of rubber bands It might have been my imagination but Wright invariably looked pleased with himself. Winstead, on the other hand, always smiled but never warmly. But my perception might have been colored by my recent experiences of the woman.

There was one picture where Winstead stood next to Arthur Wolfman and another woman who I could not identify. The inscription on the back consisted of a date in 1981 and nothing else. I set this one aside along with a headshot of the sister. There were two pictures in which Winstead appeared in a group that included Austin and one where James Patrick and Michelle Fannon were locked in conversation at the edge of what appeared to be a cocktail party. Winstead wasn't in this one and there was no caption on the back, but I wondered if she had somehow known about the relationship between the two. They were young enough, I realized, that this picture might well have been taken around the time they first became intimate. Then I found one more picture of Winstead's sister, this time standing next to Damon Wright. No surprise there except that the sister was looking sidelong at Wright and her expression suggested she had just found something disgusting.

There was nothing else of interest so I returned the box to where I had found it and slipped the purloined photos into my pocket. I did another quick pass through the house to see if I'd missed anything, then slipped out the back way, relocking the door. I hadn't been particularly nervous until then but during the last few minutes before I left, I felt remarkably vulnerable and I was several miles away before the feeling passed.

Arthur Wolfman turned up on Thursday. He and several friends had rented the Rudyard Kipling house in Vermont, known as Naulakha, for a full week. Wolfman had taken the train to Boston and rented a car. He had heard about Edison's death but claimed that it hadn't occurred to him to check in with the police until that morning. He spoke to Thorndyke at some length, the end result of which was that Wolfman could quite easily have managed to kill Edison. The six men had mostly gone their separate ways for most of the week and Wolfman claimed to have been visiting second hand bookstores on the day in question.

"At which he always paid cash," I said wryly when Thorndyke called with the news.

"Naturally. I think he actually enjoys being a suspect." The detective sounded tired or discouraged or both.

"I don't suppose anyone knows when he got back to Vermont?"

"After midnight, he claims. Says he wandered rather farther afield than he'd expected, then got lost on the way back. Everyone was asleep when he arrived so no one knows exactly when he got there. And Austin's alibi is wobbling a bit."

"How so?"

"It turns out that he called girl friend right after dinner, asked if he could borrow her car, and didn't bring it back until the following morning."

"How does he explain that?"

"Says he went to a play up in Lynn and that she wasn't interested. The lady says the same thing."

"Did he have a reservation?"

"Bought a ticket at the door, cash."

"And I suppose he knows what the play was about."

"It was *King Lear*. Upjohn is checking to see if anything unusual happened during the performance that might trip Austin up, but I'm not holding my breath." He laughed. "Rumor has it that the Captain has expressed some regret about having pre-empted the local authorities on this one."

"Poetic justice."

"So far it's the only justice in evidence."

Over supper that evening, Dusty came up with a question that had never occurred to me. "Where did Arthur Wolfman stay the night Wright was murdered? We never saw him at the Inn and he wasn't staying at the house. I remember he called a cab when they were through questioning him but I have no idea where it took him."

"He might have stayed at the Inn and we just missed him."

"There are only about twenty units and they all open onto the parking lot."

"It does seem odd. We never saw him in the diner either."

So Friday morning I called Thorndyke again, made a lame joke about installing a special hotline, and repeated Dusty's question.

Thorndyke had to refer to his notes, but he had the answer. "Wolfman slept at a friend's place in Gilsum, not far from here. The friend's name is Trevor Michaels who, incidentally, is one of the people who has been living at the Kipling house this past week."

"Any connection between Michaels and Edison or any of the others?"

"Not that we know of. I haven't spoken to him myself and I don't really have a good reason to, but I could pass it on to Ms Grayson."

"She's back from Boston?"

"Yesterday. Can't confirm Austin's story but says she's inclined to believe him. She also told the chief she can't spend too much more time on this case."

"We all have to pay our bills."

"Tibbett might hire her to stay on a bit longer if he thinks it could help, but right now it doesn't look that way."

"Doesn't seem like any of us are getting much traction."

Things got frantic at work for the next day or so and I don't think anything connected with Martin Edison crossed my mind at any point until Friday night. I was just cleaning up the dirty dishes from supper and Dusty was choosing a dvd for us to watch when the telephone rang. It was Thorndyke, calling to tell us that someone had shot Cordelia Grayson.

"She's still in the operating room and the doctor says it could go either way."

"How did it happen?"

"She was in her room at the Inn. We think someone knocked on her door and when she answered it, they opened fire. It was a .38. One bullet in the shoulder, two in the chest, two more missed completely. One of the other guests heard the shots and came out to investigate. She saw Grayson lying on the floor and ran back to her room to call 911."

"Did she see the shooter?"

"Says there might have been someone running out toward the street but she wasn't sure. It wasn't full dark but it's been raining all day up here."

I felt an immediate sense of responsibility that I knew was irrational. True, Cordelia was only on the case because I'd called her, but she'd chosen to take it and to continue after Edison's death of her own volition. I knew all that, but I still felt responsible. My first impulse was to pack a bag and drive up right away but I knew that wouldn't do any good. "I'll come up tomorrow."

"Someone up here likes to shoot private detectives."

"I'm forewarned."

"That's not always enough."

"Are you trying to scare me off?"

"Just like to have things clear."

Dusty insisted on coming along. I argued with her – it was in fact the biggest disagreement we'd ever had. My position was essentially that it was too dangerous. Hers was that an extra pair of eyes would make us safer. I told her that she would be at a disadvantage in a crunch because she wasn't armed. She conceded the point, announced that she was going to remedy that failing at the first opportunity, and assumed that would make me feel better. It had the opposite effect. Firearms tend to give people a false sense of security and that leads to taking chances they would otherwise have avoided. I held out for a long time but in the morning there were two suitcases in the car when I set out for New Hampshire.

Dusty called Thorndyke while I drove. Cordelia was out of surgery but unconscious and likely to remain that way for some time. Her chances were better than even, but not comfortably so. A permanent guard was posted in the hospital. Thorndyke had personally gone through her room at the Inn before notifying Captain Upjohn of the possible connection. He had not found anything that seemed important. Cordelia had intended to drive to the Kipling house to catch the vacationers on their last day there, and tentatively planned to visit Winstead's cottage the following morning, but there was nothing indicating that she had turned up anything new.

Captain Upjohn was skeptical that the shooting had anything to do with the Edison case and had characterized it as a robbery gone awry. I suggested that he might change his mind when the ballistics report was available. I was pretty sure it would turn out to be the same weapon that had killed Martin Edison.

We arrived late in the morning, having stopped for brunch along the way. There was still crime scene tape at the Inn when we arrived, but a very frazzled clerk checked us into a room near the opposite end of the building. I walked past the taped off area but the door was closed and there was nothing to see. As far as I could tell, there were no police officers at the site. I returned to our room and called to tell Thorndyke we had arrived. He wasn't in so I left a message.

"So what's the plan?" asked Dusty.

"I wish I could say I had a good one but the best I can think of is to follow up where Cordelia started. It looks like she struck a nerve."

"She'd given up on Austin, so we're talking Wolfman and Winstead."

"Right. I figured we could drive over to Vermont this afternoon and catch Wolfman. They're leaving Sunday so this is our last chance to get them all together."

"You don't need me along for that."

"I can't just leave you here by yourself."

"You won't be. I called Mrs. McCone. Ronald is going to pick me up at one and take me over to the house."

"What do you hope to accomplish over there?"

"Probably nothing, but I don't see any point in tagging along with you. I thought maybe if I talked to Mrs. McCone and Ronald, I might find out something new."

"Donald Mason is staying there. You could try asking him about that picture. Thorndyke is pretty dismissive of his insistence that it wasn't Martin Edison. As reclusive as he was, there are just too many people who knew him. It's much more likely that Mason was mistaken." But I wasn't really as sure as I sounded. I hadn't gotten around to developing a time line but the fact that Edison had twice changed his entire household was suggestive. "And ask Mrs. McCone if she can come up with a picture of Louise Edison."

Dusty looked me a question.

"Probably nothing, but Naomi Winstead had a sister." I had forgotten to show her the stolen pictures so I retrieved them from my luggage.

Dusty studied them for a minute. "That would be interesting, wouldn't it? It might also explain why Winstead was allowed to stay at the house rather than the Inn."

The phone rang just as I was heading out the door. Dusty picked it up, listened, said "thank you" and hung up.

"Who was that?" I asked.

"Thorndyke." She frowned and shook her head. "Cordelia wasn't shot with the same gun that killed Martin Edison."

"Is he sure? No, strike that. Of course he's sure. Well, that should give me something to think about during the drive."

I found the Kipling house without difficulty and it was very obviously the inspiration for Martin Edison's home, although Edison had elaborated considerably and did everything on a larger scale. There were two men sitting outside, neither of them Wolfman. I parked and explained who I was and one of them went to get Wolfman who showed up looking none too pleased. "I'm on vacation, Mr. Birch. It's my one chance to get away from the city and relax. What is it this time?"

I apologized, not too sincerely, and explained that I was working with the Culloden police department and that I just had a few questions. He sighed but seemed resigned and led me around the house to a smaller version of the garden at Edison's place. Mrs. McCone's place now. We sat down at a picnic table.

"Did Cordelia Grayson get in touch with you?"

"She called and asked if she could stop by yesterday, but she never showed up. Is she working with you?"

"Not directly. So you're not aware that Ms Grayson was attacked and nearly killed?"

He looked mildly surprised but not shocked. "I see. My unkind thoughts were misdirected. I assume that the attack was related to this situation and that you're taking suitable precautions."

"I'm armed, if that's what you mean."

"In your profession, I would have assumed a firearm was a standard accessory."

"You've been reading too much detective fiction. In real life, we almost never shoot anyone." Or get shot at, I thought.

"My older brother collects guns. He tried to get me interested at one time but I'm afraid I was a very bad shot and we both lost interest."

"Did Ms. Grayson give you any idea what she wanted to talk about?"

"Well, I imagine she wanted to see if my alibi would stand up. It wouldn't, of course. I freely admit that I cannot prove where I was on the night Edison was killed. I never came within twenty miles of Culloden, but I could easily be lying." He folded his hands on his chest. "Does that make me the prime suspect?"

It was hard to believe that Wolfman was a murderer, but my admittedly limited previous experience suggested that murderers rarely looked or acted the part. "You have a good alibi for the day Tracy Fannon was killed," I admitted.

"Do I?"

"Yes. She died several hours after I visited you in New York."

"Was that the same day? Well, all right then. I'm not a suspect. I find that vaguely disappointing."

"That doesn't mean you couldn't have killed Wright and/or Edison. And the girl's death might have been an accident."

"Then I'm still in the running."

I was having trouble concentrating. A vague suspicion was growing more distinct in the back of my mind but I couldn't think of a way to resolve it. "What do you know about Edison's marriage?"

"Nothing particularly interesting. I never met the woman. Louise was her name, I believe."

"Did you ever talk to Damon Wright about her?"

"I rarely spoke to Damon at all. He was polite because he wanted me to review his clients' books, but he had no interest in me otherwise."

"There's some indication that Wright was investigating Edison's past. Any idea why?"

"Perhaps he was thinking about doing a book about the great man. You know, *The Martin Edison Companion.*"

"Was he a writer himself?"

"No. I doubt he had the patience for that sort of thing. He would have hired someone to do the actual composition, but he might well have conducted some of the investigative work himself. Damon was fond of looking into other people's business."

"If he was working on a project like that, who would know about it? How could I find out if he'd approached someone with the idea?"

"You might try his partners at the agency."

Wolfman was beginning to show signs of impatience. I showed him the stolen photos but he didn't recognize Winstead's sister. Then I thought of a couple more questions which gained me nothing and apologized for interrupting his vacation. He didn't tell me not to worry about it, but I decided not to anyway. I lunched in Brattleboro and called Dusty, who told me that I was invited to supper by Mrs. McCone. Then I called Thorndyke.

"Wolfman have anything to say?"

"Nothing useful," I admitted. "How's Cordelia?" The hospital couldn't tell me anything but I knew Thorndyke would have been kept advised.

"Doing as well as can be expected. Her doctor is cautiously optimistic."

"I assume you're looking into Edison's bank records?"

"Upjohn ran them. It's routine. I don't think he found anything."

"How far back did he go?"

"I don't know. I could find out, I suppose. What are you looking for?"

"I have a feeling the motive for all of this started a long time ago." I wasn't going to tell him yet what I really suspected because I hadn't figured how it could have worked.

"I can get a copy."

"Did you find out anything about William Grant?"

"No. That name doesn't show up anywhere."

"Wright must have turned up a connection between Grant and Edison."

"Or something he thought was a connection. Wright might have been wrong, so to speak."

"If he was off base, why did someone kill him?"

"Have you abandoned the idea that it was mistaken identity?"

I hadn't consciously realized it but I had. "Pretty much. Whoever is behind this is too clever to botch something that badly."

I stopped at the hospital anyway and, as expected, they couldn't compromise patient confidentiality. I didn't know if Cordelia had family or close friends who should be notified. I was allowed to look in on her but she was covered with so many tubes and monitors that it could have been anyone in the bed. Then I drove out to the site where Edison's body was found. I wasn't looking for anything in particular but I wanted to put a face on another piece of the puzzle. It was just as remote as Thorndyke had said. I was amazed that the body had been found so quickly. I was so amazed that I called Thorndyke and asked him about the hikers.

"Susan Appleby and Sheila Gomez, students at Keene State. One's from Kentucky and the other from Texas. They're roommates and I suspect they're a couple. Spend a lot of time hiking and camping. No known connection to anyone local or any of our suspects. I think they're okay. They were really shaken up."

"Just coincidence that they found the body so soon then."

"Happens."

"I hate coincidences."

He had a little bit of news. "Winstead got herself a cell phone since she's planning to stay in Jaffrey for another week or so. Want the number?"

I did and he gave it to me. Having nothing better to do, I drove out to the Edison/McCone house well before dinner time. There was a single car parked in the driveway and I pulled up alongside. Dusty came out to meet me.

"You're early."

"I was missing you too much to wait." I kissed her and whispered in her ear. "How are things going here?"

"Fine," she whispered back. Then in a normal voice, "Come on inside. Mrs. McCone made cookies."

Donald Mason was taking a nap but would be joining us for dinner. There was a big plate of still warm snicker doodles and they were good. We ate some of them with coffee, the three of us sitting around the table. "I decided to keep the house," McCone told us. "It's been my home for a long time now and Ronald has lived here just about all his life."

"Where is Ronald?" I realized that I hadn't seen him since arriving.

"He'll be in presently. He's out in the greenhouse."

"Isn't this place rather big for just the two of you?"

She nodded. "My son might move up here when his enlistment is up. He's done his twenty years."

"Is Ronald going to stay then?"

"At least for now. Ronald has low self esteem. He's actually very smart but he assumes that he's inadequate and doomed to fail, so of course that's what he does."

"Living in a house with such a strong personality as Martin Edison might make anyone feel a little inferior."

McCone looked at me calmly and her tone was even. "Martin liked to be in charge but he didn't actually want to make any decisions. Said he'd made all of the tough choices in his life before he met me and that now he just wanted to be left alone to write, or think, or walk on his mountain all by himself. I was as close to him as anyone – closer I guess – but he never really let me inside."

"He and Ronald didn't seem to be close."

"No." She looked away and I knew that she knew.

"Does Ronald know that Edison wasn't his father?"

She shrugged. "Can a person know something and not know it at the same time? If so, that's Ronald. I don't think Martin ever told him outright but there was no intimacy there. Martin liked Tracy better and she wasn't even nominally his."

"Any idea who the father was?"

"I don't know who he is, or was, or how it happened. Martin destroyed just about everything relating to his wife before I came. I've never even seen a picture of her."

The door opened and Ronald came in. Now that I looked at him closely, I realized he was older than I had expected, close to thirty if not more. He was wearing work clothes and he crossed to the sink and rinsed off his hands. McCone offered him cookies and coffee and he accepted, but he remained standing until she pushed out a chair and looked at it meaningfully.

"I'm sorry about your father," I said.

"Thanks." He didn't meet my eyes.

"Made any plans for the future?"

He shook his head. "I guess I don't need to find a job. There's plenty to do around here if I want to keep busy."

With several million dollars coming to him from Edison's estate, Ronald was certainly right on both counts. I tried a couple of other gambits and Dusty asked him about the gardens but Ronald never said more than he had to. He wasn't unfriendly but neither was he enthusiastic. McCone's expression when she looked at him was a mixture of affection and concern.

"Well, I'd better put the rest of these cookies away or we'll all ruin our appetites." She rose and started gathering dirty cups. Dusty took some as well and they disappeared into the kitchen.

I couldn't for the life of me think of anything to say, but Ronald surprised me. As soon as the women were out of sight, he met my eyes directly for the first time. "He wasn't my father."

I hesitated, wondering if I should pretend not to understand, but my face must have given me away. "I guess everyone figured it out except me. I had to be told."

"Who told you, Ronald?" There was no point to pretending ignorance.

"He did. Mr. Edison. Told me on my twenty-first birthday and said I should keep it to myself."

I wondered then, and wonder now for that matter, why Edison kept Ronald with him. He might not have wanted the public at large to know that he'd been cuckolded, but he could have set the young man up somewhere else where he wouldn't have been a constant reminder. Edison did not strike me as the kind of man who would indulge in self flagellation. "That must have been very difficult."

"Not really. I kind of suspected."

"Have you ever wondered who your real father was?"

"No. I know who he was. Mr. Edison told me his name and that he died when I was still a kid."

I felt my pulse quicken. This had to be important. "What was his name?"

"William Grant. He was supposed to be a friend of my mother's but I guess he was more than that." Ronald's face twisted into a sad smile. "Geneva knows about me, but she doesn't know that I do so don't tell her. I think it would make her sad."

"All right." Was this the secret that Wright had uncovered? And was Wright killed to keep him from spilling the beans? If so, Edison had the best motive, but no opportunity. And who then killed Edison? And why would Edison have told Ronald if it was such a dangerous secret?

My train of thought was derailed a moment later when Donald Mason descended the staircase. He nodded toward the two of us and passed through to the kitchen where I heard him ask Mrs. McCone if he could have a cup of tea. Ronald stood up abruptly and excused himself. "I want to start the sprinklers in the garden." So I was sitting there alone when the threesome in the kitchen returned, Mason carrying a tea tray with a steaming pot.

I asked Mason a few polite questions about how he was adjusting to New Hampshire and how the estate management was going before turning to what I really wanted to know. "I understand there's some question about a photograph."

"There's no question at all. That man was not my cousin. There is a strong resemblance, I must admit. But it's definitely not Martin."

"How can you be so certain?"

"The ears are different. Martin's were much bigger and they stood out quite a bit. And the nose is wrong. Too fleshy."

"People do change."

"Mr. Birch, I was a professional diplomat for most of my career. Diplomats must be adept at noticing people, at recognizing them even after long gaps of time and after only the slightest acquaintance."

I tried to shake his confidence a bit longer but without success. The odds were that he was wrong – I had already detected a good deal of pomposity in the man. It must have been a family trait. On the other hand, he might be right and that opened up another whole chain of possibilities. But if he wasn't Martin Edison, then who was he? There was only one person missing in this story that I knew of and that man was William Grant. Was it possible? If so, why would he have told Ronald that he wasn't his father when in point of fact he was.

Dinner was wonderful. We had Beef Stroganoff and steamed vegetables, and blueberry pie and brandy afterward. I felt more than full and wanted a nap. Ronald had said almost nothing during the meal and had disappeared with a whispered apology. Mason was more talkative, but he went on about his years in Paris and Rome until it all started to blur into random noise. Dusty finally pleaded a headache and we headed back to the Inn.

We compared notes along the way. Dusty listened intently, showing surprise only when I told her what Ronald had said about his parentage. She had gleaned little from Mrs. McCone. "She says that Edison had received some threatening letters a few months ago.

He never let her see them and burned them in the fireplace. She thinks there were three but there might have been more."

"No idea what they were about?"

"No. Edison tried to dismiss them as the work of some obsessed fan, but he made a funny comment. 'Uneasy lies the head that wears the crown'. She thought it meant that he was the leading writer in his field."

"Maybe." I hadn't told Dusty my theory yet. "Let's do a quick time line."

As soon as we were in our room, Dusty grabbed a pad and pen. We both contributed dates, sometimes referring to the profiles Merrilee had provided. The list was as follows:

1945 – Martin Edison is born

1963 – Edison publishes his first book

1975 – Edison moves into the house in New Hampshire, hires Louise Bowman as housekeeper

1980 – Damon Wright marries Naomi Winstead

1981 – Edison hires Mickey Ross

1982 – Edison and Bowman are married

1982 – Damon Wright and Naomi Winstead divorce

1983 – Donald Mason visits Edison and learns that he is no longer executor of the estate.

1984 – Ronald is born

1991 – Louise Bowman dies in an apparent accident

1991 – Mickey Ross and Edith Bentley are replaced by Geneva McCone

1998 – Meredith Fallon hired, Tracy Fannon born

2006 – Damon Wright becomes Martin Edison's agent

2013 – Damon Wright looks into Martin Edison's past

2013 – Martin Edison, Tracy Fannon, and Damon Wright are murdered

We both read through it several times. "We need to know when Winstead first met Edison," said Dusty.

"Chances are good that if it was early enough, she said something to Wright – probably while they were married – which didn't mean anything at the time, but since then something happened that made it relevant and Wright decided to probe further."

"We also don't know when Mason was made executor again."

"Yes, actually we do." I pawed through the now substantial pile of paperwork we'd accumulated. "Thorndyke sent me a copy of the will." I found it. "The new will was signed in 1995, and amended in 2005 to include the Fannons."

"So what does this tell us?"

"It doesn't prove anything but it suggests something. What if William Grant murdered Louise while Edison was on the West Coast signing books. Edison returns and Bowman kills him as well, burying the body somewhere on the mountain where he'll never be found. Grant looks a good deal like Edison, but he can't chance fooling the servants. Ross and Bentley are both fired and Grant becomes the reclusive author. I imagine he would have to forge Edison's signature but as long as it was reasonably close and no one actually questioned it, I doubt it would be an issue."

"Wouldn't Ronald have noticed?"

"Ronald was seven years old, spent most of his time with people hired from the outside, and is frankly not the brightest light on the tree."

"Grant would have to be a brilliant writer. The best of Edison's books all appeared after that date."

"Not impossible. For all we know, he employs a ghost writer."

"There ought to be some way we could check."

"I think there is." I picked up the telephone and called Thorndyke. He was out so I left a message for him to call. "We know Edison was in the army. They'll have taken fingerprints. We can compare them to the ones taken during the autopsy."

"Wow! This could be big. Martin Edison's books might have been written by someone else, using the name Martin Edison."

"It would also explain why the quality was so much better after the 1980s. The original Edison was burnt out. And if there was a secret ghost writer, maybe he or she died and that's why Edison announced his retirement from writing."

Thorndyke called back and I explained my theory and what I wanted. There was a significant silence as he absorbed it. "There's nothing in his financials to suggest Edison was paying another writer, but this suggests another line of inquiry."

"If it's true," I agreed. "And it might also be worthwhile if someone talked to Wright's agency to see if they know anything about a biographical project he might have been working on at the time of his death."

"I have a friend on the NYPD who could do that. But it'll have to wait until Monday."

I had forgotten that it was still Saturday. "Fine. I don't expect him to have talked about it, but you never know."

"I have some more news. Jake over at the Inn just called to tell me that James Patrick has made a reservation for two for tomorrow night."

"He's probably bringing Meredith Fallon back." But what was her status? Her employer was dead. Would Mrs. McCone invite her to continue on at the house? Would she want to live that close to where her daughter died?

"The thought occurred to me. Let me see what I can find out about those prints. Tomorrow's Sunday though, so don't expect miracles."

I called the number I had for Naomi Winstead to set up an appointment but I got her voicemail so I left a message. Dusty had changed into something distracting by then so I gave up the investigation for the rest of the evening. One has to have priorities.

There was some good news the following morning. Thorndyke stopped by while we were having breakfast to tell us that Cordelia had regained consciousness. "She's in a lot of pain so they're keeping her doped up but she did talk to Upjohn very briefly. Not that it did any good.. She can't remember anything about what happened."

"Do the doctors think the memory might come back?"

"They don't know, but even if it does there's a fair chance she didn't see anything. The two bullets that missed give us a pretty good idea where the shooter was standing and it was a shadowy spot near the shrubbery. My guess is that whoever did it knocked, retreated into the shadows, and fired as soon as the door opened."

"We're not getting any breaks, are we?"

"Someone is being very careful. And they've also been very lucky."

"Can't count on luck."

Thorndyke nodded. "Neither can we, unfortunately."

I tried Winstead's number again and left another message. I considered driving over anyway, but it would be just my luck to get caught breaking into her house while she was out. If she went back to Connecticut, I might do that, although I wasn't sure what I would be looking for. The photograph of her with her sister bothered me and I wished I had one of Louise Edison to compare it to.

Dusty and I went over to the hospital, where we sat for a while, were allowed a five minute visit with Cordelia, who could nod but not talk. Sometimes she nodded randomly so I'm not sure if she felt any better for our visit, although we certainly did. Wolfman had given me a list of landmarks he remembered seeing on the day of Edison's death and we drove out and started checking them out until I realized that we weren't accomplishing anything. We ate lunch in Gilsum and then went back to Culloden.

I recognized Patrick's car in the parking lot when we drove in and pointed it out to Dusty. "Do you think we should knock on their door?" she asked.

We were saved from making the decision when James Patrick came out of the diner carrying what were obviously two takeout meals. He saw us a moment later and came over to the greet us. "I just keep running into you two. Still playing detective? Sorry, that didn't come out right."

"That's okay. I just wish I knew the rules of the game. Is Meredith Fallon with you?"

"Yes she is." Patrick was obviously pleased with himself. "We've always been friends but recently…" His face softened as remembered grief reasserted itself. "Well, the last few days have brought us closer together. I think we might make things permanent, or at least try it out for a while."

"It's good that you have each other," said Dusty. "I know this must be hard for both of you."

"Hardest thing in my life," he agreed. "For a while Merry just seemed broken. She had…episodes for the first few days here, and once more back in Boston. But she's all right now."

"Do you think she'd mind talking to us about the murders?" I still didn't understand how Tracy fit into the puzzle.

Patrick looked uncertain. "The police interviewed her. It went pretty well when they were talking about Wright but she went to pieces when they mentioned Tracy."

"Did they ask about Edison?"

"Someone came to see us in Boston but he was only there a few minutes. It almost doesn't seem to have mattered to her. Edison was probably going to keep her on after retiring to handle his correspondence and contract stuff, but after Tracy I don't think she could have stayed there even if he was still alive. We're only back here to pick up some of her stuff and decide what to do with the rest. She's going to move into my condo for the time being and if it works out, we might even talk about marriage."

"We wish you both the best of luck."

"Look, we haven't eaten anything." He raised his hands to show us what he was carrying. "We're going out to talk to Mrs. McCone later and eventually we'll have to make arrangements to ship whatever won't fit in the car. Mrs. McCone will almost certainly invite us to stay and I know Meredith won't want to be in that house any longer than she has to, so why don't we pick a time to meet for supper and then I won't be lying when I say we have a previous engagement."

"How about six o'clock? Does that leave you enough time to do whatever you need to do?"

"I think so, at least for what we can do today." We exchanged cell numbers just to be safe and Patrick vanished into his room.

Meredith Fallon looked as though she had lost weight, but I might have been projecting. She gave us a weak smile as she sat down at the table and kept glancing at Patrick as though to reassure herself that he was still there. We all talked about inconsequentials for the first few minutes and she seemed to relax a bit, but she wouldn't look at me directly and she almost jumped out of her chair when someone dropped a dish back in the kitchen.

We ordered and the food came. Fallon had a healthy appetite. I'm not sure where she was putting it, but maybe she was eating to avoid talking. I waited until we ordered coffee to give her as much time as possible to relax. "Did James tell you that we're working with the local police on Martin Edison's murder?"

She nodded and glanced at me, then let her eyes drop. "Yes. I was very sorry to hear that. I know that he was abrasive and sometimes insensitive, but he wasn't a bad man. He was always good to me and my daughter." Her voice didn't break. "I hope they find out who did it."

I was trying to phrase my follow up but Dusty got there first. "We're pretty sure that the same person was responsible for all three deaths."

The answer was slow coming and I could see Patrick watching her intently without being obvious about it. "I imagine that's probably true."

"Then you'll help us?"

She looked at Dusty, then at me. "If they catch the killer, is that going to bring Tracy back? Of course it isn't. So if you're asking me if I care, then the answer is no. But I'll answer your questions if I can."

I started with the death of Damon Wright. Fannon was pretty vague. "I started to go along the trail with Mrs. Johnson, but she was being so prickly that I pretended to stub my toe and went back to the house. I think she was happy to see me go. I walked through the garden and saw Mr. Wolfman get up and walk off toward the house but I'm not sure where he went, maybe the bathroom. There's a bench down in front of the house and I sat there until I heard voices and knew that people were coming back."

"You didn't see Wolfman again?"

"Not until we all got together for the press conference."

She couldn't provide anything new about Louise Edison either. "He never talked about her. A couple of times fliers came to the house with her name on them and he always made me write back to the senders if he saw them, so I usually tossed them in the trash right away."

"There were no pictures or documents?"

"I know that his lawyer had the death certificate and his accountant must have had their tax returns from back then, but I never saw any of that."

"Did Edison have any enemies that you know of?"

She hesitated and bit her lip. "Every once in a while he'd get disturbing letters. There were several bunched together a couple of months back."

"Do you know what they said?"

"Yes. I opened all of his mail. They were pretty vague and all made with letters and words cut out of newspapers. Something about paying for his sins and balancing the scales. There were three of them and they were obviously done by the same person. Then they just stopped."

"Edison didn't tell the police?"

"No. He said it was just some nut but I could tell he was upset."

"And naturally they weren't signed."

"Oh, they were. I'd almost forgotten. Well, in a manner of speaking. At the bottom of each was the word 'Davenport'. I assumed it was meant to be a person's name or maybe some town."

"Did you notice the postmark?"

"No, I'm afraid not."

I tried to think of a way to bring up Tracy's death and fortunately Dusty came to my rescue. "Was Tracy upset by the murder?"

"Well, yes, of course she was. But she wasn't hysterical or anything like that."

"Did she seem nervous, or act as though she was hiding something?"

"Tracy didn't keep secrets. She was very open with everyone." There was a catch in her voice but she kept on. "Captain Upjohn tried to tell me that Tracy had an accident but I don't believe it. She knew those trails better than any of us and she had an amazing sense of balance. We set up a tight rope for her once and she went the whole length the first time without a stumble." Her voice did tremble then and she pushed her chair back. "I'm sorry but I think I need to lie down for a bit. It was nice seeing you again." Patrick started to rise and she shook her head. "No, stay and have your coffee. I'll be all right. I just need to be alone for a little while."

And then she was gone.

"She is getting better," he said. "She wouldn't have made it past the first couple of minutes a week ago."

"She's had a rough time. A new place might help her get over things. As much as she's ever going to get over them."

Patrick looked uncomfortable. "I don't know. She was pretty settled here. Edison hinted that she could stay on permanently; I think he wanted her to. Edison didn't trust many people and she was one of the few who made him comfortable. I don't think I'd ever have pried her out of here if things had gone on as they were. Hell, I might not have realized that I wanted to."

"Sometimes it's in moments of tragedy that we discover secrets about ourselves," said Dusty. "I'm sure you'll do fine together."

"I've asked her to see a therapist for a while. She still had little episodes where she slips into the past and thinks Tracy is still alive."

"I don't think that's unusual," she said soothingly.

"I guess not. But it's scary. The day Edison was killed, she took her car and disappeared while I was fixing lunch. Didn't come back until almost midnight. Scared the hell out of me."

Dusty and I exchanged furtive glances. I couldn't see Fannon killing her benefactor, but stranger things had happened. And Patrick had just admitted that neither of them had an alibi for that evening. Would he have done that if he was guilty or thought Fannon was?

"How long are you going to be here?" I asked.

"At least a couple more days. Detective Thorndyke wants to talk to us. I put him off until Monday. You two are fine but I'm not sure she's up to a police interrogation just yet. And then we have to box up the things we're shipping and donate the rest."

"Thorndyke's okay."

But Patrick didn't hear me. He was standing up. "I think I'll go check to see that she's all right." And he was gone.

We stopped at the hospital late in the day. Although they told us to keep the visit brief, they admitted that Cordelia was doing much better. She looked greatly improved as well, with most but not all of the various attachments removed or at least out of sight. As soon as we walked in she smiled and raised one hand a few inches in recognition.

"How are you doing?" we asked in unison.

"Better than I ought to be, apparently. It hurts when I breathe but it's preferable to the alternative." Her voice was barely audible.

After a bit I asked if she remembered anything about the night she was shot. "Not a thing. I had supper on the way back, but I don't even remember arriving at the Inn, let alone being in my room."

"But you do remember what you did before that?"

"Yes, and there's not a damned thing I found out that would have made me a danger to anyone. Well, at least nothing that I recognized as dangerous. I got confirmation of some of Austin's alibi – I think we can eliminate him from that killing at least. I found out that Damon Wright had been trying to track down people who knew Louise Edison, but as far as I know he struck out. And I know that Douglas Mason hasn't been back in the States for the past ten years unless he was traveling under a false passport. Nothing there justifies shooting me."

She began to sound very tired toward the end and I could detect a twinge of pain in her voice. 'Well, we'll let you rest and get your strength back. There's a guard posted outside just to be safe so don't worry about that."

"Let me know what you find out," she said, then heatedly, "I have a personal stake in this one now."

Naomi Winstead called me that evening. I asked her if she was still in Jaffrey and then if it would be all right if I stopped by on Monday. "All right. I'll be here all day." She seemed considerably less hostile than previously.

"I won't stay long but I have a couple of questions and I'm going to be in that general area."

"I heard about that woman who was shot. The reporter said that she was helping the police with their investigation into Martin's death."

"Yes she was."

"How is she? I mean, the news made it sound as if she could die at any minute."

"Much better but she'll be in the hospital for a long time."

"Can't she identify whoever it was? I assume it was the same person who killed Martin and the others."

"We can't assume anything, but we won't know who attacked her until her memory comes back." If then, I thought, but did not say.

"I'll say a prayer for her then Do you have any idea what time you'll be coming by?"

"Mid morning if that's convenient, say around ten?"

"I'll be watching for you."

It was the most pleasant she'd ever been to me and I commented on it to Dusty. "Maybe she's starting to get nervous. Three people who attended that party have been murdered so far and one of the people investigating it nearly died as well. If she thinks her own neck is in danger, she might be more cooperative."

"One can only hope."

Originally Dusty had planned to go along with me to see Winstead, but we had breakfast with Patrick and Fannon and somehow it ended up that she was riding out to the Edison house instead. Tibbett called me just before I left, looking for an update, letting me know that they'd requested fingerprints from Edison's military files. "I think you're barking up the wrong tree. I met Martin Edison back in 1983 when I joined the force and I got to know him as well as anybody once I became Chief of Police in 2000. But you're right. It can't hurt to check it out. God knows we don't have much else to look into. Captain Uptight has been trying to figure a way to dodge the bullet on this one. He's getting no traction at all. I don't think he knows as much as we do."

"And we don't know all that much."

"No, we don't. Watch yourself, Mr. Birch. Someone out there doesn't mind shooting detectives."

I left earlier than necessary because I wanted to take my time. I do some of my best thinking while I'm on the road. There were a couple of promising threads to follow now. If the man I knew as Martin Edison had actually been an impostor, that revelation would open up whole new areas to look into. The identity of Naomi Winstead's sister was less promising but if she was in fact Louise Edison, then perhaps Winstead blamed Edison for going off and leaving his wife the day that she fell to her death. It wasn't a rational reaction, but then neither was murder.

I reached Jaffrey half an hour earlier than I'd planned so I stopped for coffee and a donut and gassed up the car even though I still had half a tank. When I finally reached the little dirt road that led to her house, I was right on time. Winstead's car was parked on the grass and I pulled in beside her.

The moment I stepped out of the car, I heard a gunshot. The sharp crack was muted by distance but unmistakable and I found myself crouching behind the still open car door, fumbling for my own weapon. There was sudden utter silence; birds and insects had frozen along with me. I lifted my head and looked around cautiously but nothing moved except one branch of a nearby tree, stirred by a breeze so faint I couldn't feel it.

When nothing further happened, I cautiously eased out from behind the door. It occurred to me now that even if it had been a gunshot, which I was now tempted to doubt, it might have been someone hunting squirrels in the woods behind Winstead's house. I held my own weapon tightly but left the safety on as I quickly ran across the open space to the front door. I rang the bell and heard it jangle inside, but there was no indication that anyone was coming to answer. I tried the knob but the lock was engaged.

My cell phone was in my pocket and I had half a mind to call 911, but I still wasn't sure that I hadn't just been jumping at shadows. I edged over to the corner of the house and peaked around with exaggerated caution. From my vantage point I could see a swathe of trees, a bit of cleared ground, and not much else. The trees were mostly pine and didn't offer much cover so I chanced moving to the rear corner and taking in a broader view of the area. There was some thick brush to one side and it was possible that someone was lurking there waiting to shoot me, but if so, why had they fired when I was clearly out of sight?

I had just about decided that I had completely misjudged the situation when I turned and saw that one of the rear windows of the house displayed a pattern of radiating cracks from what was almost certainly a bullet hole. Involuntarily I crouched and slipped the safety off. I could hear crickets now and distant bird cry. Logic told me that the shooter was gone but my heart raced and I began to sweat as I edged toward the back door.

It was unlocked and I slipped inside with a mixture of relief and agitation. Could someone be lying in wait for me? I found myself in a small pantry and I very carefully moved into the kitchen proper. Nothing seemed out of place. I considered calling Winstead's name, but that would give away my presence, assuming that my theoretical opponent didn't already know where I was. The house was silent. I glanced into the short hall, then quick stepped to the next room, where I judged the broken window must be. There was a narrow table just inside the door and another under the broken window. A good sized wooden cabinet was mounted on one wall and a small desk stood opposite. I could see someone lying on the floor amidst a scattering of broken glass. After another quick look around I slipped inside.

It was Naomi Winstead. My first thought was that she'd been shot, but she opened her eyes and looked up at me. "Get down! Someone shot at me!"

Since I was crouched well below the level of the window, her caution was unnecessary even if her intentions were good.

"Are you all right?" I whispered.

"Yes. He missed me."

"Did you see who it was?"

"No. My back was to the window."

"Could he have come inside?"

"I don't think so. I heard you come through the door just now and no one else did before that." She slowly sat up, carefully keeping her head below the window sill. Tiny glass shards glittered on the front of her shirt and jeans.

"I'm going to call the police." I pulled out my cell phone.

"That sounds like an admirable idea."

It took them a while to get there; I later learned that they'd had trouble finding the right address. Two uniformed officers arrived first. They secured the house despite our assurance that no one had come inside, but waited for back up before they searched the wooded area. Anyone who had been there could have sauntered to a car parked half a mile away by then. A plainclothesman showed up a little later, an overweight man with beady eyes named Tennison who seemed bored by the whole affair.

"Probably just some stray shot from a kid after squirrels. They come up into the woods there to shoot at tin cans and bottles. He probably ran off when he realized what he'd done."

I suggested that Winstead's connection to the recent murder of Martin Edison might be significant but I wasn't able to convince him. "That was way over to Culloden. Nothing to do with us." They did find the spent bullet, lodged in the wall, but they weren't even interested in trying to determine where the shooter was positioned and I finally realized I was wasting my time arguing and just sat down and waited for them to go.

Winstead had been cooperative but had volunteered nothing. I thought she might be suffering from a slight case of shock, although she seemed completely composed. As soon as they were gone, and they didn't stay any longer than they had to, she put the kettle on without asking me. "It's tea for me but I have some brandy if you'd rather have something stronger."

"Tea is fine." It was lunch time and I felt a vague preliminary rumbling in my stomach. "You might want to cut short your stay here. I don't think the police are going to spend a lot of effort trying to find out who took that shot."

"I won't be frightened off my own property. I have a shotgun and I know how to use it."

"I noticed the gun cabinet in the other room." It was mounted on the outside wall next to the window and was big enough to hold several firearms.

"That was left over from the previous owner. I use it to hold office supplies and keep the shotgun handy in the hall closet." She opened a kitchen drawer and pulled out a roll of masking tape. "Would you mind covering up that broken window for me? I don't want the mosquitoes to get inside."

I walked back to the other room and looked around. Broken glass crunched under my feet as I made a criss cross pattern that covered the hole and which should hold the cracked glass together long enough for Winstead to have the pane replaced. While I was there, I opened the gun cabinet. Just as she'd said, it was filled with notepads, a box of pens, a stapler and a plastic container of staples, two boxes of paper clips, some index cards, and a few other items. They were all neatly arranged and looked like they'd come fresh from the store. But probably they had. Winstead had only been here a few days.

If Winstead was upset by having someone take a shot at her, she wasn't going to let me see her reaction. She seemed calm and collected as she served the tea and pastry. "Store bought, I'm afraid. I was never very domestic. Most of the time it's prepared dinners from the microwave." I did notice that the shotgun was now leaning against the refrigerator.

I said something polite and meaningless and we sipped for a few seconds. "Did you ever meet Martin Edison's wife?" I asked at last.

She considered the question for a few seconds. "Well, in a sense I did. It was a long time ago, before I was married. In fact she was just Louise Bowman at the time. It was 1976 or perhaps 1977, just after my first book was published. Somehow they talked Edison into participating in a panel on children's literature. Three of his early books were for young readers, you know. Anyway, he wouldn't travel so the mountain had to go to Martin. They wanted to film the whole thing but he wouldn't allow that, although he did go along with audio recording. Thomas Morehead was there; he's dead now. And Alice Reynolds. Last I heard she had Alzheimer's. I guess I'm the only one left."

"So you'd been to Edison's house before."

"Just that once, but Martin and I got along famously, at least for him. When he invited me to the press conference, he told me I was welcome to stay at the house and so I did."

"And you met Louise Bowman?"

"Well, naturally, since she was the housekeeper at the time. Rather prim and proper I thought. No sense of humor. Her behavior was perfectly respectable but she had a knack for making people feel as though they were imposing. I must say I was quite surprised when I heard they were getting married. Not Martin's type at all. In fact, I would have said that no one was Martin's type."

"And you never saw her again?"

"No. As I said, I was never in that house again until the night before Damon Wright died."

I sat back and watched her face closely. "I wondered, you see, if Louise might have been your sister."

There wasn't the faintest hint of a change of expression, which was a kind of expression of its own. After a few seconds she stood up. "Excuse me one moment, please."

She went off in the direction of the bedroom and I finished my tea, wondering if I'd hit a nerve at last. When she came back, she was holding a photo album. She turned it so that I could see the pictures. They were all of the woman I'd seen in the photograph with Winstead, the woman I believed was Louise Winstead Bowman Edison.

"This is my sister, Mr. Birch."

"Are you saying that this is not the woman that Martin Edison married?"

Her reply was to turn to the very last page. Attached there was a very brief cutting from a newspaper. I leaned forward and read it. It was an obituary for Agnes Winstead, who died as the result of a stroke. The date of her death was April 24, 2001.

"I see," I said quietly as one of my pet theories evaporated without a trace.

"My family was very close," she said quietly. "And now I'm the only one left."

"I'm sorry. That must be difficult."

"Yes, it has been. I'm afraid I was never very socially graceful. I have many acquaintances and few friends. I might not have seen Martin for forty years but we corresponded occasionally and we spoke on the telephone. I will miss him."

I exited as gracefully as I could after once more recommending that Winstead take a room at a motel for at least a night or two. My suggestion was firmly rebuffed. Feelling a bit guilty without quite knowing what it was that I was guilty of, I drove back to Culloden more expeditiously than I had left. The room at the Inn was empty when I arrived but the message light was blinking and the desk clerk told me that Detective Thorndyke had called.

"My New York friend talked to the people at Wright's agency. They say that not only were they unaware of any biographical project involving Martin Edison, but they doubt very much that Wright would have involved himself in any such effort. They also have a researcher on their staff whose help Wright would almost certainly have enlisted."

"I expected as much, but we needed to ask the question. Any word on the fingerprints?"

"Not yet. It might take a while. Some of the older records haven't been computerized yet so they're doing a manual search."

"Wonderful."

I was about to end the conversation when Thorndyke spoke up. "On the other hand, something interesting has turned up in Edison's financials. It might not mean anything but it is curious."

"I'd welcome anything useful right now. One of my pet theories went up in smoke a little while ago." I told Thorndyke about my suspicion that Louise Edison and Naomi Winstead had been sisters.

"I admit that one didn't occur to me. Are you sure the obituary was real?"

"Yes, although I suppose it could be for some other person named Winstead. But it did say that she was survived by her sister Naomi."

"I'll check it out. Did it say where she died?"

"Greylawn Nursing Home in Albany."

"I'll have someone check it out, just to make sure."

"So what's the scoop with the financials?"

"Well, it seems that Martin Edison was making a regular monthly payment starting in September of 1979 and continuing until August of 1990. The amount increased occasionally and continued at the elevated level on each occasion."

"Who was it paid to?"

"It was a what rather than a who. The payments were made to Davenport Sanatorium in Keene."

I remembered the signature on the threatening letters Edison had received and told Thorndyke about them. "So it seems likely that he was paying the Sanatorium to take are of someone."

"Ahh, but who? The elusive Mr. Grant, perhaps."

"I assume you've asked."

"Afraid not. The Davenport Sanitorium went bankrupt in 1997. It failed to pass state inspections for fire codes, patient care, food preparation, and there was no handicapped access. They couldn't afford to bring things up to code and cover all the deficiencies so they closed the doors. There were only a handful of people residing there, most of them subsidized by the government, and they were all transferred to other facilities."

"Have you tracked down anyone who worked there, or found where their records ended up?"

"We're looking around, but we haven't had much luck. There were two doctors, Davenport and his wife, both since deceased. They were quite old. The records for the patients who were still resident at the closing followed them to their new quarters. No one knows what happened to the rest. Probably destroyed. One of the things the Davenports were cited for was deficient recordkeeping. I'm not having much luck finding anyone else. One nurse died and another is senile. I do have one lead, however, and I'm going to see her this afternoon. I thought you might want to come along."

"Sure. My dance card is empty today. Who are we visiting?"

"Vera Caldecott."

"Nurse?"

"No, she was their accountant."

"Might know something useful."

Thorndyke picked me up at the Inn an hour later. His car was an aging Volkswagen that needed a paint job and shock absorbers, but the engine ran fine. We threaded our way through a maze of back roads and I was completely lost within minutes. "The state road is more direct but it's full of tourists. And Mrs. Caldecott lives somewhat out of the way."

"Is there a Mr. Caldecott?"

"Not any more. Vera retired two years ago but I understand she still does a little freelance bookkeeping, and I suspect she gets paid under the table."

"So we're going into the den of a desperate outlaw?"

"Desperately lonely, I'd say. She offered to have me over for lunch but I told her I was otherwise engaged."

The Caldecott house was bigger than I expected and looked like one of those places they use to illustrate the month of October on scenic calendars. It had a full porch overlooking a rustic but well groomed lawn with a miniature Japanese style garden featuring a pagoda that was also a fountain. Caldecott must have been watching for us because she was standing on the porch within seconds of our arrival. She had a full head of snow white hair, glasses with frames that looked too big for her face, and was wearing a light sweater despite the warmth of the day, but she moved gracefully and greeted us cheerfully, shaking our hands and shepherding us inside. The house, what we could see of it, was not surprisingly immaculate, decorated with a folksy touch that stopped short of being self parody.

A large tray of obviously homemade cookies sat on the coffee table. Vera told us to make ourselves comfortable while she retrieved a silver plated tea service that looked much too heavy for her. There was coffee as well as tea. If this investigation went on much longer I was going to need to diet.

"Now what can I do for you gentlemen? When you called you mentioned the Davenport home. I've been trying to freshen my memories of that time but I don't promise anything. My memory is usually pretty good though."

"We're interested in one of the patients who was treated there, but I'm afraid we don't even know his name," said Thorndyke.

"All we do know is that the bills were all paid by Martin Edison, the writer."

"Oh yes, I do recall that. 1979 through 1990. Always paid promptly and never any questions when we raised the rates."

"Did you know Mr. Edison?"

"Never had the pleasure. As far as I know he only came out to the home on one occasion."

"How about his wife" I asked.

"I didn't even know he was married."

Thorndyke took over. "Is there anything you can tell us that might enable us to identify the patient? Even something relatively minor could be helpful."

Caldecott twisted her face as if concentrating furiously for a second. "I do recall one thing that might help."

"What's that?" I asked when she remained silent.

"Well, I know the patient's name." She looked back and forth between us. "Would that help?"

I smiled. "You're making fun of us."

"Yes I am," she admitted.

"But you do remember his name?"

"Indeed I do. His name was William Grant, but I'm afraid that's just about all I can tell you. He was a label on an account. I might have encountered him in passing on one of my visits to the wards, but I didn't go there often and no one bothered introducing me to the patients."

"Do you remember anything else about him?" I finally felt as though I could see a glimmer of light ahead of us.

"Only that he was a voluntary committal at first. After about a year the doctors agreed that he was delusional and potentially dangerous, so they moved him to the secure wing." She made a sour face. "The Davenports had a rather odd view of things, I'm afraid. There were a couple of spontaneous recoveries that I remember, but basically they were caretakers and didn't make a serious effort to cure anyone. They just wanted things to run smoothly and quietly."

"They drugged their patients," suggested Thorndyke.

She nodded. "There was a lot of that. Kept them compliant. There was no malice involved and I don't recall any actual mistreatment, although there was some neglect. I retired just before the state closed them down, and frankly I was glad to be away from there."

"I don't suppose you know what happened to Grant after they closed? Was he still alive?"

She glanced at me and shook her head. "I'm afraid not. You really need to find Polly Morgan. She was the only one there who took a genuine interest in the patients. She had scrapbooks full of pictures of them and stories about some of her favorites. I think she probably did them more good than the Davenports ever did."

Thorndyke and I exchanged looks. "Who is Polly Morgan?" he asked. "I have a list of the nurses and she wasn't one of them."

"No she wasn't. She was secretary to the Davenports, what we'd call an administrative assistant nowadays. Whenever there was a job that had been assigned to no one, she'd fill in. Polly actually liked being in the wards. She wasn't very bright, I'm afraid, but she was willing and I don't think I ever saw her in a bad mood."

"Do you have any idea where she is now?"

"No, sorry. She lived somewhere close to the home because she bicycled to work. Never married, at least not while I knew her. She'd be in her fifties now, I would guess."

We thanked her and Thorndyke dropped me off back at the Inn. Neither of us had talked much during the drive, caught up in our individual but probably parallel thoughts. Thorndyke told me he'd start the machinery moving to find Polly Morgan and I thanked him for keeping me in the loop. There was a message waiting for me, an invitation to dinner, so after showering and changing clothes, I drove out to the Edison house.

Dinner this time was completely uneventful.

Tuesday morning, Thorndyke called to tell me that they'd located Polly Morgan. "Interested in another field trip?"

"Sure. Can Dusty come along?"

"Fine with me."

Patrick and Fallon had finished packing and were making the final arrangements for shipping or disposal of her things during the day. They had not yet decided whether or not to stay over another night so we wished them good luck before Thorndyke arrived to pick us up.

"We're in luck," he said. "Polly Morgan inherited her aunt's house in Putney near the Maple Grove Cemetery. She seems more than happy to talk to us."

We found the house without trouble. It was well cared for although the yard could have used some work. Polly Morgan was a cheerful looking woman, considerably overweight, with medium length grey hair and a slight lisp. She sat us down in a pleasantly furnished den with a real fireplace and so many plants it felt like a patio. We declined the inevitable offer of coffee or tea this time. Thorndyke explained that we were trying to track down one of the former patients at the Davenport Sanitorium.

"I'll help if I can. What was his name?"

"William Grant."

She nodded briskly. "Oh, I remember William. An odd man, very moody, but intelligent. He wasn't very talkative, but every once in a while he'd say something fascinating."

"What can you tell us about him?"

"Well, he came to us in 1979 or 1980 I believe, not too long after I started. I ran the front desk at first, but there wasn't much to do so I started asking if I could help anywhere else in my free time. I hate to sit around idle, or at least I did in those days. I've slowed down a bit since then. My friend Edna says I should have kept working when my aunt died, but the money was there and it was more than I needed so I decided to take some time for myself. And I kind of got used to it."

Thorndyke steered her back to William Grant.

"He was voluntary for the first couple of years. William always made me feel kind of sad. He acted gruff a lot of the time but I think he was basically just afraid of everyone. I remember once there was a confrontation with another patient and he blustered for a while but when the other man didn't back down, he started to shake and went off and tried to hide. It was days before he would speak or mix with the others after that. Doctor Davenport, the mister that is, told me William was suffering from paranoid anxiety, whatever that was. Between you and me, I never thought either of them knew what they were talking about. They say you can send away for a medical degree through a classified ad and I wouldn't be surprised if that's what they did."

"If he was voluntary, couldn't he just have left?"

"Well, theoretically I suppose. But it wasn't that easy. The outer gates were always locked. We all had passkeys. It was supposed to be for the protection of the patients. William used to get agitated sometimes and tell them he wanted to leave, but they'd always convince him to take a sedative to calm himself first and then he'd be too sleepy and by the time he woke up his mood would have changed."

"We understand he was eventually moved to the restricted ward."

"Yes he was. I remember that the Davenports had a conference with these people who were looking after William. A man and a woman. They talked for a couple of hours and William was moved that afternoon."

"Do you remember the names of the man and woman?"

"No, I'm afraid not."

"Would you recognize them if you saw a picture?" I interposed.

She thought about it. "I don't think so. As far as I know that was the only time they ever came in. I saw the man when I brought them coffee but the woman wasn't in the room. I'm sorry but it was a long time ago."

"What happened to Grant?" resumed Thorndyke. "Was he still there when you left?"

"My aunt died in 1995 and I resigned as soon as the estate cleared. William was long gone by then."

"Did he die or was he discharged?"

"Neither. He escaped." She seemed rather pleased. "The Davenports were very upset. At first they didn't want anyone to know about it. I guess they thought their reputations would suffer if people heard that someone had gotten out of the secure ward. They hired some people to look for him but I don't think they ever notified the police. By then, of course, William really was rather disturbed. Shortly after they put him in the restricted area, he decided he wasn't William Grant after all. I imagine he hid up in the woods somewhere and died of exposure. It's a shame. He was really a gentle man."

"Who did he think he was?"

"Somebody famous. They always choose someone famous. I think he picked a writer, like Stephen King."

Dusty spoke for the first time. "Would it have been Martin Edison?"

Polly nodded. "It might have been something like that. Anyway, the real person was still alive and the Davenports tried to convince him that he was wrong, but he just closed in on himself whenever they argued with him and eventually they stopped."

I remembered something Vera Caldecott had said. "I understand you took a lot of pictures while you were working there?'

"Oh yes. I had lots of scrapbooks full of them. Some of the patients loved looking through them. They had lost themselves somewhere along the way and seeing their own images was reassuring."

"Would you have taken pictures of William Grant?"

"Oh, yes. Quite a lot of them. He was rather handsome."

"Do you still have any that we might take a look at?"

She sighed. "No, I'm sorry. There was a fire, you see, at the place where I was rooming when I was still working there. I lost almost everything. There were a few things that I salvaged and I put them in storage for a while until I had a new place, but then there was all the confusion when my aunt died and I was throwing out a lot of things she'd accumulated over the years and I guess a lot of my old stuff went along with them."

We spent another half hour during which we learned little more. Dusty managed to ferret out a couple of little things about Grant – who probably resembled Edison at least superficially – but it was mostly about the kinds of food he liked, or what he wanted to do when he was free again. Apparently he made more than one attempt to escape before he succeeded. "He hid in the back of a delivery truck once. The driver caught him before they were out the gate." None of what she remembered seemed particularly helpful.

"How did he finally get away?" Dusty asked.

"He called one of the orderlies into his room and hit him over the head with a chair. Took his coveralls and his gate pass and was gone before anyone knew anything was wrong. I always had mixed feelings about that. I mean, he really must have needed help if he didn't even know who he was any more, right? But at the same time, he wanted so much to be free that I couldn't help being a little bit glad that they never found him. I suppose if he died out in the wild somewhere, I'd feel bad about it, but then again, he didn't have much of a life where he was."

I was feeling pretty pleased with myself on the drive back. "The timing is perfect. This William Grant person was someone Martin Edison knew well enough that he felt obligated to pay for his treatment over a period of many years. At some point Grant began to identify with his benefactor so much that he adopted his identity. Then he escapes, and goes to what he thinks of as his house. He either meets Louise Edison there or out walking and when she refuses to go along with his delusion, he pushes her off a convenient cliff. Then he waits for the real Edison to get back from California, convinced that he's awaiting an impostor, and then quietly kills him and disposes of his body."

"That's quite a reach," said Thorndyke dubiously.

"No, it fits. Remember, he fired all of his household staff about then and became more reclusive than ever. The new staff wouldn't know that he wasn't really Edison."

"But how could he take over Edison's persona as a writer?" asked Dusty.

"You said yourself that his work became much better during the 1990s. The original Edison had burned out but the new one was conveniently a skillful writer in his own right."

"I've met Edison a few times over the years," said Thorndyke. "He never struck me as unbalanced."

"Maybe in his new persona, he found some kind of equilibrium. I do know that he drank a lot. Maybe that masked any minor incidents where his illness wasn't under control."

Thorndyke reluctantly granted that I might be right. "We'll have the fingerprint records in a day or two. Then we'll know for sure."

I spent the rest of the afternoon on a conference call with Barry, Steve, and Tina. I expected to stay in New Hampshire for at least another couple of days and a few things had to be rescheduled, others reassigned, and a couple of minor decisions came up which they could have handled without me but didn't want to. Patrick and Fannon were leaving in the morning so we had dinner with them that evening. The food at the Inn was reasonably good but the menu was limited and I decided that Dusty and I would have to resign ourselves to longish drives for the rest of our meals other than breakfast.

Fannon had more color in her face and even chatted a bit, both of which I took as good signs. Patrick was more at ease as well. I really hoped they were going to make it as a couple because I had the feeling that they were both very lonely. On the other hand, they were still suspects and I tried to view them objectively. Someone had killed Damon Wright, Tracy Fannon, and presumably William Grant posing as Martin Edison, and there weren't that many viable suspects.

Wednesday morning they moved Cordelia out of intensive care so we went to see her. I would describe her mood as angry and embarrassed. "I should have checked before I opened the door."

"Do you remember the shooting now?" I asked.

"Not really. Just bits and pieces. But obviously I wasn't cautious enough. I even left my weapon on the dresser."

"Don't beat yourself up. You were tired and you hadn't found out anything that would obviously put you at risk."

"But I must have found something. Otherwise, why would the killer have risked trying for me in a public place? I've been going over the previous couple of days in my mind but the only thing I can think of is that I asked a lot of local people if they'd heard of William Grant."

"Did you get any responses?"

"Not a one."

"Did you say anything to any of our suspects about Grant?"

"Only the editor, Austin. He said the name sounded vaguely familiar, but it's so generic that it was probably nothing. He said he'd ask around his office to see if anyone knew of any connection with Martin Edison, but I doubt he'll remember."

The nurse came in to do a sponge bath and we made our excuses.

"So what's next?" Dusty was obviously frustrated by what she considered our lack of progress, but I actually thought things were beginning to take shape. As I saw it, the primary motive for the recent killings was the murder of the original Martin Edison and/or Louise Edison by William Grant. Wright's poking around threatened to derail the killer's plans, so he had to go. Tracy Fannon must have seen something, or perhaps she really did just fall to her death. In any case, with the impediments out of the way, the axe had fallen on Grant/Edison. The killer had attacked Cordelia because she seemed to be on the right scent – as were we – and killing got easier with practice. I was still troubled by the fact that Cordelia and Grant/Edison had not been shot with the same .38 but there might be a good explanation for that.

We drove south and found a nice little restaurant for lunch. I had planned to ask Mrs. McCone if we could go through Edison's papers, but there had been no answer when we called the house. Then I tried his lawyer, who was in Bangor attending a conference, could not be reached except in an emergency, and no, there was no one there who could authorize us to examine Edison's file. Wolfman and Austin were back in New York, Patrick and Fannon were on their way to Boston if they hadn't arrived yet, and although Naomi Winstead was probably still in residence in Jaffrey, I had no new questions to ask her just now. I did call her cell phone and she answered immediately, confirmed that she was quite all right and that there had been no further incidents. "The local police say they're watching the area closely but you couldn't prove it by me."

So we drove back to the Inn. On the way I explained my theory about the replacement of the original Martin Edison in great detail. I could tell that Dusty wasn't entirely convinced, but she was intrigued.

Back at the Inn, we spread our growing stack of paperwork out across the bed. "Let's assume that all three deaths were caused by the same person," I suggested.

"How about Cordelia?"

"We'll consider the attack, but it's still possible that someone else was responsible. Remember, the ballistics didn't match."

We started with the Martin Edison we had met. "Obviously he didn't kill Wright or himself. That leaves him with no motive for killing Tracy either. Let's take him off the list." I moved the paperwork related to him to the dresser.

"And Mrs. McCone has an alibi for all three, although she could have shot Cordelia."

"Let's take her off the list as well." Dusty moved a thin file to the dresser. "And Tracy as well." She shifted another.

"Ronald Edison could have killed Damon Wright. The fact that he found the body so quickly is suspicious on the face of it. It's also possible that he pushed Tracy to her death. He does have an alibi for the night Edison was shot, but there are gaps long enough to weaken it."

"Motive?" asked Dusty.

"He may think he's the son of the real Martin Edison. Maybe he found out about the impersonation from some source we don't know about and decided to kill the usurper. The source might well have been Wright, who was looking into Edison's past. Ronald had to shut him up or Wrighte might have pointed a finger when Edison died. Tracy might have overheard or seen something that made her a danger. Cordelia was looking for William Grant and mentioned it to the locals, one of whom might have mentioned it to Ronald, who also incidentally inherited a small fortune."

Dusty nodded. "Okay, he stays on the bed." She looked at the other folders. "Let's take Damon's file out." She moved it. "Looks more manageable now."

"Meredith Fallon. She had opportunity all three times, although I find it hard to believe she'd kill her own daughter. In her case, let's assume that Tracy died accidentally."

"How could she have killed Edison? She was in Boston when it happened."

I shook my head. "Patrick says she took off that day in her car and didn't get back until after midnight. There was plenty of time for her to drive up here and back."

"Motive?"

I shrugged. "I suppose she might have learned about the impersonation, but it probably wouldn't have mattered to her. Edison/Grant was a good employer and had promised to keep her on during his retirement. I suppose she might have been after her share of the inheritance. Sounds weak to me, but there might be factors we're not aware of."

"She was also here in town when Cordelia was shot," said Dusty. "Patrick says they were together but he might have been covering for her."

"So let's look at him next. He had opportunity in the first two cases and his alibi for Edison and Cordelia have the same flaws as Fallon's. He had a second hand motive to kill Edison. It looks like he's going to end up with a chunk of the estate through marriage, and he may well have resented the old man's influence over Fallon. It doesn't seem likely she'd have left if Edison was still alive."

"Then he might not even have known about the impersonation."

"Right, although they might have been working together. That would take care of their mutual alibis. But again, I can't see him killing Tracy under any circumstances."

"Maybe that really was an accident."

I shook my head. "I hate coincidences."

"So who's next? How about Arthur Wolfman?"

"Shaky alibi for Wright, but he couldn't possibly have killed Tracy. Could have driven over and shot Edison, but I'm not sure where he was the night Cordelia was attacked. Let's leave him on the bed for the time being, but I'm having a hard time seeing him as the villain."

We looked at Naomi Winstead next. "Another one with a shaky alibi for Wright's death. She knew who was wearing the jacket so it couldn't have been a mistake if she was actually after Edison and she might have slipped downstairs without anyone noticing. She was mad at Tracy that day, but she has a prickly disposition. She was in the area when both Edison and Cordelia were shot."

"But someone tried to kill her. Shouldn't we be considering that as a fifth incident?"

"I'm not sure. It didn't feel like a serious attempt and it might have been just what the police said it was, a stray shot from some kid out hunting squirrels. Why not fire more than once and why not get closer to the target?"

"So we leave her on the bed."

"Yeah. I was more interested when I thought she was Louise Edison's sister, but there might be another motive."

"Hillary Austin couldn't have killed Tracy either?"

"No, and it would have taken some fancy footwork to slip off and kill Wright. His alibi for the night Edison died convinced Cordelia that he was clear. Put him with Wolfman as technically a suspect but I think we can eliminate them both."

The last folder was for the Johnsons. "I don't suppose we can trust them providing alibis for each other," said Dusty.

"Probably not, although they aren't the closest couple I've ever seen. Peggy was having an affair with Wright and Peter knew about it. Wright may have broken if off, although she says otherwise, but there's clearly a motive for each of them."

"Neither seemed to even notice Tracy."

"No, that's a puzzle in their case as well. The mysterious letter on her notepad, if it's a clue at all, could be for Margery or murder or lots of other things, but they don't seem to have had any reason to want her dead. They could have killed Edison separately or together, hoping to get movie rights from the estate. Who is his literary executor?"

"Mason."

"We don't have a folder for Mason."

"I thought Cordelia confirmed he hadn't been to the States in years."

"Not while traveling under his own passport. But he might have used a forged one. He lives alone in France and he travels around Europe a lot. His absence would not have made a stir."

"Why would he rock the boat by identifying the person in the picture as an impostor?"

"I have no idea. Why did he tell us the story about the change of executors? And for that matter, assuming it's true, why did Grant change his will back when he replaced Edison?"

"Well, Louise was dead so she couldn't serve. And if Grant really believed that he was Edison, wouldn't he want someone in the family to be named in her place?"

I thought about it. "Makes twisted sense, I guess. I knew I kept you around for a reason."

"More than one, I hope."

"Yes, but to demonstrate the other, we're going to have to move all the suspects off the bed." We did just that.

I was in the shower when the telephone rang so Dusty picked up. When I came out wrapped in a towel she told me we were being taken to dinner. "By whom?"

"Chief Tibbett. I imagine he wants a progress report."

"Well, at least this time we have something to tell him."

But as it turned out, we didn't have as much as we thought we did.

Tibbett showed up at dusk in a late model Cadillac. "My one vice," he told us with a laugh. "I don't smoke, rarely take a drink, and the only woman I ever wanted enough to stay with didn't want me." We left town, heading south, then turned west. "It's a bit of a drive but I promise you it's worth it."

Dusty and I took turns telling him our theory that Martin Edison hadn't been Martin Edison at all, that Wright had turned up information revealing this, and that he had been killed by someone who was after William Grant rather than the man he was impersonating. "It might be someone trying to avenge Edison and his wife, or it might just be some old enemy of Grant's."

Tibbett remained silent throughout our recitation. In fact, our only interruption was when my cell phone buzzed. It was Naomi Winstead. "I just wanted to tell you I'm on my way back to Connecticut. Since the local police don't want to take this seriously, I decided I should take your advice and lay low for a while."

"Probably a good idea."

"Let me know if anything turns up."

We arrived fifteen minutes later. The Cookery looked like a private house; in fact, it probably had been at one time. There were only eight tables and all of them were occupied except the one reserved for us.

The food was excellent and Tibbett didn't drop his bombshell until we had finished our meals, and ordered Irish coffee all around. "You've done a lot of legwork and you've come up with more than we could have, more than Uptight and his minions for that matter. But I'm afraid it's all been for nothing."

I had no idea what he was leading up to, but I knew I wasn't going to like it. Tibbett had the air of someone about to break bad news and, even worse, he looked like a man who knew he was defeated. "The fingerprint information arrived late this afternoon. Thorndyke was going to call but I thought I should deliver the message myself. You see, the man I knew as Martin Edison, the man who was shot to death a week ago, was in fact Martin Edison. The prints matched."

"That can't be," I said, knowing that it not only could be but certainly was.

"There must be some mistake." Dusty had adopted my theory so completely it might have been hers.

"I'm afraid it's certain. I'm not mocking you, Mr. Birch. I thought you'd really grabbed onto something. But it looks like we were all wrong."

The drinks arrived. We all drank from our cups without speaking for a long time. I was the first to break the silence. "I don't know what to tell you, Chief. We can go over everything and look for another angle to investigate." I took a deep breath. "But I'm not sure that you're getting your money's worth."

"I'm not worried about the money. To be honest with you, I've been considering dropping the matter ever since Ms. Grayson was attacked. Police officers know that there's always a chance of violence. It's part of the job. It's different for you folks."

"Are you firing us?" I said lightly.

"Let's just say you've completed what I asked you to do. You've looked into places I might not have thought of and you developed some interesting scenarios. The fact that they didn't work out is a separate issue. I'll be happy to pay for your time and there are no hard feelings."

I told him I couldn't take his money and he argued back and we compromised on expenses, for which I would send him an itemized bill, when I got around to it. If I got around to it.

We were halfway back to Culloden when the radio came to life. It was Tibbett's office telling him there was a fire at the Inn. "How bad?"

It was under control, but it hadn't been an accident.

He didn't turn on the flashers but he crowded the speed limit all the way back. We saw the flashing lights from a few blocks away but there were no visible flames and it was too dark to see the smoke. When we pulled into the parking lot we could see that one unit was completely gutted and the two adjacent ones heavily damaged. Needless to say the room that had been destroyed was the one where Dusty and I had been staying.

We stood near the Chief's car while he talked to the fire chief. Our car was still parked in front of our room. It was covered with ash but as far as I could tell, it hadn't been seriously damaged. The fire was almost out. Uniformed firefighters were in all three rooms dousing the last remaining hot spots. There was quite a bit of smoke but it was dead calm and it was rising straight up into the air. There was a surprisingly large crowd of onlookers behind the police lines. I guessed this was the most excitement they'd had in Culloden in years.

After a bit, Tibbett came back to us. His expression was grim. "Someone doesn't like you two very much."

I'd surmised as much. "How did it start?"

"Looks like someone tossed a Molotov cocktail through the window. Bottle of gasoline with a rag for a fuse is the most likely. Crude but it did the job. Hope you didn't have anything valuable in there."

Our clothing and luggage was gone. Also my laptop and all of the files we'd brought with us. "Anyone see anything?"

"Of course not. There was a big bang and people came running but no one noticed anyone headed the other way." He shifted his weight uncomfortably. "Your car was parked in front. Whoever did it probably thought the two of you were inside."

"The thought had occurred to me."

"Your car is a big singed but it should run okay."

"Are you suggesting we get out of Dodge?"

"Might be prudent. There's another motel just this side of Keene."

I shook my head. "I don't think so. I think we'll take your advice and just go home."

"I'm none too happy about having this happen in my town."

"Not your fault."

"You might want to watch yourselves for a while."

I knew what he meant. If we left, the killer might assume that we were off the case and no longer a threat. But he or she might decide not to take the chance. Providence wasn't that far away.

Fortunately I always took my keys with me when I went out. The car started right up and I headed home. We didn't talk much on the way.

I won't say that we went on with life as usual because we didn't. For the first week we acted as though we were under siege. I even paid one of our subcontractors to watch the house while Dusty was home alone and I continued to carry my weapon even though the shoulder holster chafed. On the other hand, we both had plenty of things to occupy our time. The issues I had put off while we were away had to be dealt with along with a few newly arisen, and I am happy to say we picked up three new customers that week alone. If this kept up I would have to hired another full time operative. Dusty threw herself into her writing and reported she was turning out five thousand words per day of acceptable first draft. She'd made some improvements to the fantasy world in our attic as the story began to unfold itself in her mind.

I still had the original set of printouts that Merrilee's kids had assembled for me, but the additional material Thorndyke had provided, as well as the notes Dusty and I had made, were gone forever except for the time line, which for some reason Dusty was carrying in her shoulderbag. I thought about having Steve run them through the shredder, but instead I moved them to the back of the open case drawer in my filing cabinet. Thorndyke called that same day just to touch base, express his regrets that he hadn't been able to say goodbye, and to sheepishly admit that they had no leads on the firebombing.

"How's the official investigation going?"

"Upjohn's stalled out. They've reassigned some of the resources he'd been given. Another week or two and it will be just another cold case."

"Too bad," I said. "This person needs to be locked up." But on balance, I was just as glad that I wasn't involved any more.

Two days later, Dusty dragged me back into it.

The night before she'd told me she was going to take a day off. "I have Lucinda in a nicely complicated mess but I haven't figured a really elegant way to get her out of it, so I've been stuck all afternoon. Sometimes it's best just to walk away for a while and let my subconscious indulge itself."

"It's good to be your own boss."

I thought she'd go to a movie, or maybe read a book, or even just spend a day aimlessly driving around visiting the obscure antique shops she liked so much. Maybe she did. I don't know exactly where she found her inspiration, but when I arrived home that evening, the dining room table had been cleared off and she was sitting there bent over a yellow lined pad.

"Plotting?" I asked.

She looked up at me and smiled. "You're really very good at this."

I hesitated. "Good at what?"

"Investigating. I realized that when you told me your theory that Martin Edison was being impersonated."

"Well, it was a clever idea, I'll admit, but it turned out to be completely wrong."

She sat back in her chair and folder her arms. "Not completely. In fact, I think you got everything right except the timing."

Dusty still had the timeline we'd created, but she'd added a few items to it. She asked me if any of them were wrong because a couple of them relied on her memory rather than the now destroyed physical notes. I couldn't find any flaw.

"Your original theory was that William Grant replaced Martin Edison sometime in 1991, that he murdered Edison and his wife and fired his entire staff so that the masquerade could succeed. Then he retreated from public view until a few years had passed. He was convincing in part because he probably believed that he was in fact Edison."

"That's about it. But we know it's not true because of the fingerprints."

Dusty shook her head. "That's because we had the sequence of events wrong. Look at this." She pointed to an early point in the time line. "Edison fired all of his household staff except for Louise Bowman in 1979."

"He kept her on because he was romantically involved with Bowman. In fact he married her a few months later."

"Right. They were married two months after they began to pay for William Grant's stay at the Davenport home, and shortly afterward he made her the executor of his will."

Suddenly I realized what she was suggesting. I sat down and rested my chin on my palm, thinking it through. It didn't take long. "It works," I said at last. "William Grant did impersonate Martin Edison, but he did it ten years earlier than I realized."

"And he could do it because the real Martin Edison was staying at a nursing home under an assumed name."

"Until he escaped in 1990, after which he murdered Louise and probably the original Grant as well."

"Maybe. But Grant had to have known that Edison was loose because there's a two month gap. When Louise died and the real

Edison turned up, Grant might just have disappeared. And maybe now he's back."

"Why wait for so long? And what would it accomplish? He couldn't possibly impersonate Edison a second time."

"I don't know. We'll have to ask him when we catch him."

I didn't like the sound of that. "We'll pass this along to Thorndyke, but we're not going to get involved again. Grant, if it is Grant, is playing rough."

"That's another thing. How do we know his name is really Grant? That's just the name Edison used at the sanitorium. It could be anyone."

Which was not a comforting thought. We talked about it until late in the evening and finally decided not to call Thorndyke just yet. We would both give the idea some thought, try to poke holes in the timeline, and if we couldn't, then we'd tell him our latest theory.

The more I thought about it, the more Dusty's renovation of my original idea made sense. I couldn't discount the possibility that Grant was back, but it didn't seem to make any sense. If he wanted revenge for the death of Louise – presumably murdered by Edison – then why wait so long? If it wasn't Grant – or if Edison had waited for him to return from California and murdered him as well – then who else had a motive? Someone connected to either Grant or Bowman who had belatedly discovered the truth? Or could it be something else entirely? Bowman's estate had turned four people into millionaires – Mrs. McCone, Ronald – who in this scenario was the son of Grant rather than Edison, Meredith Fallon, and Donald Mason. And James Patrick seemed likely to realize a sudden upturn in his finances if he went ahead and married Fallon, although the sizes of his recent book advances suggested he didn't need the money. Or there might be some other motive we hadn't yet considered.

I didn't see a clear way forward, but I thought we might finally be on the right path.

I had some free time at work the next day so I dug out the file and read through all the profiles. Nothing leaped out at me but when I was done I had that nagging feeling you get when you've forgotten to do something and can't remember what it was. I pushed the thought around for a bit with no success, decided to leave it alone for the time being. Besides, I had a meeting with a client who wanted help with some vandalism at his miniature golf course. Posting a guard would be expensive and just scare the vandal off, but some camouflaged and well placed infrared cameras would probably solve the problem.

The solution occurred to me on the way home. I wasn't even thinking about it at the time but one little fact suddenly occurred to me and that triggered a series of connections that pointed me at other little inconsistencies and by the time I got home I was pretty sure that I knew who had killed Wright and Edison, wounded Cordelia, and set fire to our motel room. I also knew that the shot fired at Naomi Winstead's house had not been an accident, and while I still wasn't sure about Tracy Fannon. I could suggest a reason for that as well. The problem was that I couldn't prove any of it.

I ran my thoughts past Dusty who responded with a long and very satisfying kiss. "I told you that you were wasting your talents running audits and hiring people to follow wandering spouses."

"Don't deify me quite yet. I'm sure I'm right but unless we can prove it, the whole thing is just an intellectual exercise."

I decided to sleep on it, but in the morning I was more confident than ever that I was right. I called Thorndyke as soon as I got to the office. "I think I've solved the case, sort of. But I need to have a few things checked first."

"I'm all ears."

I talked for a long time while Thorndyke made notes. I wanted him to check birth and death certificates for three people, and we needed a search of records for hunting licenses issued in New Hampshire for the past ten years. I also wanted him to get a search warrant and he balked a bit until I told him a little more about what I thought had happened. "No promises," he said. "But the Chief still has some weight around the state. I'll talk to him right after we're finished. We'll probably have to get Captain Upjohn involved."

"Life is imperfect."

I suggested a couple of more things, then let him go and looked up another number and called Hillary Austin. He wasn't in yet but I left a message and sure enough, he called back within the hour. He confirmed what I suspected and asked why I was interested, but I told him I was just eliminating some distracting side issues. I didn't trust him not to say something he shouldn't and reveal something that I didn't want Edison's murderer to know.

If everything went as I'd requested and as I expected, I still wouldn't have enough to convince a prosecutor, but it would help confirm what I believed to be true. The killer was clever and careful, no doubt about it, but no plan this elaborate could be perfect. I asked Merrilee to have someone look at one of our suspects more closely than before and she assigned it to the best of her kids, a short, skinny black woman named Carla who was majoring in computer science at Providence College.

There seemed to be nothing more I could do immediately, which meant that I was restless for most of the day. Carla dropped off a folder late in the afternoon and I glanced through it. I nodded to myself as I read further confirmation of my theory, then typed up a detailed account of what I thought had happened and why, plus a list of things that had made me suspicious once I'd had time to look at them all together. There were still questions to which I had no answers. I didn't know what had made it necessary for Tracy Fannon to die. I was pretty sure I knew why both Wright and Edison had been killed, and why the shot had been fired at Naomi Winstead's house in Jaffrey. But I couldn't prove any of it.

Thorndyke called me the following day and told me he was emailing some of the information I'd asked. None of it contradicted my theory. The search warrant was in the works and in fact the search was made the following morning after the appropriate local authorities had been brought into the loop. "There was no one home," said Thorndyke. "And we didn't find any firearms."

"I didn't really expect to but we had to take the shot."

"We did, however, find a few rounds of ammunition for a .38 revolver."

"Careless."

"I'd guess it was by accident. They had rolled down into a gap between a shelf and the wall."

"Not where it was usually kept."

"That was my thought." He paused. "It's not enough for an arrest."

"No. We're going to have to provide a little push."

I brought Dusty up to date and told her my plans to nudge the killer into making a mistake. Not surprisingly, she wasn't thrilled with the idea. "I thought you wanted me to be a little more like Sam Spade."

"I said you should project more of a romantic image to your clients. I never said you should put your ass in the line of fire."

"I'll be careful."

Thorndyke and Tibbett got the ball rolling. "It'll take a few days because we're talking multiple jurisdictions."

I was itching to get this over with and I didn't want to wait. "I have a suggestion that might simplify things." He listened, decided it was worth a try.

"I'll get back to you." A couple of hours passed before he did, but I could hear the excitement in his voice. "It worked. How soon can you get up here?"

"First thing in the morning."

Dusty insisted on coming along even though I flatly refused to let her put herself at risk. She might have argued but my bluff would sound more plausible if I was alone. We drove directly to the station where Tibbett met us himself. "The suspect hasn't arrived yet so we have time for lunch."

The Inn had reopened, but the three gutted rooms were closed up and I didn't see any sign that they were under repair. Tibbett looked at the ruin glumly and I remembered that he was part owner. "Won't the insurance pay for the damage?"

"Sure but we haven't been close to full in years. We're going to take down this whole wing and put in a new restaurant with a bigger bar."

We didn't talk much while we ate. I confess that I was nervous and Dusty knew me well enough to pick up on it. When we were done we returned to the police station where Thorndyke and a technician fitted me with a wire and a button camera. "We'll have men spotted all around. If you want help on the double say something about having car trouble on the way up."

A few minutes later Tibbett received a call that our quarry was in place. "Let's get this done," I said, sounding more confident than I felt.

I would drive my car alone. Dusty would be following with Tibbett and Thorndyke and four Culloden police officers made up the balance of the caravan. Captain Upjohn had supposedly provided ample coverage but Tibbett didn't trust him. Once we were all ready, we set off for Jaffrey hopefully to trap and arrest Naomi Winstead for murder and arson and as many other charges as the prosecutors could devise.

The other two cars dropped back out of my sight about half a mile from our destination. I turned up the narrow driveway and saw Winstead's car parked exactly where it had been last time. I was wearing my shoulder holster, but I sincerely hoped I wouldn't need it. I've never fired it at anything other than a target and it was one of those experiences I would just as soon forego.

There was no sign of life from the house when I got out of the car so I walked up to the front door and rang the bell. After a few seconds, the door opened and Winstead looked at me with what I interpreted as vague apprehension rather than simple surprise, but I was probably projecting.

"Mr. Birch. What brings you way out here?"

"I was hoping to find you. I called your house and your cell phone and there was no answer at either number."

"Well, it turns out that I've had a visit from a burglar, or more likely children or just some homeless person looking for a place to spend the night. Nothing seems to have been taken but the police asked me to come up to see if anything was missing. It's rather a mystery."

"Actually, I think I can help you with that. I know who broke in." She gave me a sharp look. "Could we talk inside?"

Although she clearly wanted to refuse, she opened the door wider. "Suit yourself. I can't offer you anything to drink, I'm afraid."

"That's all right,"

I could tell the front room had been searched and I was certain Winstead knew as well. We sat down opposite one another and I forced myself to speak with a level voice. "I have to admit that I was the person who searched your house, Mrs. Winstead."

She looked mildly surprised but not at all worried. "And why would you do something like that, Mr. Birch?"

"Because I was looking for proof that you murdered Martin Edison, of course."

Her expression didn't really change but I could see a shift in her eyes. "And what led you to believe anything as silly as that?"

"I'm actually pretty pleased with myself. You were quite clever, but you made a few mistakes and you took a few chances. I should probably tell you that I wrote down everything I know and left it with someone from my office to be opened in the event of my death."

"How melodramatic." She almost seemed to be enjoying herself.

"Well, I do remember the shotgun in the front closet."

"I took it back to Connecticut with me. I suppose I could hit you on the head with a blunt object or something similar. The fireplace tools look to be adequate."

"Shall I tell you a story?"

"By all means. I might make a book out of it."

"Let's start with Martin Edison, a troubled young man who joined the army in search of a family, only to discover that he really didn't like having many people in close proximity. He suffered from periods of intense depression and mild paranoia so the army released him. Alone but still lonely, young Martin began to create companions and entire worlds in his imagination and when he turned these fantasies into actual stories, he discovered that people would pay him quite well for the results."

"I know Martin Edison's history."

"Bear with me. In 1975 Martin bought the house in Culloden where he lived his entire life. He hired Louise Bowman as housekeeper and saw as few outsiders as possible. He was sensible enough to employ a lawyer but conducted most of his business by telephone. The lawyer convinced him to write a will and he did so, naming Donald Mason – his only living relative – as executor and primary beneficiary. Although Martin continued to write, the therapeutic value declined, or perhaps there was some other factor at work. It might well have been that Louise Bowman exacerbated his condition intentionally, or with the connivance of a third party. Let's call this outsider William Grant."

This time she couldn't entirely mask her reaction. She'd been alert all along but now I could see the tension in her shoulders and in the way she held her hands, deliberately not clenching them.

"By 1979, Martin was a wreck and knew it. He probably couldn't write. Louise may have suggested that he take a prolonged rest someplace where people understood his problems. Someplace like the Davenport Sanitorium in Keene. Desperate for peace of mind, Martin agreed to an extended voluntary stay but either he or

Louise realized that it would be a bad idea if it got out that Martin Edison wasn't playing with a full deck. So they decided that he should use a false name and as it happened, Louise knew someone who looked a lot like Martin Edison. Why not just trade places for a few months? And so it appeared that William Grant went to the Davenport home while Martin Edison continued to live in his big house, although the truth was quite the opposite. And the new Edison had to discharge all of his servants other than Louise, since they might have realized what was going on. Edison charitably paid all the expenses for the unfortunate Mr. Grant."

"You should have been a writer, Mr. Birch. You have a powerful imagination yourself." Her voice was different now, tense but controlled.

"Oh, the story gets even better. The Davenports weren't very good at curing their patients and they may even have made Martin worse. In any case, he remained for two years before he either spontaneously began to feel better or just decided that living at home couldn't be worse than living there. So he probably told Louise that it was time to end the masquerade. But Louise and William were having such a good time spending Martin's money that they didn't want to go back to the way things had been. So they had a talk with the doctors Davenport, who agreed with their assessment that their patient was clearly delusional, having decided that he was actually the noted author Martin Edison, and that he should be moved to the restricted ward. All expenses to be paid, of course. The Davenports may even have known the truth, although it wasn't necessary."

"Even if this fantasy was true, what has it got to do with me?"

"Oh, I'll get there eventually, Naomi. May I call you Naomi? I think we're going to be much closer in the future than we have been in the past." She didn't answer so I pushed on. "Anyway, the bogus Martin Edison marries Louise Bowman the following year and in due course their son Ronald is born. Ronald is largely raised by hired help, seeing little of either of his parents even though he lives in the same house with them. I suspect he was an accident. William Grant and/or Louise Bowman – since she isn't really Louise Edison – realize they are running through the assets so they singly or jointly start writing new fantasy novels using Edison's characters. Or perhaps they employed a ghost writer. In any case, the results are clearly inferior but the name is magic and they sell reasonably well, keeping the coffers full. Everything seems to be going quite well for them." I paused dramatically. "Except that in December of 1990 the real Martin Edison escaped."

"Summoned a dragon and flew over the walls," Winstead said sarcastically.

"Something like that. Anyway, he made his way back to his home and probably confronted Louise. She no doubt tried to convince him that they had only been trying to do what was best for him. Martin was restless and they walked while they talked and at some point Louise said the wrong thing, or perhaps Martin had intended to kill her all along. In any case, he pushed her over the edge and disappeared."

"She didn't die immediately, you know. They said she was probably conscious and in pain for several hours."

"I didn't know that. Anyway, William Grant was at that time out in California signing books as Martin Edison, so he clearly wasn't a suspect. As far as he knew, Louise had died accidentally. He flew back to the house without suspecting that he was in danger and at some point Martin showed up again and killed the impostor. I have no idea where the body is buried but I imagine it's somewhere on the mountain. The restored Edison fired the only two servants who might have noticed the change and hired Mrs. McCone to replace Louise. Young Ronald may or may not have suspected something at the time, but since he was treated as well or as poorly as before, he probably forgot any inconsistencies that may have arisen."

"You still haven't explained how I fit into any of this."

"Well, first I should point out the mistakes you made. I'm embarrassed to say that I didn't notice any of them at the time, which doesn't speak well about my brilliance as a detective, but I did plod through eventually. I'm particularly upset that I let you mislead me about your sister since I already knew the truth. You had two sisters, Naomi. One of them died just as you described it, but the other was Louise Winstead Bowman. Where is Mr. Bowman, incidentally? I found a record of the marriage but he seems to have dropped off the earth shortly afterward. Was he the first of your sister's victims?"

Winstead was obviously working things out in her mind. "All right, yes, Louise was my sister. But we hadn't seen each other for years until the day I attended the writers' conference at Edison's house. We barely spoke to one another. I no longer thought of her as my sister."

"What caused the break?"

"That's none of your business and it has nothing to do with Martin Edison."

Oddly, I thought she was telling the truth this time. "That might be true but you also made another mistake. You told me the gun cabinet in the other room was left over from the previous owner."

"So?"

"The previous owner was Damon Wright, your ex-husband, who refused to own a firearm. He mentioned it the day of the press conference."

"Then it must have been the people who owned it before him."

I shook my head. "The day the window was shot out, you made a point of drawing my attention to it."

"I may have mentioned it."

"So I took a look and it was filled with office supplies."

"I used it as a storage cabinet. What's wrong with that?"

"Everything in the cabinet was new and unopened. If you were moving into a new home, I could understand that, but you had come to Jaffrey to sell the property, not to write your next book. And you wanted me to believe that the only weapon you had was the shotgun, which you brandished when I first arrived, so you emptied the cabinet, carried all of your other firearms and ammunition down to the basement, and made a quick stop at an office supply shop to provide some camouflage."

"If all of this is true, why did someone take a shot at me?"

"Oh, but they didn't. You fired that round through the window some time before I arrived, leaving broken glass on the floor. Then you waited for me to drive up, fired another round out through the hole in the window, hid the weapon where I wouldn't see it, and lay down on top of the glass waiting for me to find you. I did notice at the time that none of the fragments were in your hair or on top of you, but I didn't realize the significance."

"That's all just conjecture."

"All but this." I reached into my pocket and showed her two .38 calibre shells. They weren't the ones the police had seized but she wouldn't know that. "You spilled these when you put them on the shelf. I found them when I searched the house."

"You can't prove any of this."

"I've already told you the story of Martin Edison. Now I'd like to tell one about Naomi Winstead."

"I think I've already heard more than enough." She didn't rise though and I thought she actually did want to hear what I knew. Or guessed.

"Naomi was the youngest of three sisters in a moderately well off family. Their father wanted boys, as you told me the first day we met, but not being blessed with any sons he taught his daughters to use firearms and to hurt. The oldest sister, Louise, took over management of the family business when their parents died in a car crash, but she wouldn't listen to advice and managed to bankrupt the company within two years. Relations among the three sisters cooled considerably but they still kept in touch. Several years later Naomi sold her first book, Agnes was working as a secretary, and Louise married Charles Bowman, then a few years later went to work for Martin Edison. At some point, Naomi and Louise became estranged from one another."

Winstead turned her face away to conceal some reaction but regained her composure almost immediately.

"Naomi married Damon Wright in 1980 but the marriage only lasted two years. During that time she told him about her sisters, and that she and Louise were no longer on speaking terms. Wright was in the early stages of creating his own literary agency and probably was quite interested in the connection to Martin Edison, and frustrated by how tenuous it was. He didn't pursue the issue at the time, but he didn't forget it either."

"Damon never forgot anything," she said. "He was a bastard but he was sharp as a tack."

"Several years later, Louise died in what was assume to be an accident. Did you attend the funeral by the way?"

"No. I was in Europe." Her voice shook.

"Edison began writing again, and better than ever. He allowed all of the books he hadn't written himself to go out of print. And so the years passed until Damon Wright decided to stir the pot.

He started asking questions about Edison and spotted the same oddities that I did, the changes in his writing style neatrly coinciding with the changes of personnel at his house. Oh, and Edison changed agents both times as well. In fact he did so every six or seven years from that point on just to make the pattern consistent. He probably would have done the same with his household staff except that he fell in love with Mrs. McCone and he couldn't very well fire Ronald, who was supposed to be his son."

"My nephew."

"Yes, your nephew. As I said, Wright started putting the pieces together and came to see you. He floated his theory that Martin Edison had murdered Grant and your sister and you believed it. At one point you sent threatening letters with the name Davenport as signature. You wanted revenge for your sister so you bought the house in Jaffrey so that you could follow Edison and watch for a chance to kill him. One day you nearly did. You sneaked up on his campsite and shot at him with your shotgun or maybe a hunting rifle. You even had a hunting license in case some forest ranger asked you for it. You missed that time, or maybe you were just trying to frighten him, or maybe you wanted to prove to yourself that you could have killed him if you'd wanted to. Or at the last minute you realized that Wright would know, or at least suspect, that you were responsible, so you'd have to kill him first. For whatever reason, you fired only the one shot and then you left."

"If I wanted to shoot someone, Mr. Birch, I wouldn't miss." Her voice was strong again.

"I don't imagine you would. Then Edison announced his house party and press conference. Somehow you convinced Wright to convince Edison to invite you. The one time sister-in-law perhaps? Or did you go directly to Edison and talk him into it? Either way, you were there to at least scout out the territory. When Edison loaned Wright his jacket, it was too good a chance to miss. The police had already been told that someone was trying to murder Edison – although they didn't entirely believe it – and here was the perfect way to get rid of Wright and make it look like a failed attempt on Edison. Even better, you had witnesses to prove that you knew about the borrowed jacket so you couldn't possibly have mistaken Wright for Edison. You'd never get such a beautiful opportunity again so you sneaked down the back staircase, or perhaps the fire escape, followed Wright until he was out of sight of the others, and bashed his head in."

"I'm a regular criminal mastermind, I guess."

"It was more luck than cleverness. Someone could easily have seen you outside the house. In fact perhaps someone did. Tracy Fannon was working in the back kitchen and she probably took things out to the trash bin. Did she spot you coming or going? Is that why you had to kill her as well?"

"I thought the little girl's death was an accident." There was a hint of sarcasm in her voice now.

"Did you know that she lived for a few minutes after the fall, and that she wrote something in her notebook before she died?"

For the first time I saw a hint of fear. I had struck a nerve. "The police think it's the letter 'M' but I believe they're wrong. Turn it over and you have 'W' for Winstead."

"That doesn't mean anything. It could be 'M' for mother."

I waved her comment away. "It doesn't matter. What does matter is that now there was no one to threaten your ultimate goal – the death of Martin Edison to avenge your sister." She tried to hide it but Winstead was suddenly amused and I faltered. Somehow I'd made a mistake. But I forged on. "I imagine you watched the house until you knew Ronald and Meredith Fallon were both gone. You called, planning to disguise your voice if Mrs. McCone answered, but you were lucky again. Edison picked it up himself so you didn't need to. I don't know what you told him – probably that you knew who was trying to kill him. That wouldn't even have been a lie. He agreed to meet you and you shot him three times."

"That's a remarkably unlikely story."

"It's not quite over. You talked to Hillary Austin and he told you that Cordelia Grayson was asking questions that might lead the police to William Grant. He remembers the conversation. So you went to her motel room, carefully choosing a different pistol this time, and tried to kill her. Something must have distracted you because you didn't do a very good job of it, and Cordelia is pretty tough anyway. Then you arranged the little sideshow about someone shooting at you here, and pretended to be on your way back to Connecticut while you were actually preparing to firebomb my room at the Inn. Lucky for us we weren't there at the time or this conversation wouldn't be happening. And another little oversight.

Except for Dusty and I and the police, none of the suspects knew the address of your place in Jaffrey, so how would the phantom shooter have found it?."

"You make it all sound very plausible, Mr. Birch, but I'll bet if I took the time I could come up with alternate scenarios just as logical."

"Perhaps, but they wouldn't be true."

"And you still can't prove that I was responsible for any of these deaths. The worst I did was refrain from telling the police that Louise was my sister. I was so frightened of being a suspect, you see, and that was all so long ago that I didn't think it was relevant. We weren't even on speaking terms."

It was time to play my bluff. I had half hoped that she'd blurt out something incriminating and I could call in the troops, but she hadn't. What I was about to do was very dangerous. Winstead did not appear to be armed, but there was a knitting bag on the couch beside her and I'd never seen her doing anything that domestic.

"I was walking around your yard this morning, before you arrived."

"Returning to the scene of your crime?"

"Looking for clues. You'd be surprised what people throw out in their trash. Alas, you seem to have disposed of your trash."

"I'm starting to get tired of this conversation."

"Bear with me just a little longer. I happened to notice that spruce tree way out back. The one with the pockmarks and a couple of bent nails sticking out of what's left of the bark."

"What of it?"

"Looks to me like someone nailed up a target and started shooting at it."

"I told you, the owners before Damon must have had guns. Or it might have been neighborhood kids. This place has been empty so long they probably hang around here a lot."

I shook my head. "This is considerably more recent. I looked at the marks and they kind of puzzled me. A lot of them were too ragged to be consistent with gunfire alone." I reached into my pocket and took out the spent .38 round that I'd borrowed from Thorndyke. "You missed one when you dug the others out of the tree, I'm afraid. Now what are the odds that ballistics will identify this as coming from the same weapon that killed Martin Edison, or the one that nearly killed Cordelia Grayson?" It was a complete bluff, but she couldn't be absolutely certain that she hadn't overlooked a round.

I saw that I had finally pierced her armor. Winstead glared at me with such intensity that it felt like a physical impact. I saw her hand move toward the knitting bag and tensed, but she moved it back. "What do you want, Mr. Birch? You didn't come here today just to taunt me."

"Isn't it obvious? I want to sell my silence. Otherwise I would just have gone to the police with what I know and let them take it from there."

"And how much would this cost me, assuming I accepted that what you say is the truth?"

"I'm not greedy. I know how much you make from the Poppy White books. Two thousand per month should be about right. Any more than that would raise questions. I have to funnel this through my company. You'll be a client paying a monthly retainer for confidential security services and no one will be the wiser. Trust me, I have several similar clients. In my line of work, you tend to turn up secrets that people will pay to bury. The rate is non-negotiable but I promise it won't go up and as long as you pay on time, there's no reason why we should ever even see each other again."

"You have this all thought out."

"Of course. This is the business I'm in."

"We might be able to come to an arrangement." She stood up slowly and moved a step away from the knitting bag, which made me feel much better. On the other hand, she hadn't given me anything. Even if she agreed to pay, she could claim she had just done it to get rid of me. I needed an admission of guilt, or for her to tell me something only the killer could have known.

"There's one place where my story is just guess work," I said quietly. "And I admit I'm curious. Did Tracy Fannon see you that day? Is that why she had to die?"

Winstead moved even further away from the couch and the knitting bag. She seemed almost unaware of my presence now, her thoughts elsewhere. But she answered my question. "No, no one saw me. I used the fire escape and I know another path that leads to the trails. Damon was just ambling along. I had to wait for him to catch up."

"Then why did you push Tracy over the cliff?"

"Because she went into my room to clean up and like a fool I had left my revolver sitting on the night table. I had brought it along just in case the opportunity arose, but bashing Damon's head in was much more satisfying. But I still planned to shoot Martin and I couldn't let her tell anyone that she'd seen a gun in my room. The girl was better off dead anyway. She could never have led a normal life."

I suppressed a twinge of anger. "So you lured her out for a walk and pushed her off."

"She didn't suspect me of anything. It was easy, and necessary." She had crossed the room to the fireplace and had her back to me.

I was about to speak the code words that would bring in the police when she crouched suddenly, reached into the rack of fireplace tools, and spun around to point a handgun at my face.

"I suggest that you make no sudden moves, Mr. Birch."

"I wouldn't think of it."

"It's my turn to tell a little story. There once was a man named Paul Birch whose official job was to run a private detective agency but who sidelined in blackmail. After his death, the police would go through his company's records and find a number of questionable payments. One day Mr. Birch bit off a little more than he could chew. Somehow he found the weapon that was used to kill Martin Edison. He might have taken it to the police, but what was the advantage of that? Instead he decided to concoct an elaborate and fairly convincing story implicating a perfectly innocent woman in the murders of three people. He showed her the weapon and threatened to plant it somewhere the police would find it and under circumstances that would implicate her. Coupled with his fabrication of the chain of events surrounding the deaths, it would almost certainly be enough to convict her. But he was willing to suppress that information in return for a certain monetary consideration."

I was waiting for an opportunity to refer to car trouble but since the police were monitoring the conversation, they probably already knew I had underestimated Winstead. All I had to do was keep her talking instead of shooting. "Do you really think they'd take your word over mine?"

"You won't be saying anything, Mr. Birch. You'll be dead. You underestimated my tenacity. I tried to grab the gun, we struggled, and it went off. Your fingerprints will be on it along with mine by the time the police arrive. I will be in near hysterics because I've never killed a man before. It will be a wonderful performance. I'm sorry you're going to miss it."

"You won't get away with it."

"Oh, I think I will. But before you go I want you to know how wrong you were. I hated Louise with a passion. I was engaged to be married to Charles Bowman when she met him. He was handsome and rather quiet and truthfully not very smart, but I loved him dearly. Louise saw him as a useful pawn and she quite deliberately stole him away. I swear at times I thought she had hypnotized him. She was never that good looking. None of us were, really. I only came to visit that one time because I knew they were still together and I wanted to see him. I thought that surely after a year with her he would have seen the light. But he was still besotted, lived in a rented room in that awful town, and saw her when he could. He did look a good deal like Edison but he had a moustache back then. I threw myself at him, he turned me down, and I never saw him again. Agnes told me that he'd run off. Neither of us ever realized that he'd become Martin Edison."

I was confused. "But if Bowman impersonated Edison, who was William Grant?"

She laughed. "There never was a William Grant. That was just the name Edison used when he went into the rest home. Charles Bowman ceased to exist and William Grant had never existed in the first place."

"So you killed Edison because he killed Grant. I mean Bowman."

"Yes, and I'd do it again. Just as I'm going to kill you now. I'm only sorry you didn't bring along your slutty girlfriend." And she tightened her grip and there was a single gunshot.

Fortunately it was Chief Tibbett who fired, not Naomi Winstead. It was a difficult angle through the window and the bullet only grazed her outthrust arm, but she dropped her weapon. When the door burst open, she gave a deep sigh and stood away from the fallen handgun. I received a withering look but the wound from that was pretty shallow. Dusty came in a minute later acting as though I'd been mortally injured; she was crying when she threw her arms around me, but it was relief rather than sorrow. They took Winstead outside while Thornton was advising her of her rights. I disengaged Dusty and shook Tibbett's hand, thanking him.

"It's never a pleasure shooting someone, particularly a woman, but I didn't mind so much this time. I liked Tracy Fannon."

Later that day we heard that the Connecticut police had failed to find any firearms in Winstead's house there, but a few days later a check of her finances led them to a storage locker that held a variety of handguns and hunting rifles. The shotgun was in the trunk of her car. Winstead clammed up and called a lawyer but we had the weapon that killed Edison, the one that had nearly killed Cordelia, and a tape of her confession to me, plus enough background to make a compelling case. There was a cursory search for the remains of Charles Bowman but it was more show than substance.

There was some good news in the days that followed. James Patrick and Meredith Fallon invited us to their wedding. Arthur Wolfman's next novel sold to a major publisher, but it didn't make the bestseller list. Hillary Austin got fired when his firm was acquired by some German holding company. Geneva McCone still lives in the house on Mount Brandoch. Ronald visits her frequently but he's enrolled full time at the University of Vermont. He and Cordelia date occasionally. She seems to have fully recovered. The Johnsons lost their backing for the Kenneth Roberts movie and have separated.

Dusty and I are still together. She delivered the first volume of her fantasy trilogy to her new agent, who says she has high hopes for it. The attic is going to be revamped because her hero has been exiled to a neighboring kingdom for volume two. My agency has been very busy but I confess that I've been suffering from the doldrums lately. After solving three murders and having a gun pointed at me by someone determined that I should die, the placement of security cameras, the possible embezzlement of a few thousand dollars, and the whereabouts of a runaway dad six months behind in child support just aren't very exciting.